THE
DEADLANDS
AND OTHER STORIES

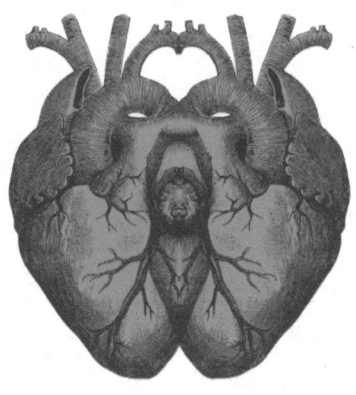

BILL BLUME

DIVERSIONBOOKS

Also by Bill Blume

Gideon Keep, Vampire Hunter
Gidion's Hunt
Gidion's Blood

Diversion Books
A Division of Diversion Publishing Corp.
443 Park Avenue South, Suite 1008
New York, New York 10016
www.DiversionBooks.com

For more information, email info@diversionbooks.com

First Diversion Books edition August 2015.
Print ISBN: 978-1-68230-016-9
eBook ISBN: 978-1-68230-015-2

CONTENTS

DRACARGE

Snarge \\ˈsnärj\\ *noun*: the remnants of a bird after being sucked into
a plane engine
Dracarge \\drā-ˈkärj\\ *noun*: same as snarge, but with a dragon
instead of a bird

The thin smear of blood on the runway of Heathrow International
Airport could be loosely translated into one very big "oops," if it
had been an accident.

My partner Kensington and I got the call a little after four in the
morning. Our flight paths crossed over the M4 just a few miles out
from the airport and our crime scene.

"You okay, Windsor?" Moonlight reflected off of Kensington's
light blue and purple scales as he flew in dizzying circles around
me. His long wings nearly hit me in the face. He's not the best flyer.
"You look a little green."

"I'm supposed to be green."

"Well, yeah, but you're a different shade of green tonight."

"It's not night. It's morning." I glared at him. "Would you fly
straight!" I can normally dodge his random flight path without
trouble, but I was on the wrong end of a fire water hangover and still
burping flames with a kerosene aftertaste. I shivered as I repressed
another burp.

"Somebody woke on the wrong side of his weyr this morning."

I kept my snout shut for the rest of our flight. Kensington
blessedly limited his flight path to a wibbly-wobbly line.

The flashing blues of first-responders marked our crime scene halfway down the south runway. I counted at least six humans standing around the mess. Most of them were dressed in fire brigade gear, waiting to wash down the runway once we'd collected our evidence and officially pronounced today's unlucky victim a goner.

"I am not in the mood to deal with these human bunglers." Heathrow, or, as we mythical creatures still call it, the Hexagram, was one big testament to human stupidity. Back in the 1950s they'd had six runways, which formed a six-pointed star. All those planes crisscrossing in that pattern had built up an inordinate amount of mystical energy. Even with the runways reduced to just two airstrips, the pent up magic still drew in the random dragon every so often. A few unlucky ones, usually the dumber lot, got sucked into a jet engine.

"So do we know the name of this morning's Darwin Award winner?" I grumbled as I landed next to the only human sporting a police uniform. This chap was bundled up in a big black coat and danced from one foot to the other to keep warm.

"'ullo there." He looked down at me. He'd pulled his flat, black hat down low, but not enough to hide a distractingly overgrown unibrow. "You must be the boys from the dragon coppers."

"Special Agents Windsor and Kensington." I all but stabbed my International Bureau of Draconic Affairs badge in his eyes. "I take it you're with the 'human coppers.'"

He held up his hands to fend off my sarcasm. "Right then, just trying to be friendly."

"Ooh! I wanna new friend!" Kensington rubbed up against the constable's leg. The human went rigid, not sure how to respond to being groped by a dragon in the fashion of a cat. It still amazes me that the Hexagram hasn't claimed my partner.

"Draco's scales, Kensington! Let's just get the samples and get out of here." The mystical energy in the ground tickled my talons. Bad enough to be in this place, but the rest of the day was guaranteed to yank the horns on my head. No worse way to end a day than visiting the surviving family members to tell them their loved one was a golden skid mark.

I say "golden" because dragons have gold-colored blood. That's also the reason my last thread of hangover-battered patience snapped when I saw the leftovers on the runway, illuminated by the spotlights on the side of the fire engine.

"This blood is red!" I hovered up to meet Constable Colorblind at eye-level.

His breath misted from him as he hugged himself against the cold. "Yes, there's blood."

"You called me out at four in the morning for a pile of snarge?" A blue-flamed burp shot out of me unbidden, and the vile aftertaste gave me a full-body shiver. I really shouldn't have stayed so late at the pub.

"'ey now! No need to torch up the place." The small shot of flame had sent all of the humans back a few steps. One firefighter ran behind the front of his engine to hide. "I saw the surveillance video, and it was definitely a dragon."

I resisted the urge to tell this airport constable he ranked just one rung above a rent-a-cop with me, even if he was technically part of the Metropolitan Police. "Oh, really? Well, I know dragon blood when I see it, and that isn't it!" We traded glares, neither willing to flinch. "Kensington, would you inform the constable what color dragon blood is?"

Not only did Kensington not answer, but I heard one of the humans regurgitating his breakfast.

The constable lost our staring match, and I saw the revulsion on his face as his eyes were drawn in the direction of the snarge.

I refused to turn my head, not wanting to confirm what I already suspected. "He licked it, didn't he?"

The constable, who turned almost as green as my scales, nodded. He stepped back as if to retreat from a rabid beast. I looked down to see Kensington walking up to me as he licked the blood from his snout.

"So what did it taste like?"

His eyelids squeezed down as he worked on his answer. "Smoky and robust with hints of iron."

"No, you idiot!" I floated down to get in his face. "What species?"

His head bobbed about in deep thought before he answered. "Gremlin."

"That's absurd!" The constable had his nerve back. "I saw the video, and I know a dragon when I see one."

"Fine, constable. Why don't we have a look at that video?"

Fifteen minutes later, five of which included me delivering a colorful lecture in dragon anatomy, we were in the security office which smelled of stale coffee. The surveillance video played on one of the monitors. The video showed a dark red, wing-shaped body flying straight at the jet engine, and then... snarge.

"Um, Windsor," Kensington's snout pressed up to the screen with his eyes crossed, "that looked like a dragon to me."

I'd watched the playback a dozen times already, and the only thing stopping me from torching the entire place was the desire to still have a paycheck at the end of my shift.

"Looks like a dragon to me, too." I didn't need to look at Constable Colorblind to know he was smirking. "Of course, I'm not an expert like some people here."

"Fine." I glared at him through the haze of smoke wafting from my snout. "It's a dragon flying towards the plane, but that's not dragon's blood on the runway."

I shoved Kensington out of the way and went through the video frame-by-frame until I found what I was looking for. "There!" The focus was perfect. I pressed my talon's nails to the screen, pointing to a small figure with flailing arms and legs flying into the engine. "That's the gremlin."

Not wanting to be proven wrong, the constable pointed to the red shape. "But that's a dragon!"

"Relax, human. You won't have to do any paperwork. This is my investigation now."

My sudden eagerness to keep the case threw him off guard. "Oh, well then. That's excellent." I could see the suspicion in his eyes, trying to understand what it was he was missing.

"I'll need a copy of that video for my agency."

"Of course." He grabbed a blank disc and set to burning a copy for us.

I couldn't wait to get that disc to our forensics unit, because I was certain I recognized that dragon, and if I was right, we'd just gotten a lead on one of the dragon world's most notorious assassins.

. . .

I tried to avoid a second visit to the Hexagram by calling the phone number for the Gremlins' Union rep, but on every try, the line would ring and then drop to static.

The sun was just finishing its climb by the time Kensington and I flew back onto airport property. We played extra nice this time, going through the front doors, a decision I regretted as we were forced to navigate a group of protesters railing against unfair layoffs by all of the airlines.

We stopped by the security office, flashed our badges and headed for the hangar where the gremlins' union had an office.

We were halfway to the hangar when I realized Kensington was talking to me. "What was that?" I shouted over the roar of a Boeing 747-400 swooping onto the runway like a drunken eagle diving after a fish. The landing sent ripples of mystical energy through the large, beige concrete squares that covered most of the airport property.

Hate this place.

"Why are we looking for a gremlin when we're looking for a dragon?" Kensington asked.

"Because we need to know who was killed to figure out who hired the dragon. We find that person, then we can—" An Airbus drowned out the rest of my explanation, and I didn't bother finishing it. A forensics tech had confirmed what I suspected when I saw the video. The red-scaled dragon caught on camera was a French-hired wing known as Henri Flambé. A guy like him only killed for pay, and at his price tag, the gremlin stain on the tarmac must have been into something huge.

We stopped in front of the closed doors to the hangar, a giant dull white monument to the shape of the box. The main doors were long walls of dark glass. I fluttered close enough to press my snout against the glass and realized they weren't tinted. The inside of the hangar was just dark.

"This doesn't make sense." Not a single bulb inside was lit. The only light was shining in through the skylights. "Where are all the humans?"

Kensington scratched his snout. "Working?"

"What?"

"Heathrow is the busiest airport in the United Kingdom and the third busiest airport in the world." He nodded with absolute certainty. "They must be working."

I didn't say anything for a moment. I'd never heard anything that intelligent come out of his mouth. "How do you know that?"

"Wikipedia is my favorite e-book."

"But Wikipedia isn't—Whatever. That still doesn't make sense." I pointed through the glass door. "This is where they work, and this place is as dead as Stonehenge at midnight."

I glanced at the neighboring hangars. Not a single plane was being serviced in any of them. There wasn't so much as a mechanic sitting outside for a smoke.

We flew around the building until we discovered a human-sized door on the eastern wall. Even with the skylights, the inside was cloaked in shadows.

"Hello!" My voice echoed off the metal walls.

"Ooooo…" Kensington did somersaults through the air. "Echo! Echo! Echo!"

The only occupants were a flat, bright blue tow truck that resembled a vice on wheels, scaffolding, and various other mechanical items parked along the walls. Office windows lined the upper half of the far wall. A utilitarian set of metal steps led up to a dark doorway.

As we reached the steps, Kensington's horns twitched and his head bopped back and forth. I also heard the music once we entered the hallway. The only light spilled out of an open door at the far end. The lights in the room flashed to the beat of the music. I couldn't think of the song's name but recognized it was Muse. A sign above the door identified this as the "Break Room."

The only man inside wore a dark blue jumpsuit. He had his back to us and was rocking his butt to the tune. He held what resembled a small, plastic guitar.

I cleared my throat to get the man's attention, but the music from his video game muted me.

Kensington danced in midair and then shouted in time with the song, "My plug in baby!"

The man screamed. All at once, he tried to spin around, rip off the video game guitar, turn off the television and place his body between us and the pile of empty cans of Guinness on the coffee table. Unfortunately, the human body wasn't capable of doing all that at once. He smacked himself in the face with the guitar, then fell backwards onto the coffee table and split it in half with a loud crash.

He thrust an arm up into the air, his hand still wrapped around the neck of the guitar. "I'm okay!" A pair of bloodshot eyes looked at us over the edge of a pronounced beer belly.

I shook my head. "Third busiest airport in the world, huh?"

Kensington was too distracted by the all the pretty graphics on the TV screen. His head still bopped in time with the music. "My plug in baby!"

I flew over to the TV and turned it off, hoping that might silence Kensington, too.

"I'm sorry." The words slurred out of the mechanic. His name tag identified him as John Smith, clearly the son of creatively-challenged parents. "I'm so, so sorry." He struggled to get up. The empty cans of ale foiled his efforts.

"We're looking for the Gremlins' Union Office."

"The office? Oh, yeah. That's Rusty's space. He's really good at Guitar Hero." He waved his hands in front him as if to diffuse some dire threat and the rest of his words spilled out like limp bullets from a machine gun. "Not that we play it a lot. Well, maybe once or twice a week. Okay, well I mean we... Um, maybe. It's not important really. Rusty really isn't very good at Guitar Hero. You know he's a gremlin, right? Always gets distracted by the guitar remote, trying to figure out how to make it work better, but just messes it up. I told him last time to just play the bloody game—"

"Sir!"

The mechanic's eyes widened. "Oh, sorry. That's right. Office."

"Yes, where is it?"

"Third door down. The sign is upside down, and it's on the wrong door. Keeps falling down and they always put it back up on the wrong door." He sniffed as tears welled in his eyes. "But Rusty isn't there. He's not ever coming back." His voice choked and the toilet bowl of his grief flushed out of him. "Poor little guy! Those little suction cup feet were really adorable, you know?"

"Mr. Smith, what happened to Rusty?" Although, I suspected the answer, I wanted to hear him say it.

"Well, he—I mean, he just. You know, the jet engine and he just went." He held up his hands, clapped them together and then wiggled his fingers in the manner of something dispersing.

"What makes you sure he's the one who got killed this morning?"

"He was the only one left." Mr. Smith fell apart. Tears ran, snot flowed and the rest of his words tumbled out in a language only an equally drunk individual could decipher. Kensington landed beside the man and nuzzled as they bawled.

I left them there and went looking for the Gremlins' Union Office. Sure enough, there was a sign hanging upside down on the second door I came to. The black, rectangular plaque incorrectly identified this as the office of the Mystical Aerial Mechanics Union. As if to prove Mr. Smith's point, the sign was covered in small holes like a teenager with a chronic case of acne.

I moved on to the third door and opened it. The room was an avatar for entropy. The desk, which was only three feet wide, had a stack of five repair manuals substituted as one of the legs. None of the other legs looked like they'd ever belonged to the same piece of furniture.

The back wall was a window looking out onto the floor of the hangar. The glass was difficult to see through because of all the cracks in it.

The walls were littered with holes. The handle of a small hammer had been stabbed into the wall on the left and a calendar hung off-kilter from it.

I landed on the desk and pulled the calendar off its mount. Flipping back, I noticed the most recent "repair" jobs were struck out. Prior to that, they were either checked off or reassigned to later dates. The work had just stopped for some reason.

A knock at the door startled me and sent me flying up near the ceiling. I expected Kensington or the mechanic. Instead, there was a woman in a red business suit. Her brown hair was pulled up into a tight bun. She was the most orderly-looking thing in the room.

"I'm here to see Mr. Rustalicus Gus?"

I showed her my badge and ID. "Special Agent Windsor, IBDA. Who are you?"

Her gaze went from me to the rest of the narrow office, likely trying to decide if this was a sign of a struggle. Judging from how she changed gears, she knew enough about gremlins to recognize this was the normal state of things. "Elaine Fife. I'm a reporter for the London Times."

I glanced at the calendar in my talons and realized 11:30 am was written and circled in red ink for today. "What were you meeting Mr. Gus about?"

"Afraid I'm not at liberty to say." She had that false sense of papal-like authority reporters sport.

"Mr. Gus was murdered this morning, so stuff it, human. What are you doing here?"

The stench of fear coming from her confirmed two things for me. One, she hadn't had a clue about the murder, and two, she already suspected the reason she was here might make her a target, too.

"He called me last night. Said he had a story about the layoffs. Claimed one of his supervisors was involved in illegal activities."

"What would gremlins have to do with humans getting laid off?"

She shrugged. "Am I in any danger?"

"Maybe."

"That's not very reassuring."

"Wasn't meant to be." I tapped the calendar. "Who knew you were meeting him?"

"No one."

I gave her my business card. "Call me if you remember something useful."

"Should I be doing anything to keep safe?"

"If I were you?" I didn't look at her as I flew out into the hall and towards the break room. "I'd lock my doors and avoid French dragons."

• • •

Not every cloud has a true silver lining. The ones that do aren't really clouds. They mark just one of many different types of "thin places" in the sky, openings to other places. Most people never see them. The best they manage is a glance of something out of the corner of their eye.

In ancient times, gremlins would slip through a thin place and go splat on the ground. Then World War II rolled around and all the planes started picking up strays.

"There!" I pointed to a cloud shaped like a whale. We'd been circling the skies over London for about an hour just to find it.

We aimed for the mouth of the whale and emerged from the brief dark grey of the interior onto the white brick road at the front gates of the Gremlin Capital.

A tall grey wall surrounded the city. A pair of black, thickly-furred gremlins guarded the gates. Each had a pair of silver horns sticking out of their heads. Their helmets reminded me of welder's headgear. One of them placed himself between us and the gates. He glared through his helmet's round glass eye holes.

"Papers." His voice rumbled and was near-unintelligible.

Kensington and I offered our badges and IDs which he held

close to his face and sniffed at through a set of narrow slits in his helmet.

"What's your business in Sprocket?"

"Death notification," I said as he returned our credentials. "One of your constables is meeting us."

"Constable F'nella just arrived." He slid his fingers into the holes of a red circle set into the wall next to the gate. He turned the dial left. The circle changed to green, and the gates slid open.

The constable met us in a small courtyard. She looked far different from the guards, no taller than me. Her horns were gold. She wore a brown, leather flight cap with gold-lined, round goggles. The face beneath was lightly-furred in a pale shade of blue. She wore a dark brown uniform. I noticed the fur on the back of her hands was a darker shade of blue and while thicker than the fur on her face, not nearly as shaggy as the guards.

"Hop in." She pointed to a wooden coach with large wheels but no seat for a driver or horses to pull it. The side door was already open with a slender, metal step for those who needed the assistance. Kensington and I took the rear seat. The constable sat across from us.

Her eyes shifted towards the ceiling of the cabin. "Coach, take us to the MAMU office building."

I grabbed the edge of the seat as the coach rolled out of the courtyard and into the city. The Gremlin Capital resembled a hodgepodge of designs, but flowed in a manner that left no doubt of careful planning. We first traveled past bland, brick structures which resembled 1930s office buildings. All manner of buildings followed: glass pyramids, steel towers shaped like DNA, cathedrals, even a massive sports arena floating in a vast lake.

Kensington blurted out excited grunts and cries with each passing surprise. For once, I agreed with him.

The next neighborhood we entered was full of tree houses connected by rope bridges.

"One of the older residential districts." The constable's voice had a harsh edge to it. Her disapproving gaze focused on my talons which still had the seat in a death grip. "Is there a problem?" she asked.

I glanced out the window at all of the traffic. The means of transportation appeared just as whimsical as the city. We passed cars and other horseless carriages. A motorbike zipped past. Some type of flat, rectangular craft with rounded edges hovered past us overhead.

"Sorry, this place isn't what I expected," I said.

"Let me guess." She bit out her words. "You didn't think anything here would work."

"Pretty much." I didn't see a point in lying. She was already ticked.

"I'll have you know that gremlins are some of the most brilliant inventors. Where do you think half of the technology in the mundane world came from?" She pulled on the goggles to her flight cap as she said, "By the First Engineer, you probably still believe all that marketing foolery that Jules Verne invented steampunk!"

"It's not like gremlins are known for improving machines."

She leaned forward, giving the impression she wanted to stab me with her gold horns.

"If humans weren't so impatient and let us finish half the work we start, they'd realize we're trying to improve their machines."

"Right. I thought it had more to do with all the alcohol they drink."

"Gremlins don't drink," she said. "Sprocket is a dry city."

That got Kensington's attention. He leaned close to me and pointed out the window at a large lake. "I don't think she knows what 'dry' means." His attempt to whisper didn't stop her from hearing everything he said.

"She means they don't allow alcohol in this city."

Kensington's horns rubbed together. "But they still have water?"

I pushed him back. "Constable, you're only proving my point. They don't have it here, so they drink it every chance they get when they're on terra firma. Half my drunk-in-public arrests are gremlins who think it's a sin to see the bottom of their glass for more than five seconds."

I sat on the receiving end of a look to kill for a lot longer than five seconds.

"Let's just get to the wrench in the gears, shall we? You IBDA boys don't usually make trips up here for simple death notifications."

After getting chilled by her gaze, I wasn't about to argue with the change in topic. "The union representative for the Mystical Aerial Mechanics was murdered this morning. Dragon by the name of Henri Flambé tossed him into a jet engine on the runway at Heathrow."

Her lips curled back and exposed her teeth. They reminded me of a rhinoceros. "If you know the dragon responsible, then why are you here?"

"He's a hired wing." My answer received an impatient shrug. "Means he's a mercenary. Someone paid Flambé to kill Mr. Gus before he could implicate one of his supervisors for illegal activities."

Her irritation vanished as she sat up. "Manganese Rahl is the head of the union and suspected in all sorts of black market dealings. Well-connected, the type who knows which gears to grease."

"How long until we reach Rahl's office building?" I noticed we seemed to be leaving buildings behind and getting closer to a mountain.

"We're almost there."

The carriage bumped as it climbed a road running along the side of the mountain. "Oh, drat." Before I could distract my partner or warn F'nella, Kensington screamed and dropped to the floor of the carriage. He covered his eyes as his tail swatted back and forth.

"What in the clockwork is wrong with him?" F'nella retreated as far back as the inside of the carriage permitted. She perched on her seat like a gargoyle to escape Kensington's tail gone amok.

"Sorry." I offered the most apologetic expression I could manage. "He's afraid of heights."

"But he's a dragon." She rubbed her temples as her eyes narrowed. "Didn't he fly here?"

"Yes, I know. Ouch!" His tail swatted one of my talons. I kicked him in the arse as recompense. "He usually has to think so hard just to fly straight that it distracts him from getting scared."

We spent the rest of the ride dodging Kensington's frantic tail. The Gremlins' Union Offices were built into the side of the mountain. Our carriage pulled into a large hangar which hid most of the sky and the drop.

Kensington walked with a recurring twitch in his tail as we followed Constable F'nella into the lift.

I noticed she hit the button for the top floor and decided to be proactive. "Glad to see we're going to the bottom floor." The constable looked at me as if I'd proven I couldn't get any dumber, but a less than subtle cant of my head towards my partner clued her in to what I was doing.

"Yes, the bottom floor." Her voice was drier than Sprocket's prohibition.

When the lift opened, Kensington sighed in relief and shuffled out as fast as his short legs allowed. The constable and I stayed a step ahead of him.

Every surface from the floors, walls, ceiling, and even the furniture was carved from the rock. The chairs were the only exception. They had a 1950s mass-produced simplicity.

We walked to the end of the hall where a secretary was typing on a computer. The keyboard looked better suited for an old Hermes typewriter, with flat round buttons and typebars that swatted only at air. He looked up from his typing with a grumble. The protest I could see in his eyes faltered when he got an eyeful of me and Kensington.

"Constable F'nella, I see you've brought friends this time." He muttered to himself, "Didn't think you had any."

She sat on the edge of the desk and glared down at him. "Save it, luddite. We're here about a worker who died this morning."

"You'll have to come back later. Mr. Rahl is in a very important meeting."

I couldn't see the constable's face, but judging from the way the secretary squirmed in his chair, he was getting a double dose of the glare I'd suffered through on the ride here. His stubby fingers crawled across the desk for the phone. He pressed the button for his boss's extension the second he had the receiver off the cradle.

"Yes, sir, I know." He kept his voice low and tried to muffle the part of the handset pressed to his ear to prevent us from overhearing whatever his boss said. "Constable F'nella is here with a pair of dragons. She says it's about a dead worker and is refusing to leave." Even with Rahl's reply muffled, I didn't miss a rather impolite explicative, because he was talking loud enough to be heard through the office door. "I'm sorry, sir. She's rather adamant."

"Oh, gum the works already!" The constable snatched the phone from his hand and slammed it down. The secretary shrieked and recognized he was better off not trying to stop her as she charged towards the door. She slammed it open. Rahl sat behind his obscenely large desk in a black leather chair boosted as high as it could go to make up for his small stature.

"Constable F'nella, a pleasure to see you, as always." He pointed to the chairs in front of his desk. "Please, have a seat."

The entire back wall of his office was clear glass, providing a magnificent view of the entire city of Sprocket. The elevation did not settle well with my partner. He screamed and darted for a door to our right, presumably a private bathroom.

"Scales and fangs, Kensington," I muttered under my breath.

No sooner had he disappeared into the bathroom than he jumped back out and the door slammed shut.

"Sorry!" he shouted through the door. He saw our stares and pointed towards the bathroom. "Already in use. It's another dragon! What are the chances of that? He's tall, red, and has the weirdest accent."

I glanced at the shut door, then to Rahl who'd gone pale as a morlock. He was struggling to crank his chair down to get away, but all he managed to do was make it easier for the constable to grab him by the tie.

"Who's the dragon, Rahl?"

He didn't get to answer. The door splintered apart in a burst of flames. A large, red blur shot out of the bathroom. Kensington got caught in Flambé's grip. As soon as they crashed through the large glass window, Flambé tossed Kensington aside.

I launched after my partner. The idiot screamed as he dropped down the cliff face like a missile.

"Kensington, flap your wings!"

I tucked my wings in tight to increase my speed. The ground rushed towards me. Kensington's flailing gave him just enough wind resistance to let me catch up. He was too big for me to pull up, even if I grabbed him with my talons. He either flew or died.

His shouts drowned out mine. With seconds left, I slapped him across the face hard enough to startle him into silence.

"Fly!" I spread my wings wide, fighting gravity and struggling to catch the wind before I went splat. "Now!" I screamed as my wings ached from the effort not to bend or break. My entire body swooped hard at the last second, close enough for me to smell the grass as I launched back into the sky.

I spared a glance over my shoulder. Kensington spun through the air in an erratic spiral, but he'd made it airborne.

"All right, Flambé." I growled as I saw his red streak going straight towards the thin place that had brought us here.

I might be round and stubby, but I'm small and fast... a lot faster and more maneuverable than some French, pastry-eating crocodile with wings. Even better, he was getting caught in all of the air traffic over Sprocket. I pushed into the crowded airspace. Propellers whizzed and hovercraft engines hummed past with the occasional curse of an angry commuter.

Flambé glared back at me. He snorted a fat trail of flames to block my path. The trick didn't stop me. Bless the IBDA and its evasive flight training.

My quarry snarled, then launched straight up. This took us out of the majority of the hovercrafts which traveled closer to the ground, but that still left us with plenty of airships and the occasional plane.

That's when he did something I hadn't expected. He flipped and dropped straight at me.

Our talons tangled and wings swatted at each other, even as we struggled to maintain our flight. I dropped into my combat training. I blocked a strike with a Wind Over Water, and countered with a Barking Tiger. He didn't relent. This dragon was a professional and disrupted my attempts to subdue him. I dodged a slash of his talon with a Crouching Knight and answered with an Ali Meets Frazier.

My efforts failed, and Flambé grabbed me in a choke hold. "Let me show you how Monsieur Gus died, no?"

I struggled to break free of his grip, but he held tight. My talons weren't sharp enough to cut through his crimson scales. His foreleg squeezed tighter, cutting off my air. I couldn't even scream. I kicked his stomach, but I was too weak to hurt him. I twisted my head and saw a commuter jet flying towards us.

"Au revoir!"

Just before he could toss me. I heard Kensington's scream, the kind he gives whenever he's spiraling out of control. I felt, more than saw, his body collide with me and Flambé. We separated. My body fell to safety, narrowly avoiding the suction of the jet's large, round engine. Flambé was not so lucky. Given his size and the amount of flames a red dragon can generate, the engine exploded as he was dissected in the blink of an eye.

An "Oops" from Kensington warned me to duck just in time as he looped around me.

"It's okay." I watched as the plane limped its way back towards Sprocket's main airport. "Long as it doesn't lose another engine, should make it down safely."

I rubbed my snout as we flew back to the MAMU offices and Constable F'nella. I was a little tender from where Kensington had collided with me, but under the circumstances, I wasn't going to complain.

• • •

By the time we reached the cliff and landed back in the office, the constable had slapped the cuffs on both Rahl and his secretary. We went with them as F'nella hauled her catch into the police station.

Rahl lawyered up, but his secretary was underpaid and bitter.

"Turns out Rahl's been dealing under the table with the human airline owners," F'nella told us in her office after she'd taken down the secretary's confession. Her office was a rather shoddy affair that left little doubt the gremlin government didn't budget much for their law enforcement. "In return for a sizeable payoff, he stopped all gremlin work on human planes. The payoffs were apparently cheaper than having to maintain the planes with their work force of human mechanics."

"That would explain all the out of work mechanics who were protesting in front of Heathrow." I tried not to let it trouble me that essentially I'd gotten those humans their jobs back by making air travel unsafe all over again. Hey, it's not my fault humans aren't meant to fly. Truth be told, I'm not sure Kensington is either, but for once, I'm glad he does, wibbly-wobbly and all.

CROSSFIRE

Half of the seats in the passenger cabin were empty as the hover-plane cleared the cloud bank. Davin Cross checked his watch. The local time was 7:15 in the morning, an hour late. A sign the pilot was scared to push the engines while crossing the Atlantic?

The plane shimmied as it descended into London. A bell chimed from the intercom. "Don't be alarmed, ladies and gentlemen. Just a spot of turbulence." The reassurance offered little comfort. The pilot's voice shook worse than his aircraft. "Please remain seated until we've completed our landing into Waterloo Station."

Davin glanced out the window at the wing's exposed power cell. The inside of the large, glass sphere crackled with brilliant blue tendrils of plasma energy.

An elderly woman two rows ahead of Davin leaned over to her husband and gripped his arm. "It's supposed to look like that, right?"

Davin wanted to grab every one of them by their dress coats and shake sense into them. The plane's power source wasn't flawed, but their lives were endangered. The real threat had a name: Novaya Zvezda, and it was waiting for all of them in London.

• • •

The boarding terminal at Waterloo Station turned out more crowded than DC's had been ten hours earlier. Davin saw a handful of steam trails evaporating into the sky in all directions. A train whistle sounded the warning of its imminent departure.

"We still use the old steam engines here in London."

The woman's voice behind him caught Davin off guard. He

turned to see she looked about his age bedecked in purple pants, black boots, and a black corset over a white blouse. Fashion had followed suit when the world returned to the old modes of energy, back when nuclear and oil resources had passed their prime. The clothing styles had refused to change when plasma energy emerged.

"I'm sorry?" He tried not to stare, even though she was a very good-looking woman. He was meeting someone else.

"I said we still use the steam engines here." She shifted her eyes in the direction of the smoke trails before looking back at him. "You are Davin Cross, right?"

With that one question, she graduated from "attractive scenery" to "person of extreme interest and possible threat."

"Yes, I am. Who are you?"

She offered her hand. "TeAhna Meercroft."

He hesitated but doubted the woman's intentions were ill. If she'd wanted to kill him by a method as subtle as a handshake, she could have stabbed him with greater ease when she'd approached him from behind.

"Do I have to ask?"

"Your friend Stephen sent me." Her brows furrowed. "He said to tell you that he still misses your mother's chocolate wings?"

He laughed. Yes, Stephen had definitely sent her. His mother wasn't the best cook on the planet, but she made buffalo wings better than anyone else, including a recipe for spicy, dark chocolate wings.

"He mentioned that you warned him to avoid London altogether if he couldn't make it here before noon, which he couldn't. His plane was grounded when its plasma drive failed its pre-flight inspection." She pulled out her watch. "Should I worry that we're left with less than four hours before that time?"

"Yes." He pointed towards the main exit, or at least what the signs displayed in big yellow letters as the "Way Out."

"I'll get us a carriage." She set a fast pace as she navigated the crowd. "Where are we going?"

His shoulder bag assaulted several people in the terminal as he struggled to keep up with her. "We need to get to a place called Nine

Elms, the power plant."

She stopped at the curb and waved down a horse-drawn carriage. "Nine Elms power plant," she said and then told Davin once they'd climbed into the buggy. "You're paying."

"Got it." He patted his breast pocket to reassure her. That's when he noticed her studying him with a perplexed quirk to her eyebrows. "Is there a problem?"

"I've been in this trade for six years." She avoided the word "spycraft" because of their public transportation. "Stephen said you were an analyst for the Agency."

"Yeah, seven years." He smiled at the slight advantage in time, but it was forced. He'd hoped for a field assignment, but the CIA apparently wanted him for his mind, not his body.

"You don't look like most analysts."

"Pale and physically unfit?"

She laughed. "Yes, quite."

He knew the stereotype of his profession. Most of his co-workers in the counter-terrorism unit wore that description like a uniform. The young ones with dreams of being James Bond or Jason Bourne fought it, but he'd seen plenty of them resign to their fate. Davin could still run three miles in under nineteen minutes and took fencing lessons to keep in shape.

"Now, let's get to the fox in your hunt." She crossed her legs. "What drags an American analyst from the safety of his cubicle?"

The honest answer would be "ambition," but odds favored she could smell that. "You ever hear of Novaya Zvezda?"

"Former Russian military, radical offshoot of the Russian Refugee Confederation, out to avenge their homeland's devastation from nuclear fallout." She shrugged. "What of them? Last mention I heard was a year ago. They were picking up mercenary work to fund their cause."

"There's a reason you haven't heard anything on them since. They found a sugar daddy."

She blinked. "Pardon me?"

"Basically, they got a corporate sponsor."

"I'd heard they'd disbanded."

Davin's gut clenched as tightly as his fist. He'd suffered through that same counterargument from his supervisor just yesterday. He'd been counting on Stephen being here to help him navigate through the hoops of working in the field. Instead, he feared TeAhna might abandon him before he'd even reached his enemy's target.

"Novaya Zvezda's leader has always known how to work the intelligence community," he said.

"Really? I wasn't aware anyone knew who led them."

"Sergey Bondarenko," he said. "Heard of him?"

She shook her head.

"Former Russian general. Made a name for himself during his country's conflict with Kazakhstan back in 2048. Nuclear fallout finished the job for him but wiped out his homeland, too. Most of the damage he inflicted came from covert ops that didn't require anyone to fire a single bullet."

She held up a hand to cut off his history lesson. "Let's get back to today's fox." She leaned away from him for a glance outside their carriage. "We're ten minutes from Nine Elms, so favor the abridged version."

Great. Ten minutes to figure out if he was breaking into this power plant alone.

"A little more than a year ago, one of Bondarenko's right hand men took a job handling private security for Tolliver Rigney. Rigney's father bought up most of the plutonium mines back when the world decided to abandon nuclear technology. He gambled the family fortune on people tiring of the antiquated power sources and returning to nuclear power. He didn't bank on the development of plasma technology. Ate a bullet when Tolliver was sixteen."

"Let me see if I can connect the dots." She sported a cocky smile. "You think Rigney is funding these terrorists out of some mutual interest which involves undermining plasma technology. I've heard the notion that the rise in plasma energy failures— rolling blackouts, faulty plasma sphere gun ammunition, and plane crashes—is an elaborate smear campaign against the technology. My agency has written it off as whimsical conspiracy theories."

"It's no conspiracy theory." He tried not to grit his teeth. "This is classic Bondarenko strategy. 'Let your enemy undermine itself,' is one of his idioms of war. The so-called experts who claim plasma tech is flawed are all funded by grants from Tolliver Rigney. Bondarenko also has his own ax to grind against the Plasma Energy Consortium. Before he went underground to form Novaya Zvezda, he denounced the consortium for undermining recovery efforts to clean up Russia's contaminated soil."

She didn't say anything to that, offering nothing but a sideways glance at him.

"You look unconvinced," he said.

"Why Nine Elms? I would have expected you to take us to Lancaster House."

At least she was up on the current headlines. "The Energy Summit that starts today at noon?" He waited for her nod before he continued. "That's why I'm positive Bondarenko will make his move here in London—today. Nine Elms operates on a massive plasma generator. If it blew up in the same fashion as the power systems in the recent plane crashes, it would take out all of London."

That grabbed her attention. Pity his supervisor hadn't seen it the same way.

"Lancaster House is just two miles from that power plant. The very experts arguing in favor of plasma technology's survival would be killed by their own creation. The headlines alone would sink the industry."

"And the plutonium mines Tolliver Rigney inherited would regain their value with a potential return to nuclear power."

"Exactly," he said. "Who do you think is sponsoring this summit?"

"Rigney?"

"He's put his enemies exactly where he wants them."

TeAhna tapped her teeth with her fingernail as she considered it. "You lack any physical evidence to support your theory, I assume, or you wouldn't be here."

"No, just facts that fit together, but if I didn't believe it, I wouldn't have come. I'm risking my career going into the field like this." His supervisor had told him to go home and take a week off to get his head on straight. Hopping a plane to London would change that to something more permanent.

She pointed at him. "You're trying to make your career, Davin. I've seen your type in my agency."

"And you know Stephen trusts me, or he wouldn't have asked you to help." He just hoped she trusted Stephen as much his friend trusted him.

She tapped his leather bag, sitting on the floor of the carriage, with her foot. "Please tell me you have more in there than documents and a clean pair of underwear."

He opened the bag and pulled out his plasma sphere handgun, wrapped in grey cloak fabric. "I'm certified as a sharpshooter with it, too."

"You ever use that while being shot at by an enemy?" She raised her hand to cut him off. "A real enemy, not part of some training exercise."

"No."

She clicked her tongue against her teeth in a sound of disapproval. "You will follow my lead then."

At least she was still with him. He just hoped he wasn't picking the wrong day in his life to play the lottery.

• • •

An ornate iron fence surrounded the entrance to the power plant at the end of Cringle Street. Most of the structure's images Davin had studied during the past few weeks had been satellite photos. Except for the four smokestacks, none of which were smoking, the drab brickwork gave the facility a look more akin to a prison, complete with a guard house at the front gate.

TeAhna exited the carriage first. "Pay him," she said without a backwards glance. She fumbled through her purse as if she expected him to come up short on cash.

Davin counted off the pounds, then followed TeAhna.

A large guard stepped out to meet her. He wore a tired, grey jacket which buttoned down the front, not that he was able to button it all the way. A rifle was slung over his shoulder. He stood on the opposite side of the fence as if the barrier granted him power.

"Can I help you two?" The guard's eyes focused more on the top edge of TeAhna's corset. What Davin assumed was a cockney accent grated against his ears. People actually spoke like that?

"We're here to see the plant supervisor about an urgent matter." TeAhna continued to dig through her purse, issuing a curse or two. Davin wondered what was so important that she was still rooting around for it.

"Sorry, no visitors allowed today." He spared a glance towards Davin, but went back to TeAhna's bosom.

"No, I have a letter from the supervisor somewhere in here."

Davin did his best to cover his confusion. Letter? What was she talking about?

She pulled out a piece of paper and held it out for the guard. He had to reach through the fence to take it from her, and the instant he did, she removed her other hand from the purse. Davin caught a glimpse of her weapon's black grip and golden gears. Two curved pieces shot out of the sides and wrapped around the guard's wrist.

"What the——?" Before the guard could pull back, a loud sizzle sounded from the cuff. His entire body went rigid, convulsed, then collapsed.

"Are you insane?" Davin grabbed his gun from his bag, not even sure if he should aim it at her or the downed guard.

"That is not the real guard."

"But how can you——?"

"The jacket doesn't remotely fit; it clearly belongs to another man. That is a plasma sphere rifle, which no civilian guard would be permitted to carry in England, and that was the most pathetic attempt at feigning a British accent that I've ever heard." She opened the gate, her gun drawn and went straight for the guard house.

"Don't touch him. I've set it to repeat the shock with any movement he makes. You're of no use to me on the ground beside him."

Davin kept several feet between him and the fake guard.

TeAhna entered the open door of the white guard house. "Poor man."

Someone had shoved the real guard beneath a desk and stripped him to his undergarments. His face and chest were charred from plasma burns. "Shot at close range," Davin said.

She knelt beside the real guard and checked for a pulse. "Must have set their guns to low power for that," she said. Close range shots risked damage to the weapon being fired and even the shooter. "Perhaps fortune will favor us, and they'll forget to reset their weapons to full power."

"There's a good chance they'll leave them turned down." Davin knelt beside the guard house, using it as cover between him and the main building. He turned one of the dials near the middle of his gun's barrel. "They don't want this place to explode before noon, so they'll be cautious until they decide they're out of options. We should do the same."

"Valid point." She adjusted the dial on her gun. He noticed it was an older model with plenty of scratches to the casings.

"You ever been inside this place?" he asked.

"No." She ran across the courtyard to the nearest entrance.

Davin kept a few paces behind her. If anyone shot at them, he didn't want to be close enough for one sphere to finish the job. He hoped the fact no one had attacked them yet was a sign they'd gone unnoticed. Then again, a shootout in the courtyard was guaranteed to draw attention, and the terrorists didn't want that.

Steps led up to a pair of grey double doors. TeAhna held up a hand for him to wait. Her face tightened as she placed her ear closer to the door, listening for movement. The stress enhanced her natural beauty. Davin reminded himself to focus. There would be time to flirt later, but only if he kept his wits about him.

She gestured for him to follow and pushed the door open. The inner workings of the power plant drowned out what little noise the door's hinges made.

Even though she couldn't possibly know where she was going, TeAhna chose which turns in the hallway to take without a second wasted. He'd heard other field agents, the better ones, speak of this. Never focus on your doubt, just focus on the mission and move with certainty.

The hallway led to another set of metal doors, labeled with bold, black letters: Plasma Core. A low hum sounded from the other side.

TeAhna crouched by the doors and waved Davin closer. "I hear voices in there. Don't recognize the language, but if I had to guess…" She quirked her brows.

"Russian," he said.

Gun in her right hand, she held up her left. Two fingers, then three, and after another moment, four. Just great. At least two-to-one odds, and Davin wondered if he really counted as one.

TeAhna gestured with her hand, indicating her plan for how they should enter the next room. Davin nodded that he understood and prayed he hadn't misinterpreted any of it.

She flung the door open, gun raised, and darted to the left, Davin to the right. His eyes took in the details like a list of notes for one of his research assignments: large plasma sphere core in center of room, multiple pipes attached to the core's base like a circulatory system, three corpses on floor, five gunmen gathered in front of the sphere and three more working the gears on the far left of the room near a desk up against a large cluster of pipes.

TeAhna fired first. The opening shot nailed a short, broad-shouldered man near the sphere. His rifle clattered to the floor as the shockwave of her shot knocked down two of his comrades.

"Oh, hell." Davin sprinted for the nearest cover he could see, praying the terrorists had their rifles still set low. If so, these pipes might survive a few shots before they burst.

He aimed low, going against all his training, fearful his shots might miss and hit the sphere, doing the terrorists' work for them.

Waves of heat from near-misses chased Davin as he ran through the cover of the coolant pipes. If they'd been at full power, the spheres would have been close enough to singe him. One pipe didn't survive the volley. Metal shrieked as it split open. Plasma fluid hissed out like liquid light.

Davin paced his shots, careful not to damage the pipes, but also to save his ammo and not overheat his gun. A lucky shot hit the rifle that TeAhna's first victim had dropped. The weapon detonated, taking out two of the other terrorists. The others had already scattered.

Davin made it to the far side of the room, placing the massive plasma sphere between him and the exit. One of the Russians shouted orders, and two of the soldiers aimed their rifles at Davin. He ran, feeling safer as a moving target. A sphere to the Russian leader's head, which Davin assumed TeAhna had fired, cooked the life out of him in a blink, his death cry cut short.

The two soldiers ran for cover. They divided their fire between where Davin had been and the direction of TeAhna's shot.

Davin hid behind a large tank of what he assumed to be water. How many gunmen were left? How severe was the damage to the Plasma Core? Where was TeAhna?

Names and surveillance images filled his memory as he associated his working knowledge of Novaya Zvezda with the men he'd seen. The one with his head charred had been one of Bondarenko's lieutenants in the Kazakhstan conflict. One of the two who'd just shot at Davin was a bald-headed, bearded mercenary named Dima Nikifor. He chastised himself. Did the names matter now? He needed something to help him survive this gunfight, not random intelligence trivia.

"Dima! Bondarenko has abandoned all of you!" Davin kept moving as his shouts went unanswered. "He knows our intelligence agencies have discovered your plans. Even if you get out of here, you'll never make it beyond the blast radius!"

"Filthy, lying dog!" Dima's voice, directly behind him, sent Davin diving for cover. Their guns fired, but neither hit the intended target. A third party's plasma sphere nailed Dima in the chest.

Someone ran up on Davin to his left. He turned, gun aimed,

but then pointed it safely at the ceiling as he realized it was TeAhna. "Bloody idiot!" She grabbed his arm, pulled him to his feet and back behind cover.

He thought to explain his logic: Dima's history indicating he'd once hunted down a fellow mercenary to kill him for bailing on him during a mission. There was also his family history. Dima harbored serious abandonment issues. TeAhna appeared certain he'd been nothing but stupid, and he wasn't sure she was wrong.

"How many more?" he asked.

"At least two."

They worked their way over to the desk, where the group of three men had been working when the gunfight started.

"Some kind of bomb?" TeAhna canted her head towards something attached to one of the pipes. Her eyes stayed focused on the room around her, though.

He studied it, a square device with three chemicals in glass cylinders. Two chemicals were clear, the third resembled liquefied gold. He didn't recognize the design, but the way the gears clicked in their patient rotations hinted at a countdown to something.

"Most likely." They'd placed it on the main coolant pipe. As he looked around, he saw more on the pipes feeding into the sphere. The plasma would overheat like the rounds fired from his gun until it reached ignition temperature. No more sphere; no more London.

TeAhna grabbed him by the arm. "Move!"

A shot blasted through the air where they'd been standing, burned through the wall and kept going. They'd reset their guns. At that power level, the heat from a near-miss could kill them just as easily as a bull's-eye.

Davin spotted the gunman ducking around the far side of the massive sphere core. They fired after him, but not close enough to take him down.

"Go left," TeAhna said. "We'll surround him."

"What about the other one?"

"Just keep your eyes—"

A plasma sphere burst through her chest. The blast hurled her across the room. Davin ran and fired blindly in the direction of TeAhna's killer. The smell of her cooked blood invaded his nostrils. His heart pounded in his chest, terrified he might die seconds behind her. Even as he hid behind the nearest junction of pipes, he saw the body of TeAhna's killer splayed on the floor—killed by a lucky shot.

Just one more, and he was home free. All the doubts he'd harbored about his ability to work in the field bubbled to the surface. TeAhna was dead because of him, and if the remaining terrorist in here didn't kill him, then he'd die with the rest of London.

"Dammit!" He clenched his free hand into a fist, fingernails digging into his palm. The pain steadied him.

"Your friends are dead!" Davin's voice boomed through the core room. He fought down the quaver in his voice, thinking back to how the pilot had sounded when he'd landed here less than an hour ago. He had to do better and poured all his anger into his words. "You've wasted your time! These bombs will never detonate! Even if you kill me, I already have a squad en route to disable them."

To his surprise, the lone Russian answered. "And you are a fool!" His voice echoed in the large space, making it impossible to identify where he was. "Even if I fail, your scientists will die!"

They had a back-up plan. Davin's mind raced through the data, trying to anticipate their scheme, but he squashed those thoughts. Survival came first.

"To hell with this."

Davin ran back to the bomb on the main pipe. A magnetic plate on the base of the device kept it in place. Would removing it cause it to detonate? He looked over at the desk and saw a clipboard. The back was metal. He slid the clipboard between the bomb and the pipe, his eyes darting over the room for any sign of attack.

He picked up TeAhna's gun, avoiding her vacant stare, and slid her weapon through his belt in case he needed the extra fire power. His opponent didn't come here to die. If he had, then he would have shot the power core's sphere by now and completed his mission kamikaze-style.

Davin set the bomb next to the double doors, the only exit that he'd seen. Time to play his gamble.

He turned the dial on his gun to full power. When he made his move, he needed to convince this guy it was time to run from the crazy American.

Davin sent several shots to the far side of the sphere, hoping to drive the Russian out the other side. His foe returned fire, but the counterattack landed nowhere near Davin. This guy was just as panicked as Davin was. The realization bolstered his confidence.

He took cover in a corner near the front of the room, giving him a clear line of sight for the doors and the bomb. Footfalls echoed, moving fast.

The glow of the sphere cast long shadows throughout the room. Davin saw the terrorist's silhouette fall on the double doors and shot at the bomb he'd planted there. The chemicals in the explosive ignited, sending fire and gold-hued smoke outwards. A wave of hot air punched into Davin's body and slammed him back against the wall.

He shook his head, restoring his senses enough to get to his feet. He peeked around the pipes to see the body of the last terrorist on the floor. The metal clip from the clipboard was buried between his eyes. Davin hoped the explosion didn't damage the equipment in here. That would be just his luck to kill all the terrorists and then finish the job for them.

Then he remembered what the terrorist had said. This wasn't finished. Bondarenko had a back-up plan.

• • •

Before leaving the power plant, Davin collected the bombs and tossed them into the Thames. He pulled his watch from his pocket, which had somehow survived being jarred in the gunfight. It was almost eleven o'clock. He needed to reach Lancaster House on the other side of the river.

Once he made it to the main road, he flagged down a cab. The horse-drawn coach's driver had to repeat his question asking where

Davin wanted to go. His ears were ringing from the bomb.

As the driver sped him to Lancaster House, Davin emptied the ammunition from TeAhna's gun. His fingers shook as he loaded the plasma spheres, which resembled small capsules in their dormant state, into the clip of his weapon.

"Keep it together." He repeated those words to himself, a desperate mantra.

His mind's eye went back to TeAhna's body. He'd put her in harm's way, but he couldn't think on that. He needed to figure out what he was riding into. Only minutes separated him from Lancaster House and another possible gunfight.

Rigney had funded the energy summit. His private security, headed by one of Bondarenko's men, would be in control of the site. Bondarenko wouldn't sacrifice his men, though. Novaya Zvezda was not so large in numbers that he could afford that kind of chess play. The security would most likely be local, civilians hired just for this event. Davin could exploit that.

The driver pounded on the roof of the carriage. They'd stopped.

Davin looked out the window. They were on the Mall. He saw Buckingham Palace at the end of the road, just beyond a tall fountain adorned with golden angels. Several other buildings lined the street, mostly obscured by trees and tourists.

"Which is Lancaster House?" he asked as he paid the cabbie. The gent pointed to a beige stone structure with a vibrant green lawn to his right.

Delegates for the summit were already filing through the front gate. He forced his way to the front of the line.

Three guards were working the gate. One wore a set of x-ray goggles with mirror lenses that hid his eyes. He pointed at Davin, the goggles having discovered his sidearm. A tall guard in a black suit and tie put himself in Davin's path. Davin noticed the butt of a handgun in a shoulder holster as the guard's black jacket shifted. "Sir, you'll need to surrender your weapon." There was no mistaking the authentic British accent for this one. That confirmed Davin's theory about the local security.

"I'm Agent Meercroft." Davin adopted a subtle accent similar to the one TeAhna had sported. He'd once heard the Southern accent was the closest to the British and hoped that would help him pass for a local. For good measure, Davin flashed the badge he'd lifted from TeAhna's purse. Thankfully, the identification hadn't included a photograph. "I need to speak with the head of your security." He kept his voice low but firm. "There's an imminent threat to the summit."

The guard studied the silver badge. Davin struggled to maintain his composure as he waited to see if this guard believed his charade. The guard's eyes widened as he whispered, "MI-6?"

"I need to speak with your superior," Davin said, "now."

"Yes, sir. Follow me."

Davin kept a step behind the guard and fought back the nervousness that demanded he engage in small talk. He wasn't sure he could maintain the fake accent for very long.

"I'm Constantine," the guard said as he led Davin across the lawn which was occupied by the summit's delegation, a parade of well-dressed men and women. More guards were posted at the doors to the building. They were also armed with handguns, the traditional bullets and gunpowder variety, unlike Davin's plasma sphere design.

"Wait here, please," Constantine said, then whispered to one of the other guards. "He's MI-6."

Davin maintained his silence while he waited. This location gave him an ideal position to observe everyone on the lawn and within the drawing room. He'd done his homework on Novaya Zvezda before coming to London, but he didn't recognize any members of the terrorist group in the crowd. His stomach, empty save for a tight-fisted knot of nerves, distracted him.

Constantine returned with an even taller man who was bald.

"I'm Captain Tennant. What's this business about then?"

Davin reminded himself to use the fake accent but not to overdo it. "Less than an hour ago, our agents stopped a group of terrorists from setting off an explosion at the Nine Elms power station. We believe they've planted a bomb here, too."

"I already have a three-man team searching Lancaster House. They started their last sweep a few minutes ago." He shrugged. "We've found nothing out of sorts, thus far."

"Does this building have a back-up generator?" Davin considered this during the ride here. Killing the scientists with a bomb wouldn't undermine plasma technology, merely turn them into martyrs, but if a plasma-powered generator were to "malfunction" and explode, that would do the trick.

"I believe so." Captain Tennant turned to Constantine.

"Yes, sir, in the basement."

"Excellent." The captain smiled at Davin as if this should somehow satisfy the matter. "Our team is down there now."

"Your team? Who picked these men?" Davin tried to conceal his disdain. The captain reminded him of his boss.

"They're independent contractors, hired separately by Mr. Rigney's private security."

That set off alarms in Davin's head, even if the captain didn't find it odd.

"Are any of them a white male, five-foot-eleven, with blue eyes and a scar running down his left cheek like this?" He traced a line with his fingertip down his own face, nose to the back of his jaw. One rumor suggested Bondarenko got the scar from a landmine. Another blamed it on a Moscow prostitute.

"Yes, that would be Mr. Clark. He's in charge of their team. Why?"

"His name," Davin caught himself about to slip out of the accent, cleared his throat and continued, "is Sergey Bondarenko. He's a known terrorist and most likely sabotaging the back-up generator to explode."

"Sir, should we alert the palace?" Constantine asked. At least one of these guards was connecting the dots.

The captain rubbed his scalp as if he might squeeze his thoughts out more quickly. "Bloody hell, please tell me the Union Flag is flying."

"Sorry, sir, it's the Royal Standard."

"Curse it! The King couldn't be in Windsor today?" Sweat rolled down the captain's brow. That's when it occurred to Davin that Rigney probably hadn't hired the best security for this event. He had to take control somehow.

"Captain, if you want to notify the Palace Guard, then I could take a few of your men to search for Bondarenko."

The captain shifted his gaze from Davin to his officers. "Very well. Yes, I'll alert the palace. Find those men, and detain them."

The captain marched out the door. Davin was tempted to tell him he might want to run but thought better of it. The task of notifying the Palace Guard kept him out of the way, and the void left Davin an opening to take charge.

He turned to Constantine. "Lead me to the backup generator."

"Yes, sir." He slapped one of the other guards on the shoulder. He was a slender man with a bushy beard. "Come on, Simmons."

Constantine led them to a side room which appeared to have been converted into a temporary security office complete with the bitter scent of coffee. They went through another door to the basement stairs.

The lower level was lighted better than Davin expected. Unlike all the work to preserve the classic décor of the upstairs, the basement had been treated to a modern, utilitarian makeover. Light grey walls helped spread the light. Exposed pipes ran along the ceiling reducing what little headroom existed to a claustrophobic level.

Constantine turned to the right. "End of the corridor."

Davin let the two guards go first. Bondarenko might realize Davin wasn't with the security detail and get suspicious. This close to the big boom, these terrorists wouldn't play things subtle.

Davin tapped Constantine on the shoulder and whispered. "Just tell them there's a suspicious briefcase in the conference room and that Captain Tennant wants it checked. If they don't fall for it, they won't hesitate to kill us. They make any suspicious moves, we shoot to kill."

"Good advice," Simmons said.

They reached the end of the corridor. Constantine nodded to let them know he was opening the door.

Green light from the generator spilled out as the door slid open. Three men stood around the device, a slender tube with a small sphere in each end and cables running from it up into the pipes along the ceiling.

One of the three men stood tall and looked from Constantine to Simmons. "Is there a problem?" The voice was deep, layered with the rumble born from years of smoke and hard-living, which made it difficult to conceal the Russian accent: Bondarenko.

Davin fought the urge to go for his gun. It would have been easier to come in guns blazing, but the small chance Davin might be wrong had rendered that option unacceptable. He kept his hands free, but ready to reach for his gun at the first hint that this would go south. Things went downhill fast.

Simmons drew his gun and fired, but not at the terrorists. The bullet went straight into Constantine's temple. Then Simmons turned for a shot at Davin and shouted, "He's MI-6!"

Everyone's guns came out. Unlike Simmons, Bondarenko and his men were packing plasma sphere guns. TeAhna's earlier question echoed in Davin's thoughts as he took aim and fired. You ever use that while being shot at by an enemy?

The temperature in the cramped space spiked as the energized spheres burned through the air. Chunks of debris exploded from the walls and floor. The blasts deafened Davin, drowning out all else with an ephemeral note that wouldn't stop.

As fast as the volley began, it ended, and it took Davin's mind a moment to process all that happened in that brief exchange. Their bodies littered the floor. Simmons' unblinking eyes stared at nothing. Davin's first shot had sliced straight through his heart. He should have realized Bondarenko would place one of his men among the hired detail.

The gunfire that followed that fatal shot to Simmons took out the two with Bondarenko. Davin had dropped to the floor. He wasn't sure if he'd done it on purpose or fallen.

He stared down the barrel of his gun and met the hard stare of Bondarenko's blue eyes. The Russian general's body shook. One of the plasma spheres had seared off his left hand.

"MI-6?" Bondarenko's voice lacked the quaver of his body.

"CIA, actually." Davin kept his gun aimed at Bondarenko.

A weak laugh, laced with blood, coughed its way over Bondarenko's lips. He spoke in his native tongue, which Davin recognized after a moment. "You're just a boy. How fitting."

The Russian crawled towards the generator.

"Don't move," Davin said.

"Or you will kill me?" He laughed again, more blood spilling onto his chest. "The future has been trying to kill me all my life. This world does not favor warriors who harbor love for what is past."

Bondarenko reached towards the generator. Davin saw an explosive, a twin of those planted at Nine Elms, attached to the device.

"I said don't move!"

Bondarenko glared at him. "I choose my end. Not you, boy."

He reached for the bomb. Davin fired. The plasma sphere struck the center of his chest. The old man slid back several feet from the generator. His body jerked a few times and then relaxed with a low hiss from the hole in his chest.

• • •

The twenty-four hours that followed were occupied with a hospital visit and many opportunities for Davin to recount his tale to MI-6. He didn't try to lie, despite the more incriminating portions of his story. He'd impersonated an MI-6 agent, defied direct orders from his supervisor and smuggled a firearm into a foreign country. Spies and their governments could forgive many things, but they never granted amnesty to liars.

After the Brits decided they didn't have any business with Davin, they delivered him to the U.S. Embassy. Once there, he was placed in a chair outside a big, wooden office door with a pair of guards who didn't place any value on conversation. The silence made the half hour he spent there last even longer.

"Mr. Cross?" A man wearing a black dress coat, vest and tie, stood in the open doorway. "I'm Ambassador Morgan. Would you join me?"

"Ambassador" was a fancy way of saying he was an Agency field director, a common practice among all spy agencies.

Davin hobbled his way into the office. A near-miss from the gunfight inside Lancaster House had burned his calf. Morgan waved off the guards before closing the door. Davin hoped that was a good sign.

Morgan pointed Davin to a less-than-comfortable chair in front of his desk. "You've had a busy few days, haven't you?"

"Are they going to be my last in the CIA?" Davin asked.

"No, they won't." Morgan smiled. "I've been asked to extend the president's gratitude for your actions."

"I noticed the Brits are covering up what happened." The morning paper didn't mention the shooting at Lancaster House or the attempt to destroy the Nine Elms power plant.

"The president and Britain's prime minister agreed to it," Morgan said.

"People need to know that plasma technology isn't flawed. They need to know the truth."

"What people need is progress," the ambassador said. "In the past, society became complacent with energy from limited and dangerous resources. People need to strive for more. These terrorists might have harbored ill intentions, but that doesn't mean we can't use their actions to do something positive. We need to push for better methods of fueling our technology."

"Nice sales pitch." Davin recognized policy-speak when he heard it. "Write that one yourself?"

"No, the Secretary of State's office gets that byline."

"So people won't be told." His pride stung more than anything else. "What does that mean for me?"

Morgan smiled at Davin from behind his desk. "It means

no parades for you—sorry, but you will be rewarded. The CIA is assembling a special counter-terrorism task force called Delphi which will have our analysts and field agents working closer than ever."

Analysts. They were sending him back to a cubicle.

"Mr. Cross, we need someone in Delphi who can speak both languages, someone who can do the analysis and lead in the field."

"Me?" Dear Lord, did he hear that right? Not only were they freeing him from his desk at Langley, but they were promoting him!

"Unless you've decided field work isn't for you."

Davin had waited seven years for this opportunity. He knew he might one day forget why he'd wanted it, but he'd never free his thoughts of TeAhna Meercroft. The scent of her burned blood and the pained expression she wore into death were painted onto the canvas of his memories.

She died to give him this chance.

"When do I start?"

"Crossfire" was originally published by Flying Island Press as part of their FlagShip Special Steampunk Issue in October 2011.

ZOMBIE WALK

Gidion Keep took advantage of a simple truth every night he hunted: people see what they want to see. To the passersby on Richmond's streets, he looked like a teenager in a loose-fitting, grey hoodie. They didn't notice the weight of a box cutter in one of his zip-up hoodie's front pockets nor the bulge of a short wakizashi sword strapped to his back.

They didn't see a vampire hunter.

He used to not see vampires like everyone else, but Grandpa taught him how to spot them. Vampires looked human enough with only their fangs for the giveaway. There was more to them, though. They didn't move like a human, just as a wolf doesn't prowl on all fours the same as a dog.

After hunting and killing almost a dozen vampires in the past few months, Gidion couldn't miss the nightwalker making his way down the steep sidewalk along Richmond's Main Street. This one knew how to blend in with the after work crowd. His black trench coat hung open, revealing a pale blue button-down dress shirt and a red tie.

Gidion didn't bother to cross the street. Even at 6:30, the one-way traffic was too crowded for a quick dash. Wouldn't be much point in it either. He couldn't just attack the vampire here, even if this wasn't the most well-lit section of downtown. The front sign to the Capital Ale House heightened the pale skin tone of his target. He wasn't surprised when Red Tie went inside the restaurant. Everything about this location made perfect sense for a vampire.

The bar here attracted plenty of singles, even on a Thursday night. The parking in downtown sucked, but this restaurant provided parking in a garage just around the corner, the direction from which the vampire had come.

Gidion had parked a little more than half a mile away in a lot beneath I-95. He liked that spot, secluded but close to a lot of the nightclubs. He'd shoulder-carried more than one kill to his car there. He wasn't going to get away with that in this location, though.

After a moment to consider his options, Gidion ran for it. If he didn't push himself too hard, he could still get to his car and move it to the parking garage in less than fifteen minutes. Any vamp that could smooth-talk some victim into leaving with him that quickly deserved his meal.

Most of his run took him past brick and glass office buildings, so he didn't deal with too much foot traffic. People driving home from work late held him up when he had to cross streets. By the time the clock tower of the Main Street train station and I-95 overpass came into view, he'd built up a good sweat even with the late October weather dipping into the forties at night.

He hopped into his grey Kia Soul and floored it.

The parking garage to the Cap Ale was cramped. Even with all the lights, it provided a secluded location for an ambush. Gidion circled the lot, trying to decide where a vampire would park to abduct someone. That was one of Grandpa's lessons: think like the thing you hunt.

The dark corner of the lot stood out. Even though the blue Rav4 wasn't the usual car of choice for a vamp, Gidion saw the perfect set up. The rectangular columns of the garage blocked any view from the street, even if there weren't many cars parked here. Tiny shards of glass crunched beneath the wheels of Gidion's car. The vampire had shattered the light closest to the Rav4.

The only thing that troubled Gidion was the car being so far from the entrance. What if the intended victim was parked closer? The vampire needed a way to get dinner to the Rav4.

Gidion parked a few spaces from the vampire's ride. He'd learned the hard way that a vampire could recognize the scent of another vampire's blood, and he'd carried too many kills in the back of his Kia to mask the odor.

He removed his keys from the ignition and cracked the door open, switching the interior light to stay off. Staying focused while he waited had been easier when he'd first hunted. He found that much more difficult now. Being idle let his mind wander to one of his best friends who died just a month ago, and more than ever, his thoughts went to the mother he'd barely known, killed when he was just four. He didn't realize he'd pulled his rabbit's foot from his pocket and started fidgeting with it until he saw the vampire run into the garage.

Gidion lowered himself in the seat. What the hell was this vampire doing? Had Gidion done something to tip his hand? Surely the stench of vampire blood from his car couldn't be that strong.

The vampire stopped by each car, going to the driver side doors. He leaned close to the door handles and sniffed. This went on for about a minute that felt like an eternity and brought the vampire closer to Gidion's car until he was two cars away, sniffing a green Ford Festiva. Gidion slid his rabbit's foot back into his pocket and pulled out his box cutter. Palms sweaty, he extended the blade. He'd hoped to catch the vampire too distracted with his own victim to recognize he was prey as well.

Red Tie took a second sniff of the Festiva's door handle and then jerked back. He cracked a smile that didn't hide his fangs. He ran for the back of the Rav4 and jerked it open. The rear door blocked Gidion's view since it opened more like a car door, hinged on the side instead of the top. When the vampire went back to the Festiva, he had something similar to a small screwdriver in his hand. He knelt down next to the rear tire for a moment, but Gidion couldn't see what he was doing. As he waited and watched, he realized Red Tie wasn't wearing his trench coat, just his dress shirt and tie. The predator must have chosen his victim and was setting the rest of his trap. He threw the screwdriver-like item back into the Rav4, slammed the rear door shut and ran out of the garage.

Gidion looked back at the Ford Festiva, trying to figure out what Red Tie had done, then realized the driver side of the car was getting lower. The tire was going flat. Gidion got out of his car, deciding it was safe to check out what the vampire had done. No way the vampire was going to lure his victim from the restaurant to the garage that fast. Gidion couldn't find a hole in the tire as he felt around its curve for where the air was escaping. Then he realized what happened; the valve stem was missing.

With the time he had left, Gidion checked the Rav4. Pulling open the rear door, he saw why the vampire liked this car. The floor mat was pulled back to reveal extra storage space in the trunk with only a pair of handcuffs in it. Great place to stash a snack with two feet or for hiding from the sun if the car broke down on the side of the road. Sure as hell wouldn't be comfortable, but comfort wasn't the vampire's concern here.

Gidion went back to his car and waited. He kept his car door cracked open.

He hoped the vampire would be back in a few minutes, but the jerk kept him waiting for an hour. In the time he'd waited, he could have gone inside and had a burger or something.

Laughter let him know it was time for kickoff. Red Tie stumbled into the garage. His arm was draped around a stick-thin guy with skin even paler than his and wearing a purple shirt with a grey tie. Purple Shirt stumbled much worse, but then again, Red Tie was faking it. Vampires ordered from a menu made up of just three letters, and straying from it could make them sick.

They stopped just before the Festiva. Red Tie pointed to the flat. Purple Shirt hunched over, hands on his knees to get a better look and then cursed.

Gidion couldn't make out what Red Tie was saying, but he saw him point to the Rav4. They walked to the vampire's car. Rather, Red Tie walked. Purple Shirt still stumbled. The vampire checked his surroundings. Gidion kept low enough to avoid being seen. He couldn't see anything as low as he was, but he knew what he was waiting to hear, the rear door of the Rav4 being pulled open.

That's when Red Tie and Gidion made their moves.

The vampire grabbed the back of his victim's neck and slammed his head against the left edge of the open door.

Gidion rushed out of his car, the door having been left ajar to make as little sound as possible. Purple Shirt shrieked, but a punch from the vampire silenced him just before he was tossed into the back. Gidion slammed into the open rear door of the Rav4, smashing it into Red Tie and sending him to the ground.

The move stunned the vampire. The myths didn't get much right about the dark gifts of the undead, making these monsters grander. They fed on the blood of the living to gain immortality and gained quick healing powers, fangs, and heightened senses, but that was about as far as it went. No super strength, no hypnotic eyes and no transformations into bats or wolves would save this bloodsucker. What made vampires appear so strong was that they didn't have a conscience, so they didn't hesitate when they attacked a victim.

As long as Gidion didn't hesitate to hurt them, that evened the playing field. He pressed his advantage. He caught the vampire off-balance, in the middle of getting back onto his feet. Gidion kicked him in the face. The sneaker's sole probably didn't hurt as bad as a boot would have, but the concrete ground to the back of the vampire's head knocked him dizzy. Parking garages offered so many unforgiving surfaces. He maintained his assault, pounding the vampire's head against the ground. The vamp made it back onto his feet at one point but was so unsteady it didn't stop Gidion from flinging him into the side of the Rav4.

Gidion glanced around to make sure they were still alone, drew his sword from his back and then finished the deed. The sword chimed as the blade met the concrete, by way of the vampire's neck.

Gidion couldn't slow down, though. He grabbed the vampire's head, ran to the back of his Kia, and tossed the head into the back. The head was the important part. According to Grandpa, an old enough vampire could survive a beheading if the head got reattached, but cremate the head and the body was worthless. The beheaded body required a lot more effort. Red Tie wasn't a lightweight. As Gidion dragged the vampire's headless torso to his car, he heard the man in the purple shirt groan from the back of the Rav4, the rear door still partially open.

At least the guy was still alive, but Gidion didn't plan to check on him. Secrecy was his best weapon, according to Grandpa. He'd learned the hard way just how true that was.

Gidion wasn't heartless, though. As he pulled out of the garage onto 6th Street, he grabbed a cell phone from his glove compartment. He had a lot of spare cell phones, thanks to the vampires he'd killed. Most of them were disconnected, but they didn't need service for Gidion to make this call.

"Richmond 911, what's your emergency?"

"I just saw a guy in a purple shirt get beat up in the parking garage for the downtown Capital Ale House. You'll find him in the back of a blue Rav4. Probably needs an ambulance."

He hung up and turned off the phone. If the cell was still active, then the cell phone company could potentially plot his location. Turn it off, and he was as good as a ghost.

He dug out his actual cell. That he was still working with a dumb flip phone while his prey used smart phones really sucked. Dad needed to join the 21st century. Having a phone with all the bells and whistles of an iPhone would be kind of useful for hunting vampires, not that he could use that argument. Even though Dad knew about vampires and had hunted them in his younger days, he'd flip if he had a clue what Gidion was doing. At least the phone worked. Grandpa answered his call on the first ring.

"You still sitting in that parking garage?" Grandpa required him to check in every hour. Part of the deal.

"Headed to the funeral home." He paused to make sure the lane was clear as he merged onto the Downtown Expressway. "I got one for the cremator."

Grandpa laughed. "Damn, boy! Not even nine o'clock."

"Yeah, this guy practically fell on my sword for me. See you in a few."

As he hung up, he glanced at his speedometer, making sure to keep it right at the speed limit. He'd been pulled over once with a dead vampire in his trunk. He didn't plan to repeat that experience.

Was just as well he'd snagged Red Tie early. He'd already done his homework, but he had a World History test and needed some more time to study and sleep so he wouldn't be a zombie in class.

• • •

Gidion's best friend Seth reached out with his arms, a blank look on his face and a loud, long moan bellowing from his throat.

The display earned more than a few laughs from people in the school courtyard. Most students at West Chester High preferred to avoid the cafeteria. Even with the weather turning cooler, Gidion and his friends preferred this spot. The courtyard was divided into a few circles of benches with bushes providing an extra barrier from any wind.

"That is such a pathetic effort." Andrea slapped Seth's arms as he turned them towards her. "I expect better from my boyfriend." She was still laughing, though.

Moments like this, Gidion felt a bit like a fifth wheel. Not that he didn't have a girlfriend, but she'd moved from Virginia to Arizona a few weeks ago. It helped that Andrea didn't annoy him like she used to. He'd made the mistake of joining her and Seth for a movie the past weekend. The movie part was fine, but when they went to a coffee place afterwards, he wished he'd driven himself instead of being held hostage to lovey dovey eyes as Andrea clung to Seth.

"Hey, I do an excellent zombie." Seth stuck out his tongue.

"You do an excellent cliché zombie. Leave the dance of the undead to a professional." She pointed to herself with melodramatic flair. "Pity you have to work tomorrow night. I think you'd get a kick out of all the costumes. Besides, who's going to take my picture if you're not there?"

She'd been pestering Seth to get Saturday night off all week, ever since she found out this year's Richmond Zombie Walk was going to be at night for the first time.

"Sorry, my boss already said there's no way. Besides, I gotta get date money somehow."

"Oh, good Lord." Gidion held up two fingers in the shape of a cross to ward off the mushiness. "You two are gonna put me in a diabetic coma."

Andrea scowled at him. "You'll live, Gidion Keep."

"Assuming she doesn't eat your brains," Seth said around a mouthful of ham sandwich.

She adopted this mock thoughtful pose as she considered Gidion. "Well, he does have a good one. Got the highest score on our World History quiz earlier this week."

Gidion made a little bow. Andrea was one of the only freshmen in AP World History and typically ruined the grading curve, but he'd been giving her a run for the money.

The herd of students in the courtyard was starting to shift and thin. Gidion checked his watch. "Seven minutes and 34 seconds before class."

Seth laughed. "What? No count for the milliseconds?"

"Hey, I have this timed out to a science. As long as I leave this spot at precisely three minutes and 23 seconds, I can make it to my desk in World History class right at the bell."

"Well, then you've got a full four minutes to spare." Seth tossed the last bite of his sandwich into his mouth, balled up his lunch bag and swooshed it into the trash can.

"He's just making sure we have time for this." Andrea grabbed Seth to place a kiss on his cheek before making a playful bite at his throat followed by zombie groan. "Later, teddy bear."

Gidion faked some gagging sounds to mock them and earned Andrea's stink eye before they headed towards their class together.

"Why don't you come to the Zombie Walk?" Andrea asked.

"Sorry, can't say that dressing up like a zombie is my thing."

"Exactly, you can take my picture while I'm walking down Cary Street with the other zombies."

Gidion knew about the annual Zombie Walk in Carytown but hadn't gone to it. He'd never been that into zombies, so the idea of dressing up like one along with dozens of others and shuffling in slow motion for more than a mile down a crowded sidewalk wasn't his idea of a fun Saturday night.

"You can't get one of the other zombies to do it?"

"No, the people in the walk aren't allowed to break character."

"I'm not sure I can go. My dad is off tomorrow night, so he's probably going to plan something." He was already irritated that meant he wouldn't be able to hunt this weekend. Dad's overnight job in Henrico County's 911 center made it a bit easier for him to get out of the house at night to hunt, but when Dad was off, he couldn't get away with it. "He's all about doing the father-son thing when he isn't working."

"Well, pooh." Andrea let it drop as they walked into class. Test time.

• • •

Dad was asleep when Gidion got home that afternoon. It was always a bit of a crapshoot which way Dad would go on his Fridays. Sometimes, he'd try to stay up and just go to bed early that night. This was one of those "get home and crash" days by the looks of it. Their dog Page was even cooperating, not barking at every kid walking down the street. That it started to rain during the last class of the day helped. No one was staying outside to make any noise to offend the German shepherd mix. She lounged on his bed as if she owned it, having pushed the blue comforter into a round pile for her pillow. She shifted her big brown eyes to look up at him and lazily licked her snout as if to dare him to make her move.

"Oh, chill out, dog. You can stay put."

He flipped the sign on his bedroom door knob before shutting his room. The sign was a picture of a blue police box with the words "The Doctor is in" above it. This had started as a bit of a joke to let Dad know when he was home, even if his door was closed.

Turning on some tunes at a level that wouldn't have Dad coming in to kill him, Gidion got to work. School stuff could wait since it was now the weekend. This was the time for some intelligence work. Most vampires he ran into these days were nomadic, living out of their car and with everything about their lives contained in their pockets.

He pulled the manila envelope from his desk drawer where he'd left it last night. Red Tie had a rather nice black leather wallet, thick with credit and debit cards. They identified him as Joseph A. Carroll, Morris Elliot III, Carlton Webster, and even Sally Mae Stephens. The Montana driver's license matched Morris, but only God and the ashes in Granpda's funeral home knew whether this was a fake ID.

On the plus side, the wallet had plenty of cash in it. Grandpa paid him a solid hundred for any vampire he killed and let him keep any of the cash in the pockets. In this case, that was a nice haul, adding almost five hundred dollars to his reward. Gidion didn't want to think how many victims Red Tie had gone through to build up this stack of bills. He'd noticed some vampires preferred to stick with cash, though. Stolen credit cards carried a risk some vampires didn't want to take, even if the nomads didn't stay in one place.

Morris "Red Tie" Elliot was rockin' the latest iPhone, lucky bastard. Fortunately, this cell didn't require a code to access it. Not a lot of apps on this vampire's cell, but he had one for his email. Gidion tapped the blue and white icon. He started with the most recent messages. The subject of the emails made him sit up even as his stomach twisted.

The subject was two words: "Zombie Walk."

• • •

Gidion called Grandpa as he was leaving his house Saturday night for Andrea's place.

"Wow. You managed to answer your cell phone."

His Luddite elder grumbled over the background sounds of a bar. "Mind your manners, brat. You picked up your 'date' yet?"

"Very funny. Yeah, I'm on my way to Andrea's now. I take it you're in place already?"

"This place looks like a damn fruit bar."

Gidion shook his head. He knew better than to argue the point.

Gidion had taken a perverse pleasure in suggesting he wait in the Burger Bach restaurant on the edge of Carytown. If everything went according to plan, he'd need Grandpa close to pick up his kills for him.

"Just understand this, boy." As Grandpa yelled over the crowd around him, Gidion was forced to pull the phone back from his ear. "You're only getting half your pay for this one if I gotta do all the heavy lifting."

"Fine. Whatever." Gidion rolled his eyes. "I'll call you later."

He reached Andrea's house a few minutes later. Her place didn't look a thing like he expected. Somehow, he'd always imagined the Templeton house being some fancy affair. When Andrea had given him the directions, she'd promised he couldn't miss it but refused to explain why.

Now, he got it.

The single-story house was a rancher made of faded brick, and it was all decked out for Halloween, which was less than a week away. The Templetons had more than a dozen jack-o-lanterns placed strategically on their property. One even doubled for the head of a massively creepy scarecrow placed in the middle of the front yard. Fake spider-webs were placed all throughout, joined with the flash of orange and green Christmas lights. Perhaps the most extravagant touch was a noose covered in fake blood hanging from a tree sitting on the corner of the property. A skeleton in an orange prison jump suit was placed on the ground with the skull on its side a few feet away, as if the corpse of a hanging victim had decomposed to the point that the head rotted off and the body dropped to the ground.

He parked in the driveway and made a quick check of his weapons. He wouldn't have a private moment after this. This must have been the fifth time he'd done inventory since getting ready to leave his house. Even though the sun was still out, he was already jumpy about tonight's hunt.

Red Tie had been exchanging email with two other nomads. These clever boys had learned about the Zombie Walk and decided to take part in it, not for the fun of dressing up but for the rare chance to feed in public view without anyone being any the wiser. Even Gidion had to admit there was a certain brilliance to it. The more he considered the task of identifying these vampires hiding among the zombies, the more he realized he was out of his element. He'd called Andrea to pick her brains about the walk and found himself drafted into driving her and taking pictures. As if this hunt wasn't complicated enough already.

He reached the door, adorned with a wreath made from fake bones. Even with all the dead bodies he'd handled in the past few months, he found himself squeamish as he reached inside that bony circle to use the brass knocker.

There was movement inside and muffled voices. As he waited, he glanced at the decorations. He bet this place looked freaking awesome at night.

When he heard the door open, he turned to face it and screamed. What lurched out of the doorway sent him scrambling back off the porch.

"Sweet Jesus, Andrea! Is that you?"

She'd dressed up as a zombified Batwoman. As far as Batwoman costumes went, it was pretty good, too. She'd found a black shirt with a red bat on the front. The rest of the outfit, including the mask was all black except for a bright red belt. Her eyes were a brilliant red that made meeting her gaze difficult. The makeup work she'd done to her face was insane. Not only had she powdered her skin white, but she'd drawn around the left side of her lips to make it look like the lips had been rotted off and her teeth were exposed. Her brown hair was hidden beneath a bright red wig of wavy curls, but the right side of the wig was replaced with exposed brains.

"What do you think?" she asked.

The most impressive part of the costume was her right arm. He leaned in close for a better look. The right sleeve of her shirt was ripped off just a little below the elbow, but instead of her arm sticking out of the sleeve, there were two bits of blood-stained bone that looked snapped in half. He reached out to touch the pointed edge of one of the bones where it looked like her forearm had been ripped off.

"How did you do that?"

A hand shot out from beneath her tattered cape and reached for his face.

Andrea laughed as he jumped back again. He fought down a growl and resisted pointing out how close she'd just come to getting sliced with a box cutter.

"Pretty neat, huh? It's actually sewn into the inside of the cape. I just have to keep my arm hidden behind my back." She spun in a circle to give him the full show.

"That is just freaky." He had to admit that he was impressed.

"Thanks!" Her usual chipper voice seemed so wrong coming from something so creepy. "My mom was in theater in college. Still does a lot of costume work for the Barksdale."

"So, this is the Gidion Keep I've heard so much about." Andrea's mom stepped out from behind her, and there was no missing the relation. Aside from a few more pounds and wrinkles, Andrea's mom had the same face shape and straight, brown hair. Andrea could have been her younger clone. Her mom smirked as she looked him up and down as if privy to a joke he'd missed.

He played nice, though. The way Dad had grilled him about being polite and saying "ma'am" and the like to Andrea's mom, he'd acted as if Gidion was going on a date. He'd pointed out to Dad several times that this was Seth's girlfriend, not his, to which Dad had simply replied, "Uh huh… Right."

At least Gidion didn't have to meet her dad. Andrea's folks were divorced, same as Seth's. He got the impression that common ground had helped the two of them get close much faster than they might have otherwise.

Fortunately, his visit to Planet Awkward ended quickly, and they were in his car heading past the various strip malls along Midlothian Turnpike.

"Sorry about my mom," Andrea said as he took the ramp onto the Powhite Parkway. The sun was near the horizon, the sky a canvas of contrast with the dark of night on the eastern half and bright red and orange hues in the west.

"No worries. My dad is the same way."

After a moment, he started chuckling to himself.

"Care to share?" Andrea asked, and even though he kept his eyes on the road, he could sense she was giving him that stink eye, which probably would have been even more brutal with those red contact lenses.

"I've never told Seth this, but my car's nickname is 'the Little Hearse.' Started calling it that after I went to work for my grandpa's funeral home." He glanced at the zombie girl in his passenger seat and smiled. "Seems really appropriate, at the moment."

She smiled, which parted the illusion of her makeup, making it look like she had two sets of teeth.

"Ew! Don't open your mouth like that!"

That just encouraged her to keep doing it, and she laughed as he avoided her face.

"You know, that's good luck." He pointed to the red bat symbol on her chest.

She looked down to where he pointed. "My breasts?"

"What? No! I mean—"

She slapped at his hand. "Relax, Gidion. I'm just messing with you."

He unzipped his grey hoodie and pulled it to the left to reveal the red bat on his black t-shirt. "In China, red bats are considered good luck. That's why I wear this shirt whenever I go out—at night." He stopped himself as he realized he was about to say he wore it to go hunting.

"Is that your way of saying you're hoping to get lucky tonight?"

"Dear God, no!" He scowled as he saw her disturbing twin smile again. "You're still messing with me, aren't you?"

"It's not my fault." She crossed her arms, which looked exceptionally weird with a third one snapped off at the forearm sticking out to the side. "You just make it too easy."

They reached Byrd Park around 6:30. The sun had slid away with a half moon left to own the sky. Dozens of zombies were gathered around Fountain Lake like some kind of union protest of the undead and decayed. Those with drinks all used straws to avoid messing up their makeup, even the ones who were drinking from Starbucks cups, steam rising in the chill air.

Andrea left him to register and get checked out by some judges. Apparently, they gave awards for the best costumes, and she was hoping to win one for "Best Pop Culture Theme." The competition looked pretty stiff. As Gidion walked through the crowd, he saw a few people practicing their zombie walk and exchanging pointers. A little girl who was probably no more than three years old with blonde pig tails jumped in front of Gidion and held up her hands as if to claw at him as she let out a loud "Roar!" Her zombie parents apologized and pulled her aside. He overheard them telling her, "No, dear. That's more like a werewolf. You want to groan."

As one of the non-participants, Gidion got drafted by more than one zombie to take a picture. That annoyed him at first, but then he realized this worked well with his plans. Since the walk hadn't started yet, very few people were "in character." Once the walk started, they'd all be walking in lurching zombie style, making it near impossible to spot the two vampires.

Gidion didn't have much to work with. The vampires knew each other well, so they hadn't bothered to say what they'd be wearing or the like. All he knew was that their names were Reggie and Elton.

He passed zombies with exposed brains and guts. One dude had used sausage links to dangle from his stomach like intestines. Some dressed as zombie versions of famous people. He spotted a Lady Gaga and a Miley Cyrus, complete with a large Styrofoam ball painted grey and dragged along by a chain for her wrecking ball. There was Tom Brady in a New England Patriots uniform with the helmet's facemask partially ripped off. Plenty of people had gone the cosplayer route same as Andrea with a Wonder Woman, a movie-version of Wolverine, two Batmen and even a Katniss Everdeen. The most insane outfit was a woman who'd taken advantage of being pregnant to not only zombify herself, but had used a baby doll which was also zombified and sticking out of her belly with arms reaching out for dinner.

"Ew, now that is the best argument for birth control I have ever seen," Andrea said as she caught up with him.

"No kidding." The costumes were so distracting, Gidion found it hard to stay focused on looking for the vampires. He still hadn't spotted them yet, and they didn't have long before the walk was supposed to start. He also had to make good on his excuse for being here and used her phone's camera to snap a few pictures of Andrea in her costume. She hammed it up, going for the heroic pose, cape held out on her "good arm" side, and then switched to zombie mode, reaching towards the camera. He scored brownie points by including the moon in the background of several shots.

Andrea was posting a few of the pictures onto her Instagram feed when a man, dressed like a zombified cubicle worker, stood on a bench near them. He shouted and waved a cricket bat stained with fake blood to get everyone's attention.

"Are you dying to get started?" The bad pun received the appropriate response. He held up his hands to pacify them. "Just making sure everyone gets a chance to practice their groans." That got more laughs than the first joke.

From there, he went through the rules and gave out the awards. Andrea was robbed, with the Best Pop Culture Theme going to the guy dressed as Wolverine. Not surprisingly, the lady with the zombie baby protruding from her stomach won for "Most Disgusting."

Gidion didn't pay much attention to the rest of it, still trying to spot the vampires. Where were they? Had they even shown? Maybe they'd chickened out when Red Tie was a no-show.

The organizer was going over the plans for everyone to drive over to the grocery store in Carytown, the official starting place for the walk. The park was just the pre-walk meet up.

"I'd like to introduce our two victims for this year's walk." The organizer pointed to a man and woman, both in red button down shirts. "As you can see, they've dressed the part of those who are about to die."

Someone shouted "Red Shirts!" even as others went for irony

and thrust their hands high in the Vulcan gesture to "live long and prosper."

Gidion had read the rules ahead of time, so he knew these were the volunteers who would get "attacked" and zombified during the course of the walk. If the vampires planned to take anyone for a snack, then it was most likely going to be one or both of the red shirts.

"All right," the organizer said. "See everyone over in the grocery store lot in less than thirty. We've got a few folks with vans if anyone needs a ride."

Dammit! He hadn't found the vampires. This was going to be a disaster, if he didn't spot them ahead of time.

"Oh, wow! Those fangs are so real looking."

He heard the woman's comment from somewhere behind him. He turned and standing in the admiring gaze of the lady were two guys dressed up as zombified vampires. One of them had gone for a Wesley Snipes version of Blade, complete with trench coat and silver stakes in holders on his hips. The other was a long-haired Brad Pitt take on Louis from Interview with the Vampire.

Surely it couldn't be this simple. Could it?

But one look was enough to know it really was. The smug bastard dressed as Louis even took the woman in hand and gave her a spin like they were on a dance floor. He dipped her and hissed suggestively at her throat.

Andrea leaned close to whisper to him. "Zombie vampires? How lame. As if that would even work."

But it did work. Even with police placed along the route, would anyone think twice when they saw a vampire bite a victim on the throat and the person dropped dead?

That's when it hit him. No one would think twice about the vampires, but if he attacked them in the open, then the cops would be on him in a flash.

"Earth to Gidion Keep." Andrea waved her hand in front of his face. "Let's go, boy wonder."

"Cute."

Andrea rambled about something on the way to his car. He missed most of what she said. He focused on the vampires and saw them climb into an older model, red van.

"Wait." He looked at Andrea in his passenger seat as he cranked the Little Hearse. "What did you just say?"

He pulled back from her red-lensed, stink eye. "I asked if you wanted me to flash my breasts at you while I was walking down Cary Street."

That left him gaping, and his eyes went to the red bat on her chest. "Uh…" Yes, he was looking at the bat. Right.

She leaned closer, as if to target a part of his body to set on fire with her glare. "You weren't listening."

"Sorry." He pulled out and managed to get a few cars behind the van. "Was just trying to decide the best way to get to Carytown." And how to decapitate a vampire in plain sight, not that he could tell her that.

As they followed the cars filled with fake, rotting corpses, Andrea told him what she'd really been saying, which was how she wanted him to take her picture during the walk.

"Hey, I'll get you some good pics. Don't worry." Yeah, right. Not like he wasn't going to be busy with a pair of blood-thirsty killers. How the hell was he going to do this?

• • •

The first waves of zombies were staggering down the sidewalk on Cary Street by the time the Little Hearse parked in the grocery store's lot. Blade and Louis were already in the line to start.

Andrea indulged in a last non-zombie show of excitement, striking a quick two-step dance with her "good arm" thrust skyward. "This is gonna be awesome!"

He grabbed her arm to hold her back, not wanting her too close to the vampires hiding in the parade. Before he could think of something to say, he saw one of the zombies in line trip. The guy had rolled back his eyes for a more vacant look, and with his eyes off the ground, he got entangled with another rotter. Seeing the decomposing dominos nearly tumble gave him an idea.

"Gidion?"

Andrea's voice jolted him back to the moment and his unexplained hold on her arm.

"Sorry, just wanted to let you know I'm going to stay close instead of running ahead and waiting for you. Okay?"

She shrugged, and then lifted the left side of her cape high in a dramatic pose. "Just make sure you get a shot of the whole package at some point."

"Sure thing."

Gidion ran ahead to position himself on the edge of the sidewalk near where the zombies were starting their mass crawl. If he thought these people looked freaky back at the park, seeing them slip into character amped that by a factor of fifty. One woman was keeping most of her weight on her right foot with her left foot kicked out at an angle to slide across the ground. That must have hurt like hell, but you'd never know it by her empty gaze. Watching her move past him covered his arms in goosebumps.

Pulling out Andrea's phone, he snapped several shots, right off. Better to get them now, while he still could. If he ended up empty-handed, he didn't doubt she'd flog him with that fake half-arm of hers.

That he'd delayed Andrea worked to his advantage. Both vampires were only four corpses ahead of her. Ironically, the undead pair were some of the least convincing zombies in the whole parade. The task of keeping an eye on them required him to walk backwards most of the way as he avoided an obstacle course of pedestrians, streetlight poles, trash cans and trees.

The planned course for the walk went down Cary Street for more than a half mile until it reached the Dixie Donuts across from the old Byrd Theater. At that point, all the zombies would switch sides of the street and head west back towards the grocery store lot. At the current pace, this was going to take a long time.

The intersections forced the participants to break character.

Gidion remembered seeing that in the rules he'd read on the Zombie Walk website. Carytown wouldn't shut down for all these people, especially on a Saturday night. The street was crowded with cars and non-zombie, non-vampire pedestrians out for all the food, drinks, and fun that Carytown had to offer.

Blade groaned, a token effort ruined by a smile that mocked the ignorant prey stumbling around them. He reached over and slapped Louis on the arm when the groan didn't get his attention. Gidion noticed a jerk of Blade's head, directing Louis' attention to someone ahead of them. When Gidion followed their line of sight, he realized what was happening. They weren't planning to go after the red shirts. The vampires were targeting the other zombies. The one that had their attention was a woman who looked to be in her mid-twenties, dressed in a dark green, sleek formal dress. Her outfit offered plenty of skin with a v-shaped neckline in the front. If the front was a lowercase "v," then the back was most definitely an uppercase "V." She'd purposefully turned the dress into a tattered mess, stained in fake blood and with plenty of rips and tears. He wondered how much powder she'd needed to get her entire body to look so pale. The only parts of her skin not pale white were the wounds, which were little more than long lines of fake blood running down from a "bite" to her left shoulder.

Despite the amount of skin the Prom Queen was showing, she wasn't the center of attention, not with many more elaborate zombie costumes surrounding her. The important detail was that she was alone. Even in a group of people pretending to be mindless monsters, Gidion could tell she wasn't here with anyone else.

No one was going to miss her if Louis and Blade turned her into dinner.

Gidion got a good shot of Andrea with her phone's camera, but as he positioned himself for the shot, he made sure to place himself near Prom Queen. He checked his surroundings as he saw the vampires push their way closer to their victim. A few shops ahead, he saw a dark gap between two brick buildings. They wouldn't have a hard time sinking their fangs into her on the sidewalk and dragging her into that narrow space.

To the vampires' credit, they at least made token efforts to look like they were shuffling forward, even if obviously doing it too quickly. The awkward walk made them vulnerable to Gidion's plan. He kept Andrea's phone held up as if trying to frame her for a picture. Just as he saw Blade make the first move to reach for Prom Queen, Gidion stuck his leg out in front of the vampire, causing him to trip.

"Oh! Sorry! Don't mind me!" Gidion made an effort to be as loud and obnoxious as possible. He even caught a few of the zombies, unaware of the life-and-death chess match taking place in front of them, break character to look his way. "Clumsy of me! I'll be more careful!"

Blade shoved Gidion in the chest. That almost knocked him down, but he managed to keep himself on his feet. Gidion didn't let that discourage him.

Louis and Blade tried to reposition themselves several times, moving from one potential snack to the next. Gidion got in the way every chance he could and was getting quite artful at it. He didn't even need to trip them. All he had to do was get near the intended victim as they were about to strike and make an ass out of himself by yelling something like, "Oh my God! It's the zombie apocalypse! Run for your lives! Save your puppies!" As long as he drew attention to where the vampires intended to strike, they couldn't risk a move.

The plan was working like a charm. He got them all the way down Cary Street without even a nibble for all their efforts. He was halfway home.

They made it to the Dixie Donuts. Police officers periodically stopped traffic to let the zombies break character and dash across the street to the Byrd Theater. The wait to cross Cary Street created a bottleneck effect and caused Gidion to lose sight of the vampires and Andrea.

The police were taking advantage of a lull in traffic to let a large group across. He spotted the bright red hair of Andrea's wig as she stepped back onto the sidewalk across the street. She slipped back into character to shuffle along the sidewalk at an appropriate zombie pace.

Gidion got held up on the Dixie Donut side of Cary Street. An officer blew a whistle to stop anyone from going across as he surrendered the street back to the cars. As he waited, Gidion looked for Blade and Louis. He searched the group of zombies gathered around him without any sign of them. Then he searched over the tops of the passing cars and spotted both vampires... right behind Andrea.

He stepped off the sidewalk to find a break in the traffic to sprint across the street.

"Hey!" The police officer blew his whistle to run him back onto the sidewalk. "Stay put, kid."

Gidion considered running back up Cary on this side of the street, to cross over where there wouldn't be an officer to stop him, but the sidewalk was choked with too many moaners. He'd have to wait for the officer to stop traffic.

If the zombies hadn't trapped him in place, Gidion would have paced. All he could do was keep Andrea and the vampires in his sights, but despite how slow the undead mob was moving, they were more than halfway to the next intersection by the time the officer let anyone across.

Gidion shoved Andrea's phone into his front pocket and ran for it, but as bad as the foot traffic had been on the Dixie Donut side of the street, the line for the ticket booth at the Byrd Theater combined with the Zombie Walk made any attempt at breaking into a sprint a waste of time. Gidion pushed his way through the crowd and nearly knocked over a half dozen people, including a guy leaning on a falcon head cane and his date wearing a dark red velvet coat.

"Sorry!"

From somewhere down the block, a woman screamed. Gidion abandoned being civil and shoved people out of the way.

He only relaxed a bit when he saw an arm reach up out of the mob. One of the red shirts getting "attacked" and zombified. Witnessing the event, Gidion realized he'd been an idiot to think the vampires would go after the red shirts. The planned zombification drew too much attention, but then Gidion realized what that meant.

All eyes were on the fake attack. If the vampires were waiting for an ideal moment to make a move on Andrea, then the perfect time would be now, with all eyes on the red shirt.

"Screw this." He was never going to catch up to the vampires on this sidewalk.

He ran between a pair of parked cars and onto the street. Cary Street offered little space between the moving traffic and the parallel parked cars. The only thing in his favor was this being a one way street, so he could at least see when he was about to turn into pothole filler. He hugged the side of a parked Prius as a large pickup with tires on steroids rumbled past him. Despite the cars, he was moving much faster this way.

Now, he needed to find Andrea and the vampires.

Once he made it past the red shirt attack, the foot traffic eased. He got back on the sidewalk as he crossed the next intersection and dodged the groaning horde. A couple stumbled out of a gourmet pizza joint. Gidion nearly collided with the lady. She was obviously drunk and screamed when she saw the zombies.

"Move it!" He pushed her aside and ran past her.

His progress stopped as he hit a zombified chain gang, complete with shackles around their ankles. Naturally, they were all as tall as Wookies. He resorted to jumping behind them, mugging for a decent look over their shoulders.

A glimpse of bright red hair and exposed brains crossing Belmont Avenue gave him hope, but he couldn't see the vampires. Had he passed them somehow?

When he reached the intersection, he stepped up onto the narrow base of the street lamp pole. He looked in all directions. No sign of the vampires behind him. A look ahead offered no sign of them either. He was about to hop down when he realized that bright red hair was missing.

A scream came from ahead of him. He jumped down and ran across the street. The zombies were swarming around someone.

He caught a glimpse of the center and saw a man in a red shirt hunkered within the mass using the cover of the undead to apply his zombie makeup.

He realized why they'd chosen this spot. It was right in front of the red brick store front to One Eyed Jacques, a game shop full of customers who could appreciate this kind of costume madness.

He pushed past the red shirt attack. This would be the perfect time for the vampires to take a victim, so where were they?

He stopped just past One Eyed Jacques. He was about to run again when he realized there was a narrow gap between the left wall of the game shop and the grey brick furniture store just past it. The moment he saw it, he knew this was the perfect place for a vampire to drag a victim. How could they resist?

There! In the dark between the two stores, he saw the movement and heard a woman's muffled shrieks. Andrea?

Panic choked him. He abandoned stealth and raced into the thin alley. The street noise, the traffic and Zombie Walk, dropped to a whisper as the musty odor of a space rarely touched by sunlight assaulted his senses.

He drew his box cutter, the space too narrow for his sword.

The vampires heard him, but the confines of the alley worked against them. The closer of the two never even had a chance to turn around. He grabbed Louis by the hair, which he realized in hindsight was luckily not a wig. A hard shove smashed the side of the vampire's head against the brick wall. That knocked the fight out of him for a split second, but it was long enough. A slice to the throat with the box cutter sealed the deal. Not an immediate kill, but the cut went deep enough to make it inevitable even as Louis's hands tried in vain to hold back the rush of blood from his neck.

Blade climbed over the woman and lunged at him. He tripped over Louis. A fast jab at the eyes with the box cutter made him flinch back, putting him off balance. The move worked against Gidion, though. Their bodies collided and they tumbled on top of Louis.

Their fall knocked the box cutter from Gidion's hands. His head cracked against brick as he reached for his weapon. A forearm thrust up against the vampire's throat saved him from getting bitten.

The strike to his head had Gidion dizzy. He couldn't register up or down in the dark. The woman on the ground screamed, drowning out everything else.

Gidion buried his knee into the vampire's stomach. Their bodies scrambled with neither able to get a final advantage.

As Gidion shoved the vampire, his hand gripped something cold and metal near the vampire's hip, one of Blade's silver stakes. It probably wasn't real silver, but it wasn't like vampires really had a silver aversion. Gidion ripped it from its sheath and buried it in the vampire's mouth. A loud gagging sound warned that the vampire wasn't dead, but he tossed about in desperation. Gidion slammed the back of the vampire's head against the wall several times until the fight bled out of him.

Gidion pinned the vampire down. He scanned the ground for his box cutter and found it, just within reach. He grabbed it and delivered the killing strike to the throat.

He pulled his hood back up before he glanced back at the vampires' intended victim. She'd stopped screaming. Now that the fight was finished, he could see it wasn't Andrea but rather the first woman the vampires had targeted, the Prom Queen in the green dress.

"You all right?" He lowered his voice and realized he sounded a bit like his father when he did that.

She answered his question with a shaky nod. The light from the street bounced off her wide eyes. She clung to the wall as she got back to her feet.

"You didn't see anything. Don't call the police, and don't tell anyone anything." He stood. "Get out of here. Go straight home and be glad they didn't kill you."

He kept his head down, hiding his face, as he forced his way past her and ran out the back of the alley into a parking lot. Certain no one was in the lot, he pulled off his blood-covered hoodie and then slid off his sword. He wrapped the sword and his box cutter in the hoodie to hide them from view. He stayed in the back lots all the way to the grocery store. On the way, he called Grandpa and told him where to find the vampires' bodies. As long as Prom Queen did as she was told, Grandpa would be able to retrieve them and take them on a one-way trip to the cremator at the funeral home.

No one gave him a second look as he walked through the first wave of the Zombie Walk to finish the trip through Carytown. He was just a kid in a t-shirt and jeans opening the trunk of his grey Kia Soul. He tossed his hoodie and weapons into the back and pulled out a small, blue duffle bag. The hand wipes helped him clean the blood from his arms and hands. He also kept a spare change of clothes in there. He got in the backseat of his car and managed to change into the clean clothes without anyone noticing.

By the time he'd gotten out of the car and up to where the zombies were crossing back into the grocery store lot, he could see Andrea's bright red wig nearing the end of the walk.

She smiled and ran to him. "That was awesome!" Her voice shrieked as she spun in place. "They're also having a dance downtown, and anyone dressed as a zombie gets in free. We should go!" He could see there was no point in arguing. She was already dancing, and if he'd learned anything about Andrea during these past few months, he knew that once she got excited about a thing, she didn't stop until she experienced it. He was too relieved to see her alive to be annoyed.

"You sure you're up for that?" he asked.

"Absolutely!"

"I'm surprised." He smirked. "You look dead on your feet."

She groaned.

THE INSOMNIAC

I've never tricked anyone out of their money. I just sell a convincing lie.

Before Momma died, she taught her "little girl" all about selling things.

Rule one is simple: never lie, but bend the truth like a stripe on a candy cane.

I see examples all around me. The way my grandma calls me "imaginative" with a nervous twitch to her lips really means I'm weird. When the sales lady at Justice says, "I'm not sure we have anything in your size," it's code for "You look fat." Even when I see the pile of unopened envelopes on the kitchen counter grow and when Dad gets the constant phone calls from automated voices with the bank saying they're calling about a personal matter, I know the bend in my father's reply. "You don't need to worry about it."

What I do doesn't require much of a lie.

I sell people on life after death.

This ain't that angels-singing-and-playing-harps, float-to-Heaven version, though. No, I give them that rotting, groaning, *Walking Dead* immortality.

Don't judge me. When my momma died two years ago, I discovered Dad wasn't what you'd call a bread winner. He's not lazy or stupid, but I definitely got my sly from Momma. Dad mows other people's lawns, which is funny, because our one-bedroom apartment doesn't have a yard.

Dad takes the bedroom. I get the sofa. It's not all that bad, because I can watch TV later than my friends. Also makes it a lot easier to sneak out in the middle of the night so I can earn some cash.

I make my money on Friday and Saturday nights at Hollywood Cemetery.

Nothing sells a product like word of mouth. That's rule number two: build a reputation that'll feed you.

That's how I ended up climbing into Terrell Oliver's black Chevy on South Cherry Street at two in the morning on a Saturday. He's a senior at Manchester High. Short as Lil' T.O. is, you'd never guess what a terror he is on the basketball court. Most guys like him come to me on a dare.

I hop onto the passenger seat and foam pokes out of a cut in the leather between my legs as if it's sticking its tongue out at me. When I look at T.O., I see that reaction I've come to expect.

"Are you kidding me?" he says. "What are you, nine?"

"I'm twelve."

He slides his sunglasses down his nose to make sure I'm not a figment. "You're Madame Absinthe?"

Really? "No, it's just Absinthe." Suppose I shouldn't complain, because that's how most of my "customers" hear about me. My name's really just Abby, but nobody wants to say they went to a girl named Abby to see her raise the dead.

That's rule number three: packaging sells the product.

I'd love to dress in some gothic gown and throw on some eye shadow, but that doesn't work so well tromping through a hilly cemetery in the dark. When I first started convincing people I could raise the dead, I tried to dress like some miniature New Orleans witch. One girl laughed in my face and told me Trick or Treat wasn't until October.

Instead, I keep it simple with a black hoodie over a BLKHRTS t-shirt. Can't say I really like the group, but the t-shirt shows a black heart on the front. I'm not talking some cute heart shape. This looks like an actual human heart. Ew. Still, older kids see it and take me seriously.

The first six months required the most work. I'd hang out at sci-fi conventions and outside nightclubs that cater to the goth crowd.

I even posted flyers with my email address printed a dozen times at the bottom for people to rip one off and take it with them. Then the reputation took over. You wanna see a real zombie, then "Madame Absinthe" is the girl to see.

"I'm still waiting." I pull out my smart phone and wiggle it for him to see the open Venmo app. I do all my business over Venmo. It's social media meets commerce. Nothing makes a teenage boy pay up faster than getting publicly shamed by a "little kid." I once posted a video of a guy running from the grave. That boy screamed like a baby racing back to momma. My giggles in the background didn't hurt the blackmail quality of the video. You bet he paid to have me take it down.

When Lil' T.O. hesitates, I cross my arms. "Seventy-five dollars now and another seventy-five after."

"Let's make it fifty up front." He smiles as if he's doing me a favor.

"Later, Lil' T." I open the door. That's one of Momma's rules, too. Don't hesitate to walk away. The minute they see you're not willing to, they'll yank your chain and drag you around like a dog tied to the back of a car.

That doesn't stop the knot that ties into my empty stomach as I slam the door shut. Most of the skeptics stop me before this point. Once I make it this far, the next step involves the crimson glow of brake lights as they put the car in gear and drive off.

That happened with my first customer earlier this night. My eleven o'clock never even let me make it into the car. They took one look at me, told me to go home, and left me coughing on exhaust fumes.

Dad doesn't even realize I'm the reason our cell phones still work. If he does, then he doesn't want to admit it. The text from the phone company we got earlier today means we're a week away from our phones going dark. Dad needs that phone to find work. If he doesn't get calls to go to people's yards, then it won't take long before we lose the cable and Internet, then the power, and then probably the house.

But I have to walk away, or I might as well not bother doing this "Madame Absinthe" nonsense.

I make it five feet from the car when T.O. climbs out of his car.

"Fine!"

I turn in time to see him shove his car door shut. He rests his elbows on top of the car as his thumbs get to work on his iPhone. Its light bathes his face in a blue glow.

A moment later, my phone chimes with a notification from Venmo. No clue how I stop myself from breaking into a dance. Probably because this isn't enough to pay our cell phone bill. I still need the other seventy-five.

"Let's go." I lead him to a set of cement steps that go down from the sidewalk.

"So, you're like some kind of necrophile?" Lil' T.O. asks as his car's lights flash to the click of his doors locking.

I do prefer the company of the dead, because too many people just turn out stupid like this moron. Just the way he says "necrophile" makes it clear he has no clue what he's really asking.

"It's called 'necromancer.'" If your inner dictionary isn't kicking in, that means I communicate with the dead.

The stairs from the dead end of South Cherry Street end at a locked gate. A flashlight shines against my back.

"Turn that off." I roll my eyes, not that he sees. Hard enough seeing in the dark without some bozo's flashlight ruining my night vision. It's not like I don't send them an email ahead of time with instructions. You wouldn't think a sentence like "No flashlights" would be complicated, but these idiots always bring one or use the light on their phones. "We're breaking into a cemetery. You really wanna bring the cops?"

"You got a big mouth for a little kid."

Oh, I do love the witty banter of the teenager. Are half my brain cells going to commit seppuku when I turn thirteen? If so, I'll stay twelve. Thank you.

"The first seventy-five gets you in the cemetery." A chain with a lock keeps people from opening the gate, but the slack leaves plenty of room. I slip through the gap in the gate and wave for him to follow. He climbs the fence. Winter gloves keep him from cutting his hands on the sharp, metal edges at the top.

From there, we go down this path until we reach the base of a steep hill.

"This better be for real." Lil' T.O. grunts as we're halfway up to the cemetery.

I smell the wet dirt. It sticks under my nails as I climb.

"Don't they have a place you can just walk inside?" Lil' T.O. means the front gate off of Albemarle Street near the office which they never lock.

"Sure, if you don't mind getting caught by the security guard."

The guard is why I wait once we reach the top near Palmer Chapel. The long, flat, grey building sits along the road that runs through the cemetery. Sometimes, the guard's van rolls by right as I make it here, but we're in luck tonight. No sign of the guy.

Lil' T.O. doesn't bother with caution. He walks to the middle of the road before he rests, hunched over with his hands on his knees. "Now where?"

"Now, we need to find someone who isn't sleeping."

I take him the long way, going in circles. The dark makes sure he'll be completely lost by the time I reach the grave I want.

"Do you even know where you're going?" he whispers.

"Yes and no."

Lil' T.O. curses under his breath.

I pass names I've come to recognize as better landmarks than the street signs. There's Ashton and McCarthy. Then I pass the Herndons and Binfords. I'm getting close, so it's time to start my show.

"I know my way around here, but I've gotta find the right body." Even as dark as it is, I see skepticism wrinkle his forehead. "What people don't realize is that we all become zombies when we die, but the dead would rather sleep. I've got to find one who can't rest. He needs to be just hungry enough…"

I stop as I reach the grave. "Oh, looks like it's a 'she' tonight."

T.O. stops just short of the grave and edges his way around the imaginary box where he assumes the casket is buried. The way he leans from the side reminds me of someone looking down into a pool. He turns his head enough to read the flat grave marker.

"Sherrilyn Austin." He frowns at me. "What makes this one special?"

I reach into the dirt and pull up a fistful of earth. Wet clumps slip free as I roll it around in my hand. "This one must walk a lot. Ground is still loose." A glance at our surroundings confirms the security guard isn't near. "A grave where the grass can't take hold shows a troubled soul."

T.O. steps back. "She's only been dead a couple of years."

I nod. "They need to be young. Skeletons can't walk by themselves." I stand and brush my hand off against my pants leg. "Even the dead need something to hold their bones together."

He keeps a straight face as I smile, but I don't miss the way he moves back to the foot of the grave, making sure to keep his feet on the grass. After bringing enough of these gawkers here, I've learned I don't need to ham it up. The more natural my smile, the more they panic.

"You ready?" I lean my phone against a neighboring grave's headstone to capture his reaction on video.

No matter how many times I do this, my body tenses as I sit next to the grave. What if she doesn't walk? The thought alone makes me want to cry, because I wasn't lying about the condition of the body. No matter how much she can't sleep, if the body isn't willing, the soul's desire means nothing.

"I expect to get paid." I glare at T.O.

My threat draws a scowl from him. "This is bull."

"If she walks, then you pay. We clear?"

"Yeah, right." He crosses his arms.

I reach into my hoodie and pull out three chicken bones. I position them in a triangle on the grave. They're nothing special, just leftovers from drumsticks Dad bought for dinner a few months ago. This is another of Momma's rules: never make up a reason for good props. Let your customer watch and make their own assumptions.

I shut my eyes as I mumble what amounts to a bunch of nonsense syllables. I practice this to make it sound natural. The need in my voice? That's not faked, though. I learned after the first few visits, the words don't matter, only the desperation that backs them.

The ground stirs. My skeptical customer stumbles back as a hand claws its way up into the night.

I stop calling. She no longer needs the encouragement. Her hand bursts into the open air. I stand and enjoy the show, not the zombie coming out of the ground, but my customer's reaction.

The dark hand grasps for purchase. T.O. wobbles right to left, looking for the trick, but he won't find any strings.

"You will pay me tonight, or I might send her or another after you."

He doesn't answer, eyes locked on the grave as the second hand bursts free. This one reaches out far enough to reveal the dirty sleeve draped along a withered forearm.

"Are we clear?" I ask.

He screams as the upper half of the body breaks loose. The sight of dirt raining from her torso and her groans send him running with a shrieked promise to pay.

"Baby girl?" Her voice comes out rougher than it used to, and that makes my heart ache.

"Hi, Momma." I hug her as her skeletal arms embrace me. I don't hold her too tightly for fear of breaking her bones. That first night I snuck in here and cried at her grave, Momma answered me.

Her body shudders against mine as she chuckles. "I missed you, Abby."

I look into her eyes and see this is a good night. Sometimes, she forgets how many times I've visited, thinking that night is our first.

The sight of her decay terrifies these teenagers, but the love in her faded eyes keeps her beautiful to me.

"You've gotten so tall." She strokes my cheek with her thumb. "Are you and your daddy doing well?"

My phone, still resting on the nearby headstone, chimes with a notification. I know what it means, and part of me relaxes. I'll be able to keep the phones on, and Dad can find more work.

"Yeah." I rest my head on Momma's shoulder. "We're doing all right."

WAIST DEEP

A trail of smoke in the distant sky gave Dale the closest thing to hope he'd seen since his travels had brought him back into the Ice Lands. He'd lost track of time, so he couldn't say when he'd last seen another man or woman. There were no more seasons to mark the end of one year and the start of the next. The four seasons had given way to the Three Deserts which never changed.

Pain stabbed into his toes with each step. The snow, which came up to his knees, had invaded his boots like a tiny army of daggers. The smoke promised a fire and warmth, so he pushed forward.

Then he heard the howl.

He stopped and readied his rifle. Whatever had made that noise sounded big. Even worse, it had come from the direction of the smoke. He couldn't say how close, though. The forest was full of trees, but they were all leafless timber. Sound travelled like the wind in this place.

His stomach ached, and that reminder of several days spent eating nothing but handfuls of snow pushed him forward. That howl meant food. The only question was which of them would get eaten, him or whatever monster had made that noise.

The sun was moving low, barely visible behind the overcast clouds, when he reached the source of the smoke. He'd hoped to find people and shelter. What he found was disappointment.

Small patches of flame still burned on the bones of what had been a house. Whoever had called this gutted wreck home must have been here a long time. They'd built a wall out of ice. The ingenuity to make the ice bricks impressed him, but it didn't stop whatever created the gaping hole in the wall. Four men lined up shoulder-to-shoulder could have walked through that opening.

He waited with his rifle in his hands behind the trunk of a large tree. Whatever creature had cried out earlier, it had stayed silent since. Chances favored it was busy gnawing on the former occupants of the cremated house. A trail of red dotted the snow heading north from the opening in the icy fence.

Deciding he was alone, Dale trudged through the snow to the opening. Up close, he couldn't decide if the tracks belonged to one large animal or many smaller ones. He wasn't sure which was worse, and "animals" was being optimistic. About the only thing man shared the Desert of Fire with were the Wraiths. Only the sky and the dead homeowner knew what creature had spontaneously spawned from the ice in this place.

He'd hoped there might be enough of the house left to give him a place to stay the night, but that hope died fast. The house's charred skeleton didn't look likely to survive the night. Sunset was minutes away. He wouldn't survive the night without a fire, but the light might call back whatever had ruined this place. The chimney still stood, like a middle finger salute to the gods and the home's destroyer. He decided to take his chances and use the fireplace for its intended purpose.

As he came closer to the chimney, he realized there was fresh smoke coming from its top. A faint glow emanated from the mouth at its base. The warmth called to him, and he ran the rest of the way.

He expected to find a fire, but the only thing that occupied the inside of the chimney was that warm glow. The light was coming from below the ground.

The floor of the house had burned away to reveal a stone foundation. If there was a lower level, then he didn't see a way to it through the stone. Against his feet's wishes, he stepped back into the snow and circled the foundation. He found a door leading down into the ground on the far side of the chimney. It had to be a storm cellar. The house where he'd grown up had one of these. When the earth tilted, his family had survived the first few weeks in it. As the oceans and land masses shifted, they'd been forced from their home.

Only within the past few years, at least he assumed it had been that long, did the world seem to settle.

Dale slung his rifle over his shoulder to free his hands. He touched the door and was shocked to realize it was made of metal. The builder must have found it somewhere near here. An entire city might be hidden beneath the snow in this mountain range. The surface of the earth was rewritten too much to know where any nation or city had stood.

He pulled the door open and jumped back in time to avoid taking an arrow in the chest.

The unexpected attack sent him sprawling into the snow. He scrambled to get his rifle back in his hands, but he knew he didn't have a chance. "Stop! Wait! I'm human!"

Two figures darted up out of the ground and stared down at him along the shafts of their drawn arrows.

"It can talk?" the smaller of the two said.

The big one next to him didn't say anything. He just held his bow and arrow ready with a pair of arms as thick as some of the tree trunks in this forest.

"Please, don't." Dale gave up on his rifle and held up his hands in a show of surrender. "I'm not an 'it.' I'm human, same as you."

"If you're human, then why is your skin so dark?" The smaller one seemed to be the only one who did any talking.

"You never seen a black man?"

"What's a 'black man'?"

Wasn't that just his luck? These ignorant hillbillies were probably going to kill him. The only thing that had kept him alive this long was that they spoke the same language.

"Listen, I'm human, same as you. I just have a different skin color. I'm guessing you ain't ever seen any Latinos either?"

The confused look on their faces answered that. Actually, only the small one looked confused. The big guy didn't seem to know any expressions beyond dull intensity. Despite the difference in size and demeanor, they looked a lot alike, down to the same scraggly, red beards. Probably a safe bet they were related.

"I'm just looking for some shelter for the night," Dale said. "Wasn't expecting to find anyone in there, not with the state of things up top."

The quiet one looked at his little brother and shrugged. Nice to see there was a brain in there, even if he didn't say much. The small guy nodded, and they lowered their arrows.

"What's your name?" the little brother asked.

"I'm Dale. You two?"

"I'm Tor." Then he pointed to his big brother. "This is Zalm."

Zalm offered a hand and yanked Dale up.

"Just you two?" Dale asked as he picked up his rifle and slung it over his shoulder.

Neither answered. One look at Tor said it all. They were it, as of a few hours ago.

Dale pointed to the cellar's open door. "Why don't we go inside, get warm, and—"

A howl echoed from the North. He didn't need to say anything else to get them back in the cellar. Wasn't the biggest space, especially with "Paul Bunyan" in there, but then it definitely wasn't built for comfort.

"You boys build this?"

Tor busied himself with the fire. "Our parents built it. Mom was a construction worker before the world broke."

That explained a lot about the place. Dale wished he could've seen it before everything burned. Now that he wasn't worrying about getting impaled by wooden arrows, he realized these two guys looked young. They probably were born after the world shifted.

"Where did you come from, Dale?"

"Texas, originally." The blank look on Tor's face was a mirror of Zalm's and added to the family resemblance. "I've been all over. Was born just five years before everything went to shit. My parents stuck mostly with the ocean, but my stomach never took well to life on a boat."

Tor stared at him with wide eyes. "Is it true? The stories about the leviathans?"

"I've only seen one. Was on a boat that was part of a small fleet. What I saw looked like a sea serpent. Split the biggest ship right down the middle. Only two ships out of five got away. Crew of the ship I was on mutinied, killed the captain and sailed for land." He decided it might be best to leave out the part where he shot the captain in the back of the head with the same rifle that was in his lap. "Ship wrecked on some coral a mile short of the coastline. My parents didn't survive that. Only a handful of us reached land. We must have landed smack in the middle of the Desert of Fire. Damn well-named place, too."

Tor offered him a water skin. Must have thought he was thirsty by the way his voice cracked. Just the memory of that place roasted him.

"Man came through here about a year ago," Tor said. "Claimed there were creatures made of flame. We weren't sure whether to believe him. He wasn't a good man."

"Desperation can make a man do bad things."

"He hurt our mother." Tor didn't need to say more than that. His tone said plenty. Dale remembered more than one man getting tossed overboard for trying to force himself on a woman.

"Well, he wasn't shittin' you. The wraiths live in the lava. One climbed out of a pool right in front of me." That was the last night he'd seen any of the shipwreck's survivors. They scattered when the wraiths attacked. In his dreams, he still heard the wraiths' wails, the sound they made when they chased him up the rocks. For all he knew, he was the only survivor.

Dale took another chug from the water skin and handed it back to Tor. "Barely any water to be had down there. Had to drink my piss just to stay alive long enough to get out of that place."

Tor glanced down at the water skin with a sudden look of disgust. "Here." He handed it to his brother, who didn't seem to share his apparent concerns about backwash.

"Anyway, was a long time ago." A howl to match the feeling in his soul sounded from beyond their hidey-hole. "So what is it you two have planned? You gonna rebuild or you gonna move on?"

Tor looked up at the cellar door.

"Gonna kill it." Wasn't Tor who spoke, though. That answer came from the big guy, Zalm.

"Damn, didn't think you could talk."

Zalm didn't answer. He took a chug from the water skin and gave it back to his brother.

"He can talk." Tor put the water skin away. "Just doesn't make a habit of it."

"So what was it that tore through here?" All Dale could think was how much food a beast that big might provide.

"We didn't get a good look at it, but it had black fur." Tor stabbed the logs with a poker. Fire was fine. The boy was probably hiding his tears. "Was as big as the three of us combined. Mom and Dad had gone hunting. She didn't come back. Dad said it killed her. He got us in here just as it broke through the fence. Dad slammed the door shut to save us."

Dale pointed at the bows and arrows they'd propped against their chairs. "You really think you can take down something that big with those?"

Tor didn't answer. Zalm shrugged without a hint that he had any doubts.

"Haven't seen much food up here." Dale's tone made it clear he was making a proposition.

Tor looked back at him and crossed his arms. "There aren't a lot of animals, but Dad taught us how to hunt what there is."

Dale patted his rifle. "Let's just say this baby has some serious punch, lot more than those arrows you're using. If I help you kill that thing, you willing to split the meat?"

The brothers exchanged a look. A shrug from Zalm settled their silent debate.

"All right," Tor said. "We'll head out in the morning."

The thought of meat warmed Dale almost as much as the fire as he went to sleep.

• • •

Keeping up with those two boys about killed Dale. His clothes weren't as well-suited for the snow, and the brothers weren't half-starved. Their parents had somehow carved out a life in this place. Killing this thing wasn't just about a single meal. Dale needed to convince these boys he was worth keeping around. He wasn't dumb enough to think he could survive in this place by himself. His rifle had caught more than one meal since coming into the Ice Lands, but his ammunition wasn't limitless. Unless he found a fresh supply of ammo, he was going to starve. He'd already considered taking his chances back in the Desert of Fire. At least that place had some lizards a man could kill for food.

A clear sky helped. They'd been spared any fresh snow overnight, so the tracks were easy enough to follow. Dale just had to keep up with these two kids who were keen to pay back the thing that killed their parents. That they kept going uphill didn't help.

About midday, they stopped. Dale had fallen behind, so he was glad to have a chance to catch up. The two kids weren't resting, though. Something had them bothered.

Dale planted the butt of his rifle into the snow and held onto the barrel while he caught his breath.

"What's the problem, juniors?"

Tor pulled off a knit cap and wiped some sweat from his brow. "No feeding site." He pointed to the tracks in the snow. The spots of blood had stopped, so he guessed their dad had either run out of blood or maybe the blood had frozen. The drag marks were clear enough.

"What's that mean?"

"There's no sign that it stopped to feed." Tor hesitated on that last word.

Dale was too tired to put his brain to work. "So why is that bad?"

Big dude Zalm answered. "Feeding babies."

"What?"

Tor put his cap back on. "We're worried it's dragging the body back to its lair. If it's doing that, then it might be to feed babies."

"In other words…?"

84

"We might be dealing with more than just one of these things."

"A pack of giant, black-furred monsters." Dale hung his head down. "Well, on the bright side, that's more food for us. Who knows? If they're young enough, maybe we can try to domesticate them, cultivate a herd."

The quiet one's eyebrows pushed together as he stared down at Dale. He didn't need Tor to translate the look on his brother's face.

"Yeah, I know, but it's fun to dream." Dale groaned as he stood straight. "So what are we thinking here? We calling it quits?"

Tor glared at him, his body shaking with his anger. "Are you scared, old man?"

"Hell, yes." Dale laughed, but there was no hiding the edge of fear behind it. "We're talking about a bunch of big, hairy monsters! If you aren't scared, you're a damn idiot."

Zalm grunted, his gaze shifting between the two of them. With a simple roll of the eyes, he walked between the two of them and continued to follow the trail in the snow.

"We've sacrificed more than half of our daylight." Tor shook his head. "Too late to turn back, and there's no adequate shelter between here and our homestead. We have to move forward."

Tor followed his brother. Dale leaned on his rifle and took a deep breath. He'd allied himself with a pair of teenaged maniacs. What was worse was that it really was too late to turn back.

• • •

The path turned steeper and moved into the mountains. All feeling had fled Dale's feet, and his face, wrapped in a long scarf, felt as if it might crack if he touched it. Muscles ached as he struggled to keep up with the hell-bent youths.

To make matters worse, snow started falling. Their clear trail in the snow was vanishing. Dale realized that even if he did try to turn back on his own, he'd be lost. The sun was hidden behind the clouds, and the brightest part of the sky was vanishing behind the taller mountains to the west.

"I'm gonna die following these fool boys," Dale muttered to himself. He tasted blood coming from his chapped lips.

The only good news was that the brothers had stopped again. Tor waved for him to catch up. What the devil did this boy think he was doing, looking for a good spot to do snow angels?

Tor took a few steps towards him and shouted over the wind. "There's a cave, a little higher. Spotted it earlier, before the snow started. If we can make it there before sunset, we can—"

A howl shook the mountain. Tor raised his bow and arrow. Dale drew his rifle.

"Goddammit! How did it get behind us?"

"It must have circled around to trap us." Tor canted his head for Dale to get behind him. "Follow Zalm. We have to make for the cave."

Dale didn't move. "What if the cave is this thing's home?" He searched through the snow for something to shoot, but all he saw was a shifting veil of grey. Their visibility was little more than twenty yards.

"Doesn't matter." Tor walked backwards, not bothering to wait for Dale. "We're too exposed out here. At least the cave might give us some cover."

"I'll bet its last meal thought the same damn thing."

Dale didn't try to go backwards. He'd fall on his ass doing that. He turned and ran, not that it was much of a run. He was fighting uphill with half of his legs sinking into the snow with each step.

A low growl vibrated through the ground. Dammit, it was close.

The only other thing Dale heard was his panicked breaths. His heart pounded, and his chest ached. He cursed God for his life in one thought, and with the next, prayed for Him to save it.

A crosswind struck him from the east. The same snow that slowed him also saved him from falling, but he had to stop to regain his balance. Tor struggled past him.

"Here! Hurry!"

Zalm's shout was answered by the unseen beast's growl. An arrow shot past Dale and Tor and into the void behind them.

Dale looked over his shoulder. A shadow loomed behind them. A second arrow flew into that dark shape, and a sharp roar of pain and rage ripped through the descending night.

He turned, pressed the butt of his rifle into his shoulder, aimed and pulled the trigger.

The shot thundered loud enough to drown out the wind. The shadow retreated, disappearing without any hint as to which direction it had moved.

Tor shouted after him. Dale couldn't decipher what the boy was saying. He just responded to the urgency in his voice and ran for the cave. The black maw in the mountain's side beckoned. Just before he reached it, a light flared within the black.

The light revealed Tor's shape by the edge of the entrance. His bow and arrow were held ready. Dale ran past the boy. As soon as he made it inside, his feet betrayed him. He fell on his back and slid deeper into the cave. How he managed not to crack his skull open, he didn't know.

When he stopped sliding, he realized the floor of the cave was a flat sheet of ice. He wondered how that could possibly occur naturally.

He whimpered as he rolled over to get back on his feet. The brothers guarded the cave's entrance. Their breath trailed into the darkness beyond. A torch, which Zalm must have lit, was stabbed into a pile of snow.

Tor's head bobbed as if searching for a different line of sight to help him see the monster hidden in the snow. "Did you hit it?"

"Not sure." Dale fumbled with the rifle. He dug a shell from his bag and loaded it like a blind man without thumbs trying to play "Pin the Tail on the Donkey."

As soon as he loaded the shell, a black shape shattered through the opening. The beast slammed right into Tor and dragged the boy deeper into the cave with him. Zalm fell without shooting an arrow. The torch skidded across the ice. Somehow, it stayed lit. Dale shot at the dark shape. The blast deafened him.

His shot missed. The entrance, weakened by the monster's

arrival and Dale's stray gunfire, collapsed.

Tor gasped under the weight of the animal. Blood ran down from his mouth and a wound hidden beneath the beast's paws on his chest. The creature snarled at them, giving Dale his first good look at it.

The shape of the thing resembled a wolf, but even on all fours, it was taller than Zalm. Wet, dark fur covered most of its body. Its stench was less like a wet dog, and more akin to rotten meat. Mange had reduced the right side of its face and snout to open wounds coated in bloody, pale yellow puss swimming with maggots. The eyes didn't match. The left was big with a yellowish-brown iris that seemed perfectly natural for a beast of this kind, but the right was more like a human's with a small, pale blue iris floating in a sea of white.

The eye resembling a wolf's exploded into a bloody mess. One of Zalm's thin wooden arrows buried deep into its socket. The shot didn't kill it. The beast yelped, but didn't retreat. Its massive body lunged at the larger brother.

Zalm didn't get a chance to shoot another arrow. The collision of their two bodies shattered his bow. The string snapped with a comic "boing."

Dale scrambled to reload as he ran to Tor. The boy wasn't as bad off as he'd looked. The cuts to his chest looked superficial. The blood coming from Tor's mouth gave him a manic look as he stared dumbstruck at the battle between his brother and the beast.

The two slid across the icy floor. Zalm's left hand held onto its throat by a thick patch of fur. The giant wolf's rear paws scrambled back and forth, unable to get a good footing on the ice with Zalm's weight keeping it off-balance. The beast shook its head, but the boy refused to be shaken loose.

Dale forced his attention back to his rifle and kept muttering the same two words to himself, "Shoot it."

Tor launched a volley of arrows. The slender shafts stabbed into the wolf's side. They drew blood, but they didn't slow the wolf's assault on Zalm.

Dale hesitated. The wrestling was too chaotic, and he didn't trust himself not to shoot Zalm. He needed just one opening.

Zalm punched the side of its face with his free hand. The repeated strikes made a sickening squishy sound as his fist smashed into that diseased flesh. A strike to the semi-human eye startled the animal, and gave Dale his opening.

He pulled the trigger, felt the kickback into his shoulder and watched as the side of the wolf's throat burst open. Blood sprayed out, but the wolf wasn't finished. Zalm lost his grip. The beast bit down at Zalm's head. Blood covered the boy's bearded face, and it was difficult to tell how much of it was his own.

The wolf's grunts and growls turned to a gurgle as Zalm's thick hands grabbed the top and bottom of its snout. He screamed and the muscles in his arms shook as he stretched the snout open far wider than its jaw was ever meant to. Bones cracked. A desperate sound bubbled out of the wolf's throat and then went silent as the jaw surrendered with a loud snap to Zalm's strength.

The mangy corpse collapsed on top of its killer.

Tor ran to his brother. He screamed his brother's name, but Zalm didn't answer.

Dale retrieved the torch, which had somehow managed to stay lit through all this. He carried it over to where the others were. Tor was struggling to shove the beast off of his brother, but the corpse wouldn't budge. He was about to offer his help, but as he brought the firelight closer to Zalm, he saw it was too late.

The side of the boy's throat was ripped open. Blood flowed out in a tiny stream and joined the tributaries coming from the wolf's to form a red, frozen lake around their bodies.

"Tor." Dale touched the boy's shoulder, but he jerked away from his hand.

"Help me get it off!"

Dale stepped back. "He's gone." He lowered the torch so that the flames were closer to Zalm's face and that open wound. The eyes were empty, the body too still.

Tor screamed and pounded at the side of the beast that had

robbed him of his family. Dale wanted to say something to help, but there weren't any words for it. He'd taken it little better when his parents died. How many times had he asked himself if his parents might have lived if only he'd stood by their ship's captain instead of blowing out his brains? If they'd had the captain, could they have avoided that deadly crash on the reef? He'd never know.

Death never made sense to those left behind.

Dale left Tor to work through his grief. He raised the torch for a better look at the cavern. No sign of any giant wolf cubs. He didn't see the bodies of Tor's father or mother either. They didn't find the body while following the wolf here, so what happened to it?

A groan echoed through the cave. Dale looked at Tor. The boy's sobs had stopped, and he was turning in a slow circle, looking just as confused as to what had made that noise.

Tor drew an arrow. Dale shoved another shell into his rifle, none too simple a task with a torch in one hand.

Could it be the wind? He looked back at the collapsed entrance. It was sealed. Then they heard the groan again, as if someone was straining to do something.

"That doesn't sound like an animal," Dale whispered as he walked back to Tor's side.

Tor pointed to the far end of the cavern, a place where their torch's light hadn't reached. As they drew closer, the light reflected off the icy surface to reveal a narrow passage.

Dale led the way with the torch. Only after they were deep into the tunnel, did he realize he should have let Tor go first. If they ran into trouble, he couldn't shoot his rifle and hold the torch at the same time. Nor could Tor shoot past him.

Nothing to do now. All they could manage was to press forward and pray nothing attacked.

The grunting grew louder. Whoever it was sounded in pain. Was it possible this was Tor's father? Could the man actually still be alive? Dale didn't dare voice the hope for fear of being wrong. Instead, he moved faster to get to the source of the grunts. More than once, he nearly fell on the icy floor.

The passage widened into a vast grotto. The ceiling was so high, he couldn't see it. There were several other tunnels scattered throughout the space. The walls were all ice carved into a variety of images. One resembled a snake and another a wolf. A third image contained fire in the rough shape of a man.

The strangest thing was in the center of the room. A man.

He wore nothing from the waist up. The man's muscular, bare back was to them. The skin, riddled with scars, was so pale that it blended into the cave. Long black and grey hair flowed down just past the shoulder blades. Pained grunts continued as the body jerked slightly. His movements suggested something encumbered him, and as more of the torchlight reached the man, Dale realized the bottom half of his body was missing. No, not missing. Closer still, and he saw what this truly was, a man trapped in the ice from the waist down.

Just before Dale could think to say anything, a loud scream came from the man in the ice. He was hunched forward, as if trying to pull himself free. Something snapped, and the noise reminded Dale of how it sounded when Zalm had split the wolf's jaw apart. Then a rip formed through the man's body where it touched the ice. Flesh and bone snapped and cracked but didn't bleed.

The strain in his cries heightened as his body cracked in half. The top half pulled free from the bottom, but no blood or foul matter spilled out. The place where he pulled apart was frozen.

A sigh of relief moaned from the half-man. He crawled forward but then stopped. He went still and silent, like a deer who knows it's in the sights of a hunter.

The head turned. The hair hid most of the face, but a single eye could be seen glancing back at them.

"Don't mind me." His voice was deep and smooth, not rough like all else about him. He grinned in a show of bright teeth. "Ah, you resemble my wolf's gift."

The strange half-man wasn't talking to Dale. The words were directed to Tor.

"Here, you can have this part back."

The stranger flung something big at them. Dale scrambled to his left and ducked as an arm flailed just over his head.

Tor screamed. "Father!"

Dale turned and looked down at what the half-man had thrown at them. It was the top half of another man, only this one hadn't survived losing the bottom half of his body. Even dead and frozen from his drag through the night, the family resemblance was unmistakable. The half-man had just thrown the upper portion of Tor's father at them. Black blood and other dark gore oozed from the bottom of the half-corpse.

"What the hell is this?" Dale shouted.

The half-man didn't answer. Instead, he lined up his body with the bottom half of Tor's father. His spine snaked out from the frozen bottom of his body and reached into the waist. The spine went taut after it hooked onto something within the other body. Then he pulled together, and a long luxurious moan issued from the half-man who was now whole.

"Oh, that is so much better."

Dale had already dropped the torch in his shock. He held up his rifle and aimed at the new monstrosity before him. He wasn't sure if he should shoot. Part of him didn't want to because the decision to shoot this thing was too much like accepting what he'd just seen had actually happened.

The stranger stood, and as he turned to face them, it was clear the bottom half of Tor's father wasn't exactly a perfect fit. The upper half's flesh had to bend inward like a shirt tucked into a pair of pants that were two sizes too small.

"What are you?" Dale asked. "What the hell is going on here?"

The stranger smiled at him, and for a moment, the flesh on his face seemed to move. Then Dale realized what he was really seeing. Two more pairs of eyes were opening. Two were on its forehead and two more on its cheeks.

"I'm sorry, but I thought my coming was something explained to your kind long ago." He stalked towards them. "I am the Trickster, and this is the time of Ragnarok!"

The torch burned out, plunging them into darkness. Dale fired his rifle. The shot provided a brief flash of light to show him the man with six eyes as he lunged forward. Then the darkness fell again. There was pain, and for Dale, the world finally ended.

"Waist Deep" was originally published by Seventh Star Press as part of their anthology The End was Not the End *in March 2013.*

I AM SAM

"You gotta wonder what she did in a past life to deserve that," a uniformed officer says as I arrive. Officer Jonville looks close to tasting his midnight dose of coffee a second time. I'm not known for my forgiving nature with rookies like Jonville who can't stomach a homicide. He escapes unscathed by me, save for the image of this woman's corpse that will stay lodged in his brain until retirement and beyond.

For once, I'm in little better shape. The only reason I'm not moving around the room gathering evidence or out questioning neighbors is because if I take one step from my spot on that hideous, lime green carpet, I might faint. Thank God the crime scene techs aren't here yet, they'd probably make me move.

I don't need a forensic to know what happened here. This woman and her husband were doing what happy couples do. Then in the best moment, hubby screamed as if someone had ripped the skin from his face. She didn't know what happened, asked him what was wrong. He grabbed the first thing he could get his hands on, a cheap digital clock, and smashed her head until she looked like an elephant stepped on her. Then he wrapped his hands around her throat and strangled her, squeezing the life out of her like a bug between two fingers. I've seen worse, but until this night, I've never witnessed the murder as it happened.

"Investigator Willis," Jonville says, drawing me from my distraction, "found her wallet on the nightstand. She lived here. Her name's—"

"Stella."

"Yes, sir," he says, with the obvious question showing on his face, "Stella Washington. You know her?"

I don't answer. Hell, I still can't stop staring at the body on the bed. Jonville shows some brains to go with his brass badge by not asking me a second time.

Sweat's running down my forehead, and despite a chill in my soul, I can't stop it. My armpits have been raining waterfalls since two o'clock this morning. I woke up a half hour before my pager went off, and somehow I knew the murder in my dream would be waiting for me at 10528 Dawndeer Lane. I've worked in the violent crimes unit with Henrico County Police a third of my life with a "batting average" of .800. I've seen enough shit to give toenails split ends— severed hands, autopsies on bodies that have already seen the bad end of a meat cleaver, even watched a man committing "copicide" take 19 bullets from three police rifles and two pistols at point blank range. Stella's face ranks low on my gore list, but as I look over at the dresser mirror, I can still see her husband looking at himself and screaming her name like a bad stage actor imitating Brando.

"I'm not her," I whisper, remembering the last thing he kept saying before I woke up. He sounded like he was trying to convince himself.

"Sir?"

"Forget it, Jonville." Damn, I need a cigarette. "Has anyone seen the husband?"

"No, sir."

Finally confident I can walk without falling on my face, I retreat to the front yard. Blue lights on five squad cars light up the cul-de-sac like some uni-colored, outdoor disco. All three local news stations are positioning their live trucks, eager for news that hasn't already been recycled half a dozen times over the weekend for their Monday morning newscasts. The public information officer can deal with them when she gets here. I can make out faces peeking through the curtains of their two-story residentials. The good folks in the Raintree subdivision aren't getting much sleep this morning.

I sit in my car and surrender to the need to shake. Fifty-five words per minute and I'm resorting to hunt-and-peck to use the mobile desktop in my beige ninety-four Ford Crown Vic.

All it takes is a matter of minutes, and I know enough about Stella's husband to write a book about him. Yes, Big Brother is watching, and I'm using his computer.

Samuel Washington, born October 18, 1979, has made it into more than one police report. I read them all. Sam's what we call 10-96. That's police talk for "one crazy fucker." In the past ten years, he's tried to kill himself at least three times. Sam's a diagnosed schizophrenic, but until last night, he's never tried to hurt anyone else. Guess the voices in his head just don't like him much even if they don't know the razor goes down the road, not across the street.

Damn son of a bitch. I want to kill him, not because of what he did to Stella. I'm pissed because I can't get him out of my head. Every detail refuses to leave like a bad dream should. The way it felt being inside her, how easily her face bent and bled... sensations that make my skin turn the same shade as the unstained portions of the bedroom carpet.

Get out of my head!

Maybe I'm turning into the "psychic detective." If this is the rest of my life, I might join Sam on the seventh floor of St. Mary's Hospital. That's assuming I don't kill him on sight. Maybe we can get a two-for-one special on a padded room.

Two knocks on the roof of my car scare Sam out of my head for an all-too brief moment. I turn to see Sergeant Helen Caster staring at me as if I were a two-headed fish she just pulled out of the James River.

"Hey, Sal," she says. "Is it that bad in there?"

"Nah, probably just your usual domestic bullshit, the last one for this couple." I'm not sure what else to say. I'm not known for keeping my thoughts to myself. Hell, this morning, I've got thoughts to spare that aren't even mine.

"You must be going soft then, Sal. You look awful."

"Just ate some bad fish," I say.

Helen's the one who gets to talk to the reporters. She's one of the better public information officers we've had. Knows what to say

THE DEADLANDS: AND OTHER STORIES

to the vultures, but knows even better what not to say. I'd kill for her
gift at the moment. That nightmare, Sam's nightmare, keeps playing
like a DVD player set on repeat. I'm not sure what I can tell her
that's based on facts and not the movie rental in my mind.

"Any suspects?" she asks.

I look straight at her, scared to even open my mouth. Helen's
staring at me, and I can tell her concern about me is changing from
good humor to true worry.

"Sorry, hurting for sleep," I say, forcing my best smile. "My
guess would be the husband, but nothing solid on that. We'll have a
better idea once forensics gets in there and does their magic. Lady
got clobbered by a clock. Probably will get a decent print off of
that. No one knows where the husband is. Last thing anyone saw or
heard of him was the guy running out of the house in nothing but
his boxers screaming like an opera singer stepping on nails. Man's a
freaking loon."

"You on dayshift today?"

"Yeah, gonna be a 24-ounce cup of coffee day."

My usual jokes relax her concerns. She's already smiling again,
a nice smile, too. I'm even responding in kind, but as soon as she
heads over to the house to get her own take, I'm nursing my aching
head with my hand.

My day's just starting, and come eight o'clock, I'm going where
all the crazy people go.

• • •

If you're nuts and you live in Henrico County, Virginia, then at one
point in your life you'll find yourself taking a car ride to Woodman
Road. A few blocks down from I-295, planted amid lots of
evergreens, a two-story building with tall windows and a brownish-
orange brick exterior that smacks of "government building"
practices the ultimate in discrimination. If you aren't crazy, then
Henrico Mental Health doesn't want a damn thing to do with you.

After twenty years with the county, you can bet I've found

myself in here more than I would like. Wish I could say it was only to drop off the crazy people, and I suppose that's true. Unfortunately, I've dropped off myself a few times, too. After ten years of getting into killers' heads, it's hard not to lose it. Part of me wonders if I finally have gotten lost where the buses don't run, and there ain't no coming back.

First time I came to bare my soul, they sat me down with a man. I got up and left with just a "goodbye." Yeah, it's sexist, but somehow I don't mind a woman thinking I'm crazy. I figure most women think I'm a mess anyway, so it's not as humiliating.

I've known Elena Carter for five years. She's been with Mental Health about as long as I've been investigating murders. They cram her and three other psychiatrists into one room and make them share that space while they supposedly never discuss their cases with each other—right. She's the only one in the office as I walk in there. Guess the rest of the mind readers aren't in yet.

"Morning, Sal," she says. Then she gets a look at me. "Bad dreams again?"

I don't know how to answer her. Second time in the same damn day, I'm at a loss for words. Elena's convinced that I secretly want to kill myself. She won't say it, but some things you can just tell from what a woman doesn't say.

For a good year, I kept dreaming that someone was chasing me through the county depot just down the road from here, and I couldn't find my gun. The guy cornered me in one of those big huts where they keep sand for icy roads. I'm flailing in a huge pile of sand, and I can't seem to get free. I charge him, we struggle for the gun and, suddenly, I see the other man's face.

I'm looking at myself. The guy with the gun is me.

Then the gun fires straight up into my head, and I wake up thinking it's time to find a new job.

That was five years ago, the thing that finally forced me to sit down and be the 10-96 in this place. Like going to a one-man AA meeting. Hi, I'm Sal, and I secretly want to kill myself.

"I just need to pick your brain for a moment," I tell her. She

THE DEADLANDS: AND OTHER STORIES

knows what I'm asking. The way her plump face screws up, I can tell she's not happy about it either. I've done my homework, and one of the reports on Sammy mentioned he and I have something else in common—the same shrink.

"Let's go across the hall," she tells me.

She doesn't say a thing to me until we're in "the room" with the door closed. Very little seems odd about the room at first. The sea foam green walls create a soothing mood with comfortable chairs and a coffee table, but no couch. The room is a nice place to hang out once you get past the video camera hanging from the ceiling in one of the corners, the lack of any decorative objects that might serve as blunt objects and the fact everything is nailed to the floor.

Elena blends in perfectly with the room in her gray pantsuit. Come to think of it, she never wears anything that clashes with this room. Can't help but wonder if that's on purpose or one of those "subconscious" things Elena and her pals love to talk about.

"Is this about the murder this morning?" she asks.

"Well, at least I know you have something worth sharing," I say. She's not the only one quick at reading thoughts.

"You know I won't discuss anything about my clients," she says, but I can tell she's hurting to talk.

"Tell you what," I say. "Why don't we just sit down and discuss the finer points of schizophrenia? You can offer me a lot of examples. You know how slow we police boys can be."

I'm still getting a dirty look, but there's also that hint of thanks for offering her the way out she needs. We take our seats. Me, I get the purple chair.

"Let's keep this simple," she says. "Schizophrenics hear things—voices, typically. The voices can say anything and everything. I once had a man in here who eventually killed himself, because he kept hearing what he called demons telling him to hurt others. Sometimes, the voices aren't remotely consistent." Her tone changes on that latter point. I get the message. We're talking about Sammy.

"One day it's a little girl crying because her mommy is dead. The next, some man named Ted is espousing the proper technique for chopping up human remains to conceal a murder. Even more frightening, the voice sometimes turns out to be a neighbor or a close relative."

"Why would that be frightening? I hear my mom nagging me all the time," I say.

Elena isn't laughing.

"Imagine you hear them saying personal things, things no one else could possibly know, and it turns out what you're hearing is true. Imagine you have a dream about your neighbor breaking his arm, and then wake up to him knocking on your door because he needs you to drive him to the hospital."

She has my attention now, and I'm reminded of waking up a half hour before my pager started tap dancing across my nightstand.

"What are you saying? Sam Washington is some kind of clairvoyant?" I've completely forgotten I'm supposed to be pretending we aren't talking about him. Elena looks ready to pop my hand like some nun with a ruler.

"What I'm saying," she says through gritted teeth, "is that schizophrenia isn't a single illness. It's a broad term for several similar yet different problems."

"And what do you do to help a person like that?" I ask, and I'm not sure if I'm asking for Sammy or myself. Elena lets the question hang out there, and I can tell those eyes, the same brown as the wooden chair she's using, aren't missing that something else is behind that question.

"I can counsel someone, even prescribe medication when needed. Unfortunately, some people can't be treated."

"Why not?" Sure as hell don't like that last prospect.

"Sometimes, they aren't imagining things," she replies as if that shouldn't be all that shocking a thought.

I'm trying not to laugh. She's not being funny; I'm just nervous as hell.

"Sal, there are a lot of theories about schizophrenia, and they aren't all the kinds of things any self-respecting psychiatrist places in research papers."

She doesn't intend to say more, and after this morning, I need her to. God help me. My chest is fluttering like a hummingbird, and my legs don't feel like they could support my shadow if I stood.

"Tell me more," I say, "please."

"Sal, are you all right?" She's been in my head too many times not to know I'm not doing well.

"I just need to know more."

Elena knows I'm lying. She's got her head tilted to her right in this "don't bullshit me" look. Bless her heart; she lets it go. "Some people like to call it telepathy, necromancy, or psychic powers. Probably the more accepted of the 'exotic' theories is memories."

"Excuse me?"

"Memories from past lives," she says. "We're talking about reincarnation."

I feel like someone just hit the "ctrl-alt-delete" in my brain. "You're kidding, right?"

She's still not laughing, and I can tell she's searching hard for how to say what she's got brewing in that head of hers. I live for baseball, but a game seven in the world series with the Yankees down by one in the bottom of the ninth doesn't make me this anxious. I'm starting to sweat again, and that's not good in this small room since my deodorant stopped working before I even got to the crime scene.

"If reincarnation is real, why do you think it must be a linear thing?" she says. "What law of nature dictates that you die on August tenth and start the next life August eleventh? It might well be more like die in 2004, be born again in 1607.

"Sal, all I know is that I don't have a better explanation at this point. Our goal is to save everyone, but we never make it an expectation. We're just like you. We need explanations for why bad things happen to good people." She pauses there as if struggling to say something important, but what she finally offers me won't help me find Sammy. "One thing I will tell you about Samuel Washington is that he is a good man, and if he's actually done what you think he's done, then as bad as what happened to his wife is, I'll wager what he's seen or heard is even worse."

I'm not her.

The bottom drops out of my stomach like a trap door as I remember Sammy's scream, and his words are taking on a new meaning. The one thing that still doesn't make any sense to me is why Sammy is in my head.

I'm not him.

• • •

My next stop needs to be PSB, our little abbreviation for the Public Safety Building, what most would call the police department. Unfortunately, a shower and a change of clothes takes priority. That and I'm not really ready to see any of my co-workers just yet. So I take a right out of the parking lot to Mental Health. I live in the East End, so it's back to I-295 I go.

"617 to radio," I call into the communications center.

"Unit 617, go ahead," a radio dispatcher with a squeaky voice replies.

"Show me clear from Mental Health."

"Eight-forty-two hours."

Good God, not even nine o'clock. I'm gonna need more coffee.

My Crown Vic coughs as I pull out onto Woodman Road and head north past the county depot. I keep asking myself where I would go if I was Sammy. I gotta end this investigation before I really do lose my mind. Last time I felt this bad was after a bad batch of sangria at a Christmas party two years back. That I'm sober this time around isn't encouraging.

The traffic light at Woodman and Mountain catches me as the dispatcher assigns a unit to a call about a guy on a bike riding down 295 near Woodman. Thank God I'm not a road unit anymore, dealing with that kind of bogus call. Of course, I might not have killers in my head either if I was still dealing with crap like that.

Looks like the biker decided to ditch the interstate. I see this navy blue three-speed pulling off the exit ramp from 295 South. What a freak. The guy on the bike is wearing this long-sleeved white button-downed shirt with the sleeves rolled up. And the shorts on this guy are these ugly red and white polka dots. The closer he gets, the stranger he is. He's on a woman's bike, with the middle bar sloped downward, which I've never understood. Seems like that design makes more sense for a guy considering we're a lot more sensitive between the legs. The guy's hair is a mess, like he doesn't own a hairbrush or something.

Might as well spare the road unit coming to find this guy. Besides, I could use the distraction. "617 to radio."

"Unit 617, go ahead."

"Radio, let the unit responding to the biker on 295 know he's gotten off the Interstate at Woodman. He can cancel from—"

The bike rolls past me, and I see this panicked look on the guy's face, like he's seen the ass-end of hell. Those aren't shorts. Those are boxers, Sammy's boxers.

"Radio, keep the other unit coming!" I yell into my radio like some rookie getting ready to enter his first pursuit. "Subject is southbound on Woodman approaching the depot!"

There's this hellacious pause while my excitement probably gives the radio dispatcher a heart attack.

"Radio is 10-7!" the dispatcher answers. That basically tells everyone on the radio to keep his trap shut unless he's coming to help. Not that everyone and his brother doesn't step all over each other trying to respond. The radio sounds like a digital accordion with all those guys transmitting at once. I'm just trying to get my car's blue light flashing and u-turn at the same time without getting into a wreck.

The radio finally clears up as Sammy's feet start moving faster than a man stomping grapes. "Radio, subject is wanted reference incident on Dawndeer Lane. He's wearing a long-sleeved white shirt with red and white shorts. All units responding, use caution! Subject is 10-96."

He's got about as much chance of outrunning me on that bike as I do of losing the spare tire around my waist. That doesn't stop him from trying. The idiot veers left off of Woodman.

"Subject just turned into the south entrance to the depot!" I radio all the guys coming.

In my head, I'm already filling in the blanks. Sammy's been a busy boy. Stole a woman's bike, some clothes, so why the hell come here?

I'm turning into the depot in time to see him go into a parking lot to the right, just behind a long, dirty white garage capable of housing up to twenty cars. Two long rows of white police cars, yellow ambulances and fire trucks split the lot in half. Gravel and bits of glass grind beneath the wheels of my car as I jam the accelerator to the floor. Got to get ahead of him!

He looks over his shoulder. I'm about to overtake him.

The son-of-a-bitch slips between two fire engines halfway down the row of cars.

"Dammit!" I've got to go around the entire row of cars. No way to know which way he's going until I get to the end of the row.

Need to update my help that's on the way. "Units coming to the depot, he's ducked between some of the fire engines. I need the first two units on scene to block the north and south exits. Don't let anyone out!"

That won't stop him from jumping a fence, but he'll lose the bike if he does that. Make a run for it, Sammy. Try it on foot. We've got tracking dogs. Again, I can't help but ask myself, what the hell is he doing here? Why would he steal a bike to just to ride all the way out to Woodman Road?

I finally round the end of the line of parked vehicles. My car clears the last one, a huge fire truck, and I don't see him. "No!" How could he disappear like that?

Time for another update. I grab my radio again. "I've lost him. He might have double-backed for the south exit! Anyone on it?"

"Unit 243," one of the uniforms says. "Sal, I've got it covered. I haven't seen him come this way."

"Unit 271. I've got the North entrance. All clear."

I hit the brakes and get out of the car. Where is he? Then I spot the bike on the pavement, behind a chain link fence over near one of the sand huts. Damn things look like big brown coconut shells with tall, open doors.

"617 to units responding to the depot," I say. "I think he's ducked inside one of the sand huts."

I turn off my car and slip the keys into my front pants pocket. You'd be amazed how many rookies abandon their car with the keys in it for a perp to run back and take it. I pull out my forty-five caliber Glock from the holster on my right hip and get out of the car. The sunlight reflects off my gun's silver finish, and the black grip already feels slick in the morning heat of August. My mobile radio goes on my left hip. There's this orange button on it for an officer to hit if he gets in trouble. I'm hoping I won't need it.

I approach the sand hut with my gun held ready and can't stop myself from asking the question once more. What are you doing here, Sammy? This time, I figure it out. He's trying to go where all the crazy people go: Mental Health, the one place he knows he can get help. This is the first time since the job jaded me that my heart goes out to a killer. I've spent less than twenty-four hours dealing with something he's probably wrestled with all his life, and that he's held it together this long is something I'll probably never understand. I no longer want to see him die for invading my mind. I want to help him, if I can.

"Sam!" I call out. "I know where you're trying to go. Let me take you there." I step in front of the entrance to the sand hut, and I see him scrambling in vain to reach the far side of that pile of dirt. He stops, going perfectly still like a possum in the trash when you turn on your porch light.

"I'm Investigator Willis with Henrico Police," I say. "Sam, I know what happened with Stella. I know why you're scared. You can trust me."

Sammy walks down the sand, slipping in it. He's gotten so far up the pile that getting down keeps getting him stuck, and déjà vu hits me so damn hard that I'm not ready when he charges me. My arms must be twice as thick with muscle as his, but he's desperate. He's going for my gun. "Sam! Let go!" I stare down the barrel of my own gun, and the nightmare of five years' past comes back to me. I was here. I am here! I don't want to die, dammit!

"No!" The metal digs hard into my skin as I struggle not to let go. I can't let him take the gun, but his hysteria is beating my strength.

Sammy's finger grabs the trigger. The gun jerks loose in my grip, and an explosion hammers my ears and sends an ache shaking straight down into my arms. Everything goes quiet, like a mute button flipped on inside my head.

• • •

Later that day, I'm still on Woodman Road and back in that damned sea foam green room with Elena. Somewhere else, some coroner's cutting open Sammy to make sure I'm not lying about how he died even as I'm spilling my guts here.

"It was the dream," I tell Elena. "Only this time, I saw it through my eyes instead of Sammy's. I was dreaming about him dying all that time, not me."

My ears still hurt from the echo of my gun. I can only make out half the questions Elena's asking me, but I don't miss this one.

"You said you know why Sam killed his wife. Why?"

I thought him being dead would take away the memory of it, but Elena's question makes me relive the murder again. "He just wanted to get her out of his head. They climaxed at the same time, and he remembered how she felt, saw it through her eyes. He was Stella before he was Sam, and when he realized it, he couldn't take it."

"Killing Stella didn't take away her memories, though," Elena says, "did it?" She's blending into the room again, and that's fine by me. I don't want to see how she's looking at me.

"Not for him, and not for me." Sammy's memories are still alive in me. How many more times will I remember how he killed Stella, and the look on my own face as I watched him die? "It's funny, really."

"What do you mean?"

"Sammy was desperate to get here."

"I wish," Elena says, then stops short. I finally force myself to look her in the eyes, and there's no judgment for me there. She's too busy crying for Sammy. "I wish he could have made it, that we could have helped him."

I start laughing, and she must think I'm the most heartless bastard with a badge.

"You still don't get it, do you?" I say. "Sammy did make it here. I am—I was Sam."

"I am Sam" was originally published in Spinetingler Magazine *(www. spinetinglermag.com), Fall Issue 2006, Volume 2, Number 4.*

GIDION'S ASSASSIN

The deadliest weapon of any predator is patience, and Jun Ts'ao was very patient.

Even in a city as densely populated as Hong Kong, a vampire did not simply vanish. Nomads were expected to present themselves to the local elders if they stayed more than a single night. In the past three weeks, at least four vampires had gone missing. That could only mean one of two things: a power play by one of the local covens... or a hunter.

Jun spent two weeks tracking her prey. She started with the victims. The first to fall belonged to the Kowloon coven. One of the Islanders had vanished next. From there, a nomadic visiting the Sha Tin District had left without paying his respects to the local elder. Then another Islander was lost.

Like a bird of prey, she chose the best perch to find her target. The Narrows was well-known among the vampires of Hong Kong as a place to meet. Any hunter worthy of the title would find this place. The cramped café had earned a reputation as a popular night-time snack stop for travelers filled with an ever-changing assortment of scents that at one time would have made her mouth water but only offended her immortal stomach. Mandarin and English in yellow and pink chalk dust covered the blackboard on the left wall. The menu promised soups, dumplings, and various items appropriate for the tourist eager to try authentic late night Siu Yeh, but the true delicacies of the Narrows were standing in the line, foreigners no one would miss.

She watched the customers from the second floor of the restaurant. Her table was set directly above the front door and in front of a window overlooking the street. On her instructions, the staff had placed a burned bulb in the light fixture above her table. In favor of the true clientele, the management kept the restaurant dimly lighted, and the added darkness made it easier for her to see inside and out.

A heater with a fan was placed on the floor in front of the counter and set at a 45-degree angle. The scent of each customer floated up to her for inspection. For four nights, she'd sifted through the mortal filth of more than a hundred different nations, but even before the man in the black pea coat and silk lavender scarf stepped in front of the fan, he aroused her suspicions. The nail in the coffin was the black, slender tube he carried by a shoulder strap. Little doubt as to what he kept in there, and it wasn't rolled canvas or blueprints.

She took him for a westerner, because of his white skin. He was alone. His attention was drawn not to the chalkboard menu but to the front and back of the slender restaurant. She pulled deeper into the shadows as he studied each customer and assessed his possible escape routes. A man with a gaze that hard did not seek companionship, only blood.

He stepped up to the counter. Jun's lips twisted in disgust as she caught his scent. Cologne like brandy and the tang of body odor were bad enough, but they could not mask the stale scent of dead blood on his coat. Only the red ichor of a vampire could produce that odor, a foulness that reminded her of rotted citrus fruit, but this man's stiff movements marked him for a mortal.

The server at the counter asked for his order in English, but the man in the pea coat waved off the mistake. His tongue slaughtered the Mandarin language as he ordered one of the spicier dim sum items. His accent suggested he was French. Yet another sign he was a hunter, trying too hard to fit in, an effort for which most French tourists were not known.

Jun opened her Jin Yong novel and read as the hunter chose a table near the back. Much to her irritation, he devoured his meal in the manner of one who eats to live. She could hardly criticize, having made quick work of a young man earlier this evening. Part of her payment from the local coven was a guaranteed meal when she demanded it. Hunger was a distraction that drove so many of her kind to foolish, impatient, and often final mistakes.

Within minutes, the Frenchman had finished his meal. He covered his mouth with a closed fist to muffle a burp. Her lips curled with amusement and a touch of envy. She remembered attending a Rangers football game with her friends when she was mortal. The Rangers had kicked three goals, and for each score, Jun and her friends had chugged their sodas and issued boisterous belches to celebrate. Since becoming a vampire, she'd been unable to make that sound, nor had she observed another vampire do so. She knew that was an odd thing to miss from her mortal life, but that was it.

The Frenchman strode out of the café. He had not even had the decency to wait long enough for her to finish the chapter she was reading. She shut the book and slipped it into her small shoulder bag.

She pulled on her grey coat and darted down the spiral staircase. The hunter had disappeared before she could see which way he went, but it didn't matter. Even in this urban jungle, choked with the stink of exhaust fumes, uncollected trash, and piss, her heightened senses picked up the trail of that bloodied pea coat. No doubt, he'd made every effort to clean it, but vampire blood was just too distinctive.

Jun checked the time on her phone, which was 1:07. Plenty of night to go. She strolled in the direction of her prey. Let him walk and tire himself another hour or two. For that matter, nothing required her to kill him tonight, no matter how eager the local covens were to have this finished. Her pay was no more or less, if she waited another night or another week. Hong Kong's elders were impatient, and that made them poor negotiators when it came to her contract. She could follow this Frenchman to his lair. Only the shadows knew what treasures of information she might uncover within his home.

She tracked his scent down crowded streets bathed in bright neon and through alleys so dark that even daylight must rarely touch the ground. She didn't fear being interrupted by any of Hong Kong's thieves. Most girls of her diminutive height and size would attract an attacker, but she rarely did. Predators recognized their kind and kept a respectful distance. This was not something she gained from becoming a vampire. The one who brought her into the long night against her will swore Jun must have been born with a vampire's eyes, the kind that said to "Fuck off or die." She proved him right by cutting off his head a year later. She was made for the hunt, and she didn't care how long she took to set her traps.

Even without seeing the Frenchman again, she knew she was still close. The fool made it all too easy, only affirming her desire to track him to his home. She could let him go out to hunt tomorrow night and plunder his sanctuary, perhaps kill him at the end of his patrols when he'd be most tired or maybe set a trap inspired by some useful bit of information she might discover in his home. The possibilities made her giddy.

Her mind had traveled so far into the next night that she almost missed the spike in the Frenchman's scent. She stopped in the middle of an alley with the distant, flashing lights of a sleepless city for her only source of light.

The Frenchman burst from the shadows of a dumpster with his sword drawn. Jun retreated to avoid his swing. If she'd gone any slower, her head would have been rolling along the ground in a puddle of rainwater and her own blood.

He pressed his advantage, forcing her back and keeping her off-balance. The killer in her yearned to launch at him, risk the blade and bury her fangs in his throat. That's why she'd fed earlier, to better suppress the thirst that drives her kind. Instead, she ran.

The Frenchman cursed after her. He'd not expected this. He was used to hunger-driven fools drunk on their power. There was a reason the vampires of this world would pay her handsomely to rid them of their troubles. She did what they could not.

He chased her up the alley. His longer legs allowed him to keep up, but she had the advantage here. The dark blessing in her blood prevented her from tiring, and he'd already spent half the night on his feet to set this trap. He wouldn't gain on her, and within a minute, she would be in the stragglers at Hong Kong's Temple

Street Night Market.

Red pennant banners strung from building to building across the street marked her imaginary finish line. Even the most diehard shops had closed up by now, but enough people were here to deter the hunter.

She stopped in the middle of the street and turned to see the hunter standing at the edge of the alley. His chest heaved with the effort to catch his breath. He'd abandoned the black tube he used to conceal his sword and hid its long blade behind his back.

"Oh, poor, Frenchie. What's wrong?"

She smiled and flashed her fangs. His glare warmed her heart. She strolled back towards him, leaving only twenty feet between them.

"It has been a long time since a hunter surprised me." She was pleased to see his surprise as she spoke in flawless French. She'd spent a year hiding in the Paris catacombs after slaughtering her original coven. Odds favored none of the pedestrians passing between them would understand a word of what they said, allowing them to speak without innuendo.

"Come back into the alley, and I'll show you a few more surprises, beast."

She admonished him with a "tsk tsk" as she shook her head. "I now hold the advantage. Why would I sacrifice that?"

"What advantage? You can no more attack me here than I can you."

"Neutral ground." She studied him more intently now that she could. In the Narrows, she'd been limited to brief glances. He was easily twice her size. She couldn't match him for strength. The way he held himself and assessed his surroundings displayed a well-trained intellect. A direct confrontation could go either way, and he must have sensed it.

"My advantage," she said, "is time." She reached into her coat and pulled out her cell phone and opened the app for her camera. To him, it probably looked as if she was making a show of checking the time. "The sun will not rise for another four hours."

"I can stay awake past sunrise. Feel free to stay up with

me, little girl."

She loved mortal arrogance, especially when he didn't understand the real game being played. She snapped five shots of him with her phone, then flipped to the clearest one and zoomed in on his face.

"Four hours to sunrise, but I need only one minute to send your picture to every vampire in Hong Kong." She held up the phone for him to see himself. The only difference in the picture and the man was the sudden blanching of his skin and the intake of breath that exposed his panic.

"Even if you survive this night, you will never again walk these streets in safety."

He looked up and down the street, likely trying to gauge his chances of daring an attack here and getting away.

"Do not be foolish." She wagged a finger at him. "I am not without mercy, though."

"A vampire knows nothing of mercy." The way he barked out the words drew the attention of the human cattle passing between them; even if they couldn't understand his words, they recognized his barely-restrained anger. A few looked from him to Jun, but none stopped to interfere.

"I make you an offer, Frenchie. Give up the chase tonight, and I will wait until tomorrow night to send this. That will give you until sunset to leave Hong Kong forever."

She turned her back to him and walked away. When she glanced over her shoulder, she saw him still standing within the mouth of the alley. She could read the curse on his lips before he stalked back into the darkness.

Jun sprinted for the next corner and ran as fast as she could to make it around the block. This was not the moment for patience.

She ran back into the alley from the end opposite of the hunter. The shadows concealed her as she stayed close to the wall. The fool was walking, taking time he did not have and allowing her to return to where he'd originally ambushed her. His empty tube rested on the ground, waiting for him.

A dumpster different from the one he'd used provided cover for her. The black tube he used to conceal his sword was on the ground on the other side of the alley. Footsteps let her ears measure his approach as she reached into her shoulder bag and pulled out her dart gun. Frenchie leaned down for the tube. He cursed as he grabbed it by the shoulder strap.

Her eyes saw much more easily in the dark than his could, and that gave her the time she needed to aim her dart gun. She would only get one shot. Even though the weapon wasn't as loud as firing a bullet, the loud snap made enough noise to expose her. She wouldn't have time to reload.

The dart buried into the side of his throat. She held in a bark of delight for the lucky shot, because while the weapon was quite effective, its accuracy wasn't as reliable as a sniper rifle. He ripped the dart out of his neck less than a second after it struck, but it was too late. He tossed the dart aside and screamed as he lunged at her with his sword. She dodged his attack. Once more she ran from him, but this time, she only did so enough to avoid his swings.

In less than a minute, his attack became sloppy and slow. She only needed to step to the side to avoid his weak attempts. Then the swings stopped as his battle turned from killing her to simply breathing. His sword clattered from his hand to the asphalt. Eyes bulged, staring at her as he dropped to one knee and then collapsed until his breaths stopped altogether.

She picked up his weapon, savoring the feel of it. The blade of the katana was a thing of beauty, but the hilt was ugly, wrapped with the same kind of black tape used for the grip of tennis rackets. This sword was custom-made for practical use, not for display on a mantle.

"Curare." She knelt beside him. "The dose in that dart will paralyze you for several minutes, strong enough to stop your lungs. What I love most about curare is how it leaves you completely alert as I kill you."

She lifted his sword, preparing for the killing blow.

"For the record, I do know mercy. I just choose to ignore it."

She slammed the sword down. The blade slit through the flesh and bone, making a sucking sound as the Frenchman's head popped free of his body. It rolled away, stopped only by his large nose.

The task of killing him complete, she rifled through his pockets. Odds favored she wouldn't find anything all that useful. This man was trained. All she found was a thin wallet with no pictures or identification—only cash. His lair might have provided a hint to where he'd received that training, assuming his passport wasn't a fake. She might have auctioned off that information to any coven eager enough to start a war with the hunters.

Even a few short years into immortality, she had learned knowledge was much more than power.

Knowledge meant money, which a vampire without a coven needed to survive.

She used Frenchie's pea coat to wipe the blood off the sword. She returned the weapon to its carry tube and slung it over her shoulder along with her bag.

Before she left, she snapped a shot of the beheaded Frenchman and sent it to the head elder in a text with a simple message, '*Contract complete. Make final payment.*'

She didn't worry about the coven failing to send the money. The second contract she'd ever taken was in Madrid. She was shorted on the final payment. She only sent one reminder a month later. During the next six months, she moved onto other contracts, but then she went back to Madrid and killed the coven's elder. After that, she sent another letter demanding payment from the coven's new elder. The successor proved wiser than the predecessor.

As Jun walked back to her hotel room, she used her phone to check her email. She had three job offers, but the one that caught her attention was one from an American. Strangest of all, the request was from a man. Almost all coven elders were women, but this wasn't a request from a coven. This was from a nomadic vampire about an entire city's coven that had been wiped out. The job offered the least money, but she'd never heard of a hunter wiping out an entire city's coven. She wanted to look into that hunter's eyes and take his measure.

By the time Jun had shut the door to her room and drawn the curtain to block the rising sun, she'd already decided she was going to Richmond, Virginia.

THE LADY IN THE LOCH

If Nerise had to guess, she would have wagered this man died in his sixties. The fingertips of his right hand were gnarled and scarred. The left arm was missing, neatly severed by something so hot that it had cauterized the wound. The grey beard reached to the middle of the man's chest in a haphazard manner devoid of dignity. Not even death and the thin light from a single lantern could smooth the lines of stress written across his face.

She didn't want to believe this had been her husband. Wayne had disappeared in the dark waters of Loch Morar two months ago.

He'd been twenty-eight.

A man wearing a black suit stepped into the lantern's light on the opposite side of the examination table. "Are you convinced?"

Nerise wanted to rip open Edgar's throat for asking. His words held the edge of a smirk. At least he wouldn't have to go far if she killed him. They were in a morgue.

She held Wayne's limp hand. Yes, she was convinced it was him. Despite all that insisted otherwise, too many things proved it was him: the curve of his lips, the thin patch of hair at the center of his chest, and the two moles clustered together to the right side of his abdomen.

His death tore her heart apart. They'd met at the university, married shortly thereafter. Their love for the lore of Camelot brought them together, and their search for the reality behind the myth had stolen him from her. She'd assumed her tears were exhausted, but she found herself fighting them.

A fan, efficiently feeding frigid air into the room, rattled to life within the walls of the Dundee morgue. With the 20th century just a few years away, the Scottish university had spared no expense to equip itself. That Edgar had brought her here in the dark hours after midnight without anyone to grant them permission suggested his master had provided the necessary funding. He could do whatever he wished here, even conceal the discovery of her husband's body.

Edgar lifted the sheet back over Wayne's corpse. "The body washed ashore a few days ago."

She leaned against the metal table for support. "We already held the funeral."

His mother had worn a black, high-neck dress almost as stiff and cold as her glare from across the empty casket. She'd often railed at Wayne about how improper it was for Nerise to have a profession, that she might never have any grandchildren. For the first time, the accusation stung. Knowing she would never see his smile again on the face of a son or daughter wounded her soul.

"My employer is still eager to see you fulfill your contract, Mrs. Mackinnon." Edgar checked the time and then slipped his pocket watch back into his vest. He lifted his charcoal frock coat from a chair where he'd tossed it upon their arrival and slid it back on. "Especially in light of this new find."

"The contract was with my husband. I signed nothing."

"I have a copy of the document in my carriage, if you wish to review it. The terms of the agreement were with your husband and you. From a legal standpoint, he signed for you both." He slipped on a pair of black gloves. After he picked up the lantern he'd placed by the door, he led her out of the room and up the stairs.

"If you think that just because someone found my husband's body on the shores of Loch Morar that I'm going to drop everything and go back to work for you, then you are sorely mistaken."

"Let us speak to the point. You are incorrect, and on many matters." His boots echoed on the stone steps. "If you do not carry out your contract, then my employer will sue you for the advance, the majority of which we both know you have spent.

"No doubt, the college of archeology will deny you tenure at the university in London. To say your reputation was ruined by the manner of your husband's death would be an understatement. This leaves you without income.

"But most of all," Edgar stopped at the top of the stairs and looked back at her, "you wrongly assume where your husband was found."

She stopped mid-climb and clung to the railing. "He drowned in Loch Morar."

"He was lost in Loch Morar, but—and this is the best part." The bastard paused, savoring her panic. "Your husband's body was found on the shores of Loch Ness, more than fifty miles from where he disappeared."

The unnaturally advanced age of his body had been shock enough, but this left her without words.

"All I require from you at this time is the answer to one question. Certainly not whether you will go. We both know you will." Edgar lifted his lantern to better illuminate the arrogant indifference on his face. "Where do you wish to continue your search for Excalibur, where your husband was lost or found?"

• • •

Dull blue skies and what passed for warm weather in September mocked Nerise's mood. Three days had passed since she'd seen her husband's body. Holding his hand one last time had not brought her closure, nor did coming to the rocky shores of Loch Ness where his body had been recovered.

Edgar lifted the top part of her new dive suit over her head. This one fit much better than the one lost with Wayne. They'd been forced to share the same suit, and he'd been several inches taller. She still remembered the violent jerk on the umbilical line. The motor feeding air to him had bounced across the sand and splashed into the water before the taut line went slack. The line she'd reeled in had been cut by something too sharp to be natural.

She grabbed the helmet, in Edgar's hands, to stop him from putting it on her. The memories of that last moment with Wayne and his cocksure smile made her feel trapped.

"I need a moment. I can't breathe."

"Mrs. Mackinnon, I assure you that the air pump is the most advanced of its kind."

Nerise wondered if Edgar's employer had stolen the design and the equipment. They'd never met "Master A. Dexter." Wayne once suggested Edgar might be Dexter. After the past few days, Nerise was convinced he wasn't. Edgar was just a well-trained attack dog.

He slipped her helmet on with precise movements. A pair of clicks let her know he'd locked the helmet in place, limiting her view of the world to a round circle of glass. The air pump rumbled to life, which she felt more than heard.

"You have an hour of air." Her helmet muffled Edgar to a whisper as he yelled over the generator.

Her boots slipped on the wet rocks as she lumbered into the water, but she refused to ask for help. The surface of the loch smoothed beneath her feet after about two dozen yards.

The blue-green filmy waters covered her, making it difficult to see more than twenty yards ahead. Small, dark shapes flitted through the water to escape her invasion. Her teeth clenched as she struggled to keep her breathing steady. The sky turned to a blurry image with the sun a wavy, bright spot.

She reached up and tugged the umbilical thrice, the signal to turn on her helmet's lamps. This close to the surface, the extra light wasn't necessary, but knowing the light was there would calm her. A soft hum vibrated through the helmet as the bulbs came to life.

When she and Wayne had started these underwater explorations, she'd enjoyed this. She once teased Wayne that she might toss a sword into the water for him to find. The first place they'd explored had been Loch Katrine. Night fell by the time they'd given up. They took advantage of the darkness and solitude, making love on the shore. She'd insisted on concealing their act beneath a blanket. When they were done, breathless and limp with exhaustion, they'd stared at the water and debated what Excalibur might have really been. Neither believed it was a magic sword. The weapon's many names such as Excalibur and Caliburnus all hinted at connections with ancient worlds and perhaps lost technology, but Nerise and Wayne never agreed on a theory to justify its significance within Arthurian legend.

Wayne's ghost felt distant. Within this metal suit, she sensed the world had excised her like an unwanted limb.

She came across the wooden remains of a small boat, rotting in the patient onslaught of currents and time. The sunken ship blocked her path, and as she walked around it, she was startled to see another light to the left of the ship. As she neared the source, she realized it was her reflection on a silver, metallic surface.

She should have seen something of what the reflective object was. Instead, she only saw ripples. The alteration in the water made no sense. The ripples resembled the tiny waves from where a rock might break the surface, but the pattern of the ripples was perpendicular to the floor of the loch.

Then she saw the edge of the uncertainty, shaped like a heptagon. It was taller than her. Her reflection bent inwards.

Nerise's heart still raced, but anticipation and excitement replaced her fear. She stepped around the shape that rippled like water but was not. From the side, the shape curved in and out, reminiscent of the top half of a chalice on its side. Her mind played through stories of the Holy Grail, and she scolded herself for jumping to conclusions.

A drop of sweat threatened to fall into her eye. She reached up to wipe it off and remembered just before her hand could strike the front of the helmet that she couldn't do that. The closer she came to the liquid chalice, the warmer she got.

She moved back in front of it. What was she to do with this? She had no means to record it, nor was it some lost relic to be collected and categorized. The only option was to study it as long as her oxygen permitted and write down every detail when she returned to shore.

What would Wayne have done if he'd come across this? Had he? She felt the compulsion to brush fingers along its surface. She didn't doubt he would have. She reached for it, but not to test the surface tension. She needed to know what happened to Wayne, and that meant doing what he would have done.

Her fingers dipped into the center of the heptagon and pressed forward without any more effort than the water of the loch. The only difference was the warmth filling her fingertips. The pattern of the ripples didn't change. The liquid steel refused to acknowledge she existed.

She tried to pull her hand back and couldn't.

Her struggles pulled her deeper into the chalice. Her boots dragged in the sand in a losing match of tug-of-war. She screamed and cursed. The hold of the chalice pressed on her forearms.

Then her body launched off the bottom of the loch and into the metal liquid. She screamed her husband's name. She couldn't decide if she hoped he might hear, or if she was praying to God that her soul might find Wayne in death.

Heat and darkness engulfed her. A current captured her and turned her into a blind torpedo.

Reality blinked. The pressure crushed the breath from her lungs. Then she was prone on the shore.

This wasn't Loch Ness, nor Loch Morar. Gold sands shined enough to hurt her eyes. She dipped her gloved hand into the beach to scoop it up. The grains spilled out between her fingers, not sand but tiny metal shavings. Even through her helmet, she heard the tiny clinking sound as each grain rejoined the land.

She rolled onto her back on the water's edge. Her arm shook as she lifted it to block the sunlight. The yellow-white ball she had known all her life was replaced by a white-blue one amid a backdrop of pale red.

As she sat up, she saw no trees, no grass, no animals. Beyond the gold shore, crystalline spires of all size and colors thrust from the ground to create a rainbow-hued forest. Beyond the crystal spires, massive cliffs and mountains of hard, grey rock buttressed the sky.

Then she heard the scream.

The closest thing to match the rage within that scream was

a carriage horse Nerise once saw go berserk in the middle of London's streets. The beast of burden had worn a wide-eyed mask of frothy panic and smashed in the head of the carriage driver as he attempted to calm it.

The weight of her dive suit made getting upright a slow process, despite her desperation. She fought for leverage in the metal sand to get to her knees and then her feet.

Just as she stood, one of the distant crystal spires shattered. The sound was delayed, reaching her seconds later. A flame shot into the sky from the same location, followed by another shriek, the sound of giant, rusted gears grinding against each other.

Where could she go? Had her husband been forced into this same choice? Could she get back to Loch Ness? Where was she? How had her husband survived this environment to reach an old age in a place that appeared to be made of nothing more than metal and rock? Her mind chased too many questions and refused to settle long enough for her wits to choose a course.

Another crystal spire, one much closer to Nerise, shared the first one's fate. The fractured sound of its destruction reached her faster this time.

She needed to get back, but when she turned to look at the lake, she received her next shock. The "water" was nothing but the shiny grey liquid that brought her here. When she'd been sucked into the chalice, she couldn't see anything, even before her umbilical snapped and her lamps went dark.

The land shook beneath her feet as more spires shattered at her back.

Her breath grew thin, and she realized she didn't have her umbilical to feed her any fresh air. The remnant still attached to her helmet flapped against her back.

Her fingers fumbled for the clamps to her helmet. She needed to get it off long enough to get some fresh air into her suit. The wind hit her, and she was overcome by nausea. The air carried an offensive tang of steel and iron that reminded her of blood.

The direction of the wind changed, and she smelled something that was decidedly not metal.

She turned and looked up into the burning eyes of an abomination.

The mechanical creature resembled a dragon with a long snout and neck. Wings stretched from its back with a steel framework and membranes of pale leather. The tips of the wings stabbed into the ground as the massive body lurched forward.

She stumbled back into the silver water.

The monster's neck curved down with a violent grinding of gears. The head stopped a few feet from her. Its hot breath slid over her with the stench of kerosene.

Small forearms reached from its upper torso towards her. The dragon's fingers weren't metal. Each finger was comprised of an arm taken from men and women and attached to a steel palm. The stolen arms held enough life that the human hands remained animated. The human fingers grabbed at air in a desperate need for contact. Glowing wires, slightly visible at the point of contact between the metal and flesh, pulsed with a glow that changed from crimson to white. Nerise stumbled deeper into the lake, up to her waist.

A voice as strained as the motors within this beast then spoke.

"Are you the Future King?"

Her lips shivered in silence, because no answer seemed right. Would this monster kill her if she said she wasn't?

Only when she saw the nearest of the fingers/arms did she manage to speak. Her revulsion was overpowered by loss. She recognized her husband's silver ring, engraved with "Caledfwlch," the Welsh name for Excalibur.

She reached out to his amputated arm. His fingers coiled with hers, his touch alive and warm. Was a piece of Wayne's soul here?

"This one." She ran a finger across the etched letters in his ring. "What was his answer?"

"He said he was not." The power of its voice made her release Wayne's hand. "He ran from my children."

Water sprayed up around her as lithe figures dropped from the sky and surrounded her. They stood a head shorter than her. Black wings folded in to surround and protect their slender bodies and created the illusion of cloaked women.

"And if I am the Future King?" Saying "no" wouldn't end well, but that didn't make "yes" a wiser choice.

"Are you?"

So much for being clever. The children stepped closer. Their wings parted enough for arms to reach out. Each child had four arms, two of metal and two of borrowed flesh.

She couldn't run. Only dumb luck might help her find the "chalice" on this side.

Nerise forced herself to look up at the metal dragon.

"I am."

"Let us see if you are true."

The dragon's neck twisted and creaked as it reared. A roar capped with flames burst from its snout. Wings reached wide into the sky. As the blue sunlight reflected off them, she recognized what animals had died to provide the leather patchwork for the wings' membranes: humans.

The children's many hands latched onto Nerise. They ripped her suit apart. Inhuman shrieks drowned out her screams.

"Drink, Future King! Draw from the bosom of the lake and receive her judgment!"

The children shoved her face into the lake. Pain stabbed from inside her chest as the metal liquid flooded her throat. Hot pain sliced through her right shoulder, and a second darkness fell over her mind, as her arm was severed.

• • •

The next time Nerise washed upon a shore, the ground was rocky and cold against her naked body. The blue light shining on her came from the moon. No sooner had she awakened than Edgar's discourteous hands grabbed her and jerked her to her feet.

The lamps of a carriage blazed to life, blinding her. She was pitched forward and landed on her knees next to the now silent generator that had empowered her lost dive suit.

The silhouette of a man stepped in front of the lamps. "I must say that I am very pleased."

As he neared, she saw his skin was pale. A blond beard framed a well-defined jawline. The most striking element was his eyes. The irises were shiny and silver, glowing in the dark. His suit and tie were grey, as if chosen to match.

"Master Dexter?" Nerise asked.

His smile reminded her of a tiger ready to feast. "We have passed the need for formality. Call me Amhar."

He knelt in front of her and took her right arm into his hands as if to cradle a holy relic. A sigh of awe misted into the night air.

"It has been so long since I saw this on my departed father, the King."

Her eyes widened as they took in the work of metal the children and their mother had given her. Even in the night, she could make out the engraving on the forearm. The letters were unknown to her, but she could see how easy it would be to interpret them for the many names given to it in ancient texts. At one angle, the alien markings resembled Excalibur, and as the light shifted, they changed to Caledfwlch.

"Look, Edgar." Amhar grabbed her chin to tilt her head back. "I've not gazed on the eyes of another Fae-Touched since my father's betrayal."

He laughed as he stood. "Of all of Artur's children, only I inherited the gift of the Fae's waters into my blood. Excalibur should have fallen to me, the true Future King. He buried me alive after I tried to take it. By the time I found my way out, that fool Mordred had killed Father and exiled this blade and scabbard to the water."

She smiled at him. "You weren't buried as a punishment, Amhar. Your father knew the Fae would demand all of the lake's water back. He wouldn't let them have you."

At Nerise's command, a blade burst from beneath her metal wrist as she lunged at Amhar. The weapon glowed hot and bright. Edgar placed himself in her path to protect his employer. Gun raised, he fired a shot at her chest. Nerise felt the bullet strike her breastbone, but the bullet bounced off her flesh like the tap of a finger.

Before Edgar could fire a second shot, her blade separated his head from his body without a drop of blood. The heat of the "sword" cauterized the wound. His bowler hat landed on its top next to the frozen look of shock on his severed head.

"Impressive." Amhar clapped. "A pity I already know Excalibur's secrets, far more than I imagine the Fae have had time to teach you. The weapon will be mine, and you will die before the sun can rise. Thank you for bringing it."

"The Fae warned me you might be able to take Excalibur from me, so I brought something else back for you." She pointed up. "I brought them."

From above, the grinding shrieks of the children issued with amusement.

"They've come for what Artur refused to return."

Amhar's screams echoed over Loch Ness as the children descended. They clawed at his body and threw him into the waters, drowning his cries.

BORROWED SHADOWS

Daniel Black had never feared the dark. The light scared him much more, even now that he was a teenager. He had a good reason for his peculiar fear, because he was born without a shadow.

As he limped down the sidewalk on Cary Street, he avoided lingering in the path of any street lights. He wasn't worried about people not seeing a shadow. The worry was them seeing that the shadow stretched out on the sidewalk didn't match.

He passed a couple who did their best not to make eye contact with him. His plain black cane made people more uncomfortable about staring for too long, and for those who were rude enough to stare, they usually focused on the cane and not his shadow. That's why he used the cane, not the two-inch advantage his left leg had over his right. He wore a heel lift to compensate for that.

The sidewalk wasn't crowded. The Carytown part of Richmond was made up of local businesses, most of which were closed after nine, especially on a Thursday night in February.

He'd only been forced to park his car a little more than a block from his destination.

He stopped in front of the veterinary eye care office. The windows were dark. He leaned against the olive green building for support as he zipped up his jacket. The brick wall chilled his back. His main worry wasn't the dropping mercury. He just wanted to be sure no one was watching him.

A narrow, dark space separated the green building from its red neighbor.

This was Purgatory Alley.

He first visited this place when he was seven. Even then, he understood this wasn't the safest place to go. Not everything that came out of these shadows was a friend.

As soon as he stepped off the sidewalk and into the alley, the street noise dropped, muffled like a dream. Shadows thickened, and he had to push his way through them. Whispers taunted from every direction. Flat darkness obscured the brick walls, making the alley look bigger even as it provoked claustrophobia in Daniel.

"Baxter, you there?"

A figure slipped out of the black wall, cutting Daniel off from the sidewalk. He tensed.

The first thing he ever saw emerge from these walls had threatened to rip his shadow from his body.

Daniel relaxed when the darkness formed a familiar head with glowing neon green slits for eyes.

"Thought you'd never get here, kiddo." Baxter was one of the first friendly shadows Daniel met in Purgatory Alley. He had a human shape to him, but Daniel got the impression that wasn't what he really looked like. Baxter probably made himself appear that way to avoid scaring him. He was the one who explained to Daniel that he had a borrowed shadow. When he got put together by whatever Higher Power does its thing, a shadow got left out. Whether that was intentional was anybody's guess. In order for Daniel to come alive, a shadow had to be added.

"Sue me. I have parents. Had to tell Mom I was running out to get a folder for a term paper I've got due in English next week." Sadly, that wasn't a lie, and now that Mom knew about it, she'd probably hound him until he finished it. "What's so urgent that it couldn't wait until tomorrow night?"

Baxter leaned in close and lowered his voice to a whisper. "Word is out. Someone wants you dead."

"Me? Why would anyone want me dead?"

"Doesn't sound like their beef is with you." Baxter shrugged. "Sounds like a personal issue with your shadow."

"Feng?" He looked over his shoulder at his borrowed shadow. Within the alley, Feng took on more substance. His eyes blazed bright red and his head had taken on that samurai helmet shape he adopted whenever he felt threatened. Feng wore the helmet a lot in chemistry class. Daniel really hated that teacher.

Daniel and Feng had never been able to talk, not in the traditional manner. He couldn't decide if Feng was just the silent type, if it was a language barrier thing, or if Feng was mute.

Baxter had said that was unusual, even though most borrowed shadows never spoke to their owners.

"Feng, who's after us?"

He hoped Feng could at least relay the answer through Baxter. Shadows had their own way of talking. Daniel had asked Baxter how "shadow speak" worked, but despite several attempts, none of his explanations had made much sense.

Feng's response was to shrink, which Daniel had learned equaled with feeling shame.

"That's not helping, dude." Daniel looked back to Baxter. "So do you know who it is?"

"Don't have a name for you, but it's another borrowed shadow."

"Here in Richmond?" Daniel's voice cracked. "What are the odds of that?"

"Chances of a person being born without a shadow are pretty thin. Only about 2,000 people with borrowed shadows in the whole world. That's still a lot of people, but most of them never even realize they're borrowing one."

Daniel glared back at Feng. "Yeah, well it's kind of hard not to notice when you've got the shadow of a dead samurai stapled to your back." Thankfully, Feng didn't always have the helmet on, but despite his best efforts, he always looked much too big to match Daniel's thin frame. His shadow made more sense for an NFL linebacker.

"So who is this shadow attached to?" Daniel asked Baxter.

"Sorry, kiddo. Don't know that either. What I do know is that this shadow aims to take you two out this weekend."

"I appreciate the warning." They slapped palms, which made a soft *woosh* sound as Daniel's hand passed through the semi-substance that was Baxter.

Daniel walked to the edge of the alley. He looked to make sure all was clear and stepped out onto the sidewalk.

He passed beneath a street lamp on the way to his car. Feng spread out ahead of him. Still had on that stupid helmet, too.

"You and I are going to have a long talk tonight," Daniel muttered.

He just hoped if he was going to die this weekend, the killer could get it over with before Mom made him work on his term paper.

• • •

By the time Daniel returned home, it was almost ten. Mom gave him the evil eye.

Fortunately, he'd thought to give himself a cover story for being gone so long, which was why he showed up with a café mocha.

"I sent you a text to tell you I was going by the café." He'd even asked if they wanted him to get them anything. Was it his fault they never kept their cell phones with them? It would be just his luck to get grounded and then murdered all in the same weekend.

"And yes, it's decaf." He held up the cup to display the mark on the side, not that they could probably read the barista script from across the room.

Having survived parental interrogation, he retreated to his room and closed the door.

Once in there, he tossed the bag with his term paper cover onto the bed along with his cane.

He turned off his overhead light, sat at his desk and clicked on the tiny desk lamp. It had one of those metal ice cream cone-shaped tops with the bendable neck. He twisted the lamp's top so that the light pointed at him. The silhouette of Feng's upper torso appeared within a circle of light against the far wall. When he'd been little, he'd do this sort of thing and laugh for hours at all the silly things Feng would do to entertain him.

Daniel noticed Feng was no longer sporting the helmet. He had the hair knot thing going on now.

"So what's the what here?" He'd learned a long time ago that they could have a conversation like this. Feng could nod and shrug, and while Feng couldn't or wouldn't exactly speak to him, Daniel could almost feel some of his shadow's thoughts. Sometimes, the connection worked stronger than others. Whenever Daniel felt threatened, Feng pulled in real close and could even prompt a reaction from him. His parents still told the story of how, when he was a baby, he punched and broke Grandpa's nose when Grandpa did the old "I stole your nose" trick. Apparently, Feng didn't find that very funny.

"Any idea who you've got so ticked, they'd come back as someone's shadow just to even the score?"

Feng shrugged.

"Really? Dude, seriously!" He slumped forward in his chair and groaned. "I mean, how many people could you possibly have ticked off when you were alive that they'd hate you enough to want to kill me, too?"

Feng drew his sword, a dark line that he swung with ease. Daniel could almost hear his voice, but it wasn't like a whisper. It was more like the raw thought itself shifting from the shadow into his mind.

"Killed many enemies, huh?"

Feng nodded.

"Just great. So you don't have a clue which enemy this would even be." He grumbled to himself, "Guess it's not like it would've really helped a lot, but still."

Daniel had a hard time imagining his shadow killing anyone when he'd been alive. Sure, he'd been a sword-wielding samurai and all, but this was also the shadow he'd watched dance and pantomime on his wall like a Saturday morning cartoon when he was three. He often wondered what made Feng choose to be attached to a white kid in the middle of the 'burbs in Virginia. He'd asked Baxter, but the best answer he ever got was that it was "Something honor demanded... maybe."

"So what's the plan here, chief?"

Feng stood tall, crossed his arms and capped it off with a firm nod of the head. Daniel guessed that just meant to "Stand ready" or something like that.

"You think we need to take this seriously?"

Another firm nod.

Daniel's stomach clenched. The worst thing he'd ever dealt with were bullies at school, not that many of them bothered him. Even most bullies wouldn't mess with a "cripple."

Apparently, it was bad business in the bully trade. For those bullies with fewer scruples, he could usually disarm the situation with a few jokes at his own expense. Unfortunately, he didn't think he'd get any laughs out of whoever was coming here to kill him.

• • •

Daniel had hoped a good night's sleep would make his troubles seem less oppressive.

That might have worked if he hadn't kept waking up all night. Just getting to sleep took more than an hour each time he tried. His mind wouldn't shut off, obsessing on all the things he didn't know about this person determined to kill him.

By the time he was exhausted enough to sleep, it was time for school. He'd almost fallen asleep during the spelling test in English, and he was pretty sure "paradocks" and "psychilogical" were the closest he'd come to spelling anything right. He didn't do much better in his Trigonometry class.

"Ahem, Mister Black?"

Daniel blinked as he looked over at his Trig teacher Mister Garibaldi, who was staring at him over the rims of his glasses. Drat! Had he fallen asleep? He didn't think he'd closed his eyes, but he'd completely zoned out. He looked at the problem displayed on the Promethean board.

What were they even going over in class today?

"I'm sorry, Mister Garibaldi." Daniel sat straighter and wiped the bit of drool from the side of his mouth. "What was the question?"

"Would you be so kind as to tell the class if these two functions on the board are inverses?" Mister Garibaldi's eyes narrowed. "That's assuming, of course, you're quite done admiring the back of Miss Winston's head."

That earned more than a few snickers, and he saw Allison's body stiffen in the chair in front of him. Just perfect.

He cleared his throat to stall for time as he studied the equations. Given the mush between his ears, all he read was *gibberish plus gibberish divided by more gibberish*. He'd have had a better chance of making sense out of it if he was dyslexic. Then Allison tapped her pencil on her desk two times. God bless her.

"No, sir, they're not." He forced as much certainty into his voice as he could and prayed Mister Garibaldi didn't ask him to say why.

"Very good." His teacher pushed his glasses back up the bridge of his nose into non-glare mode and looked at the person who'd laughed the loudest at the earlier joke. "Miss Pindler, perhaps you'd like to explain why he's correct."

Class ended a few minutes later. Thank God it was lunch time. As soon as he shoved his books into his locker, he was going off-campus to get a Mountain Dew or maybe even a Red Bull. He needed something to wake himself up if he was going to survive his last two classes.

"So where are you buying me lunch?"

He turned around to find Allison standing there with a smirk on her face.

"Buy you lunch? What?" He shook his head, trying to catch up with whatever she was talking about. When had he told her he was buying her lunch?

"For saving your gluteus maximus back in Trig." She threw in a head bob move as if this should have been obvious. "Come on. If we hurry, we can make it to the Burger Doctor."

"Oh, all right."

They'd been best friends since fifth grade. Allison was pretty cool for a girl. While all the other girls were into dresses and dolls, she and Daniel were pretending to be ninjas in her backyard and talking about Star Wars. They were *not* in a relationship, though. He'd said those exact words to Dad back then. Dad had found that hysterical and still loved to refer to Allison as "That girl you're *not* in a relationship with." Everyone through middle school was convinced they should go out together, mainly because she was one of the few girls shorter than he was. They were juniors in high school, and now even she was taller than him, if only by an inch.

"So what's your deal, pickle?" she asked between bites of her plain double hamburger. "You look like road kill, and Feng has been wearing the helmet all day."

He just placed his head on the orange table they'd taken inside Burger Doctor. It was slightly greasy, but that didn't stop him from letting his forehead linger there for dramatic effect.

"Yeah, well Feng is part of the problem." He spelled out the whole rumor about another borrowed shadow in town to settle some old score. She was one of the few people he'd ever told about Feng.

The first time he'd told a friend had been in third grade. That guy had made a comment about Daniel's shadow being so big, but Feng had refused to perform when Daniel had explained why. Daniel had been really cross with Feng about that, but when that supposed friend turned into a jerk in middle school, he was glad Feng hadn't played along. He'd told his parents when he was three, of course, but even though they'd made a few comments about his shadow over the years, they fell into the "Total Denial" camp. Most people did, but Baxter had warned him there were those out there who were in the know. Some of them would think Daniel was possessed and might even try to kill him.

Despite the risks, Allison had received the Feng seal of approval.

"So what are you going to do?" Allison had stopped eating.

"Hide in my room all weekend." He laughed. "What else can I do?"

Allison didn't meet his eyes. She drew circles in her ketchup with a French fry. "Well, I guess that's probably best."

What was her problem? It wasn't like this assassin was coming after her.

Then he remembered. The Byrd Theater in Carytown was holding a midnight showing of *Army of Darkness* tonight. The only reason Allison was being allowed to stay out that late for it was because she told her parents that Daniel was going with her.

"Well, maybe not all weekend." He stopped for a big bite of his burger. Thankfully, all this mess with Feng wasn't hurting his appetite.

"Daniel, it's okay." She was still drawing hieroglyphics in her ketchup, though.

For a girl he wasn't in a relationship with, she sure did know how to play the guilt card.

Truth was, he was a little bummed, too. He was really wanting to see *Army of Darkness* in the theater.

"You know, if this other shadow knows I'm here, then it probably knows where I live, so not staying there might actually be safer for me."

She didn't look up, but she smiled. "That's a good point." She finally took a bite of her fry.

They shut up and wolfed down the rest of their lunch so they could get back to campus in time for fifth period. He was in a much better mood, thinking about the movie. That he'd be going with Allison, who looked a lot prettier these days, had nothing to do with it. Right.

• • •

Daniel spent the time between school and going to the movie in his bedroom. He left the blinds in front of his desk cracked just enough to let him see down onto the street. The longer he watched for any suspicious cars or pedestrians, the more he realized he knew jack about the people who lived in his neighborhood.

They lived in one of the nicer sections of the West End, and a lot of women were power walking past the house while the sun was still out. As the sun went down, he realized it was way too dark outside to see if anyone or anything suspicious was out there.

Besides, he knew better than most just how well a person with a borrowed shadow could hide.

He needed to figure out what he was dealing with. If he could manage that, then maybe he'd have a better chance of spotting an attack in time to stay alive.

The more he thought on it, the more he decided the person coming after him must be younger than he was. After all, this was a shadow chasing Feng, suggesting Feng had gotten here first. Even with his shorter leg as a disadvantage, he hoped the age difference might even things out.

Contemplating what might be hiding in the shadows tonight had turned Daniel into a paranoid mess by the time he picked up Allison.

"My, my, Monsieur Black, aren't we looking dapper," she said as she climbed into the passenger seat of his car. "Wow, you even broke out the falcon."

She patted the silver-plated falcon head at the end of his cane.

"Just dressing for the occasion. I don't want to get killed tonight."

He scanned her yard and street for anyone suspicious. There was a red sports car pulling to a stop in front of the house across the street. Yeah, he was on full alert.

"Ahem!"

He looked over at Allison, who had this really unpleasant curl to her lips.

"What?"

"You really are hopeless. You realize this, right?"

"Huh?" He looked at the front of her house, the yard, and back at the red car with some guy climbing out and walking up the driveway of the house across the street. Had he missed something?

"If you have any hopes of ever having a girlfriend, you need to learn to repay a lady's compliment."

He shrugged. "Well, you always look nice." She made a habit of dressing "classy but eccentric," as she liked to call it. She was wearing a dark red velvet coat over a black tuxedo shirt and black pants.

She sighed and rolled her eyes. "So not the point. Just drive."

"Sorry, I'm a little focused on not ending the night as a chalk outline."

"I don't think this guy is going to kill you inside the Byrd."

She had a point. After all, that was part of the reason they were still going to the movie.

After a few minutes of the silent treatment, Allison apparently decided he'd suffered long enough. "I've been thinking over this whole thing with Feng's assassin."

"Yeah?"

"Well, how has this guy even found you?" she asked.

"It wouldn't be difficult to narrow down the city. There aren't a lot of borrowed shadows out there. All you have to do is go to a 'shadow well' like Purgatory Alley and ask around. Finding out Feng and I are in Richmond probably wouldn't take long at all."

They found a space on top of the parking deck behind the movie theater. Not too far to walk, thankfully.

They strolled past several people on their way to the ticket booth. He watched for anyone whose shadow didn't match. With so many people and all of them moving around, that wasn't so simple a task.

Once the movie started, he relaxed a bit. He decided it wasn't likely for anyone to try anything while the movie was playing. Several rows in the front waved their hands in the air as the opening credits started and shouted, "Hail to the King, Baby!"

Allison shouted, too. "Give me some sugar!"

"You're a nut." They were both laughing, though.

Halfway through the film, Allison made a bathroom run. He'd never known her to make it through an entire film without at least one pit stop. That was why they'd made sure to get her a seat on the aisle.

"Don't let anyone take my spot." She didn't wait for his reply.

He didn't expect to have to make good on her request, but less than a minute later, someone with pale-white skin dropped into her seat. Daniel guessed this guy must have been in his twenties. The darkness made it near impossible to see what his shadow looked like, but Daniel knew right away this man had to be the one with the borrowed shadow. His eyes were solid black spheres, not a bit of whites or iris visible.

"Greetings, Feng."

Daniel said nothing. He was too stunned by what he was seeing to think of anything useful, much less pithy. He'd expected someone a lot younger and smaller than this.

"You picked a weakling."

The stranger's accusation drew him out of his silence, but he sensed Feng touch his shoulder, a request for him to not bite at the bait.

"We're in a public place. You really think you can kill me here?"

The black-eyed man glanced at the rows in front and behind them. "It's dark, but you're right. Meet me at Purgatory Alley in five minutes, and be certain you come alone and tell no one."

"Why should I?" Even as he asked the question, Daniel already suspected what the answer would be.

"Because if you don't, we'll kill your girlfriend." The black-eyed man stood and pointed at him. "Five minutes."

Those last two words were loud enough to earn a "Shhh!" from someone in the row behind them. The black-eyed man was already running out of the theater, though. Daniel chased his assassin and saw him climb into the back of a black Ford Taurus waiting out front. The door closed, but was open long enough for Daniel to see Allison in the back. Daniel shouted her name, but before he could reach the car, it sped away and around the next corner. His only consolation was that she didn't look hurt, just scared.

The Byrd was on the same street as Purgatory Alley. Five minutes. Did he run for it, or try to get his car and drive it?

RUN!

The voice in his head startled him, but the instant he heard that one word, he knew whose voice it was.

"You've been holding out on me," Daniel said.

Feng was right, though. He ran for it. As running goes, it wasn't going to break any high school records. He couldn't risk that he might trip and injure himself. He had to reach Purgatory Alley before the black-eyed man hurt Allison.

"Who is he?" Daniel asked between gasps.

Ishida Masanari. He was a samurai and fought beside me. Feng's voice was both new and yet familiar. Daniel recognized the tone of shame in that voice. Then he realized what Feng had said, this was a fellow samurai. How did that make sense? He was expecting this to be an enemy.

He is our enemy, Feng said, apparently reading Daniel's thoughts. *Ten of us learned about borrowed shadows, that we could find a form of immortality through them.*

Daniel let him roll with the history lesson. He tried to absorb the details as he darted down the sidewalk. There were still people outside, but not enough to slow him. He just had to avoid plowing into someone.

We had agreed to meet after we had taken over our hosts.

That stopped Daniel short of his destination. He was standing just beneath a street light about a hundred feet past the Can Can restaurant. Feng, wearing his helmet, was looking up at him from the sidewalk.

"You mean they possessed them?" He paused to catch his breath. "Like some demon!"

Yes, but I cannot do this to you. It requires the shadow to condition his host from an early age. I chose not to steal your life. Feng's arms spread out in a desperate gesture, a plea.

"And that's why these other samurai want you dead?" He wiped the sweat from his forehead before it could drop into his eyes.

We agreed to meet on a specific date.

"And when you didn't make that date, they thought you'd betrayed them?"

Feng answered with a nod. *So it would appear. I am sorry.*

"They're going to kill me and Allison, aren't they?"

Doubtless.

"Then we better hope all nine of them didn't come hunting for us." Daniel ran again. "Don't suppose you have a plan?"

One with slim hope.

• • •

The brief stop near Can Can allowed Daniel to reach Purgatory Alley without being completely exhausted.

He felt that familiar grip of semi-solid shadows as he stepped into the alley. The far end of the narrow space opened into a back lot for the businesses which had closed hours ago. As the lot came into view, he saw the black Ford Taurus. Ishida was standing in front of the car, flanked by two others. All of them were older than Daniel and looked like a bunch of Navy SEAL wannabes. The windows on the car were dark and tinted. He hoped Allison was in there, but there was no guarantee they hadn't dropped her off with someone else.

Daniel was breathing heavily and rested his weight on his cane.

Having the benefit of a car ride, Ishida stood tense but rested. A single light in the alley was shining down on them. Daniel realized the three in front of the car didn't cast any shadows.

They are within them, Feng whispered. Could these others hear Feng speak to him?

In the better light, Daniel saw their eyes weren't pure black, but a sea of colliding black winds, some darker than others.

"When you did not show in Tokyo, brother, we were worried." Those weren't the exact words Ishida used. Daniel assumed he'd spoken in Japanese. Feng whispered the translation to him.

"I'm not a threat to you." He tapped the black heel lift on the bottom of his right shoe with his cane. "We aren't a threat."

"Shut up, boy!" The snarl that contorted Ishida's face required no translation.

Daniel's fear set his heart pounding, making him lightheaded. He forced out the words Feng had told him to speak and tried not to think on the fact that Allison's life and his own were at stake.

"I will offer you one chance to release my friend and leave in peace. Do this, and we will never threaten you."

Ishida brought his hands together in front of him. Shadows shifted and formed the shape of a katana within his hands.

Somewhere in the back of Daniel's mind, he couldn't help but think that looked so cool. The other part of his brain was screaming to turn tail and run.

Put your trust in me, Daniel.

"Not much choice." He stepped backwards.

He felt more than saw Feng envelope his body like armor formed from darkness. This wasn't a possession like the others. This was protection and partnership. It was more than that, though. He could sense Feng's will and battle-trained instincts pushing his body and enhancing it to make up for his disabilities.

Ishida lunged at him. Daniel twisted the falcon head on his cane and the black stick slid apart from the handle to reveal the blade of a sword.

He countered Ishida's attack. His arms moved faster than his own thoughts. Whispers of Feng's memories filtered through his mind, including a sense of calm familiarity. War had been his borrowed shadow's life, and even in a second life, war had found him.

They used both parts of the sword cane, the blade and the stick, to defend themselves from Ishida. Panic kept Daniel moving, ducking left and right. The muscles in his arms burned.

What kept him in control and alive was Feng's calm. Even after so much time, this was just another sword fight among hundreds.

Then Daniel felt one of his swings connect. The stick of his cane cracked against Ishida's temple. The black-eyed man's jaw dropped, turning his lips into a round "O."

Feng's voice cried out. *Strike!*

Daniel kicked. His foot slammed into Ishida's knee with a crack. The black-eyed man fell to the ground with a guttural scream.

The other two came after him. Daniel struggled to deflect their shadow swords and was overwhelmed. One of them cut his left forearm and knocked the stick of his cane from his hand.

Even worse, Ishida was back on his feet. His injured leg swelled, bones clicking as if shifting back into place.

All three attacked now.

Into the alley! Even screaming, Feng sounded in complete control.

Daniel gave up on the sword fight and ran into the alley. The shadows floating in the narrow space nearly tripped him. He hoped they would do the same to Ishida and the other two.

Stopping short of the sidewalk on Cary Street, Daniel turned and faced Ishida. The alley made it impossible for more than one of them to attack him at a time.

Ishida wiped at a line of blood running down the side of his face. "Run, and your girl will die!"

Daniel held up his sword and looked past Ishida to see the other two had followed them into the alley.

"I'm not running." Daniel smiled.

Ishida's rage shifted to wide-eyed horror as he realized they'd walked into a trap.

"This is home court advantage."

A humanoid shape with green eyes darted out from one of the walls. Baxter wrapped fingers around Ishida's throat. "Say good night, Gracie."

Dozens of shadows erupted from the walls and surrounded all three of the black-eyed men. Baxter's other fingers extended and morphed into a pair of tentacles which grabbed the dark winds in Ishida's eyes and ripped the shadow from the body. The screams of all three men were muffled with no hope of reaching anyone on the street.

Startled, human eyes appeared where the spheres of shadows had once been, but they were lifeless eyes. All three bodies collapsed to the floor of the alley. The attacking shadows retreated into the black walls, taking the shadows of the three samurai with them.

Daniel stepped over the bodies and into the back lot. Feng was still in place as his armor when he pulled open the back door. Allison screamed through a gag that was duct taped into place. She struggled to pull away from him, but her arms and legs had been zip-tied together.

Feng peeled back now that they knew no one else was in the car. Allison relaxed once she saw his face. He helped her get free.

"They're dead," he said. "Are you all right?"

"They didn't hurt me." She scrambled out of the car and hugged him. This wasn't the first time they'd ever hugged, but it was probably the first time being that close hadn't felt awkward. He'd thought they were going to die.

They decided it would be better not to be around when someone found the bodies and went straight to Daniel's car. He didn't take her home right away since getting there early would raise too many questions.

He told her what had happened in the alley, how Feng was now talking, why the other samurai had wanted him dead and how the heat of the fight had distracted them from the potential dangers of entering Purgatory Alley.

Shortly after they'd stopped by a drug store to get something to cover the cut on his arm, they were driving back to Allison's house. "Are you worried the others might come after you?" she asked.

"Yes." His laughter betrayed his fears. "But Baxter plans to pass the word along to leave me and Feng be, and that if any of the other samurai show their faces in Richmond, they better not expect a warm reception from the shadows here."

They said little else until they pulled into her driveway. "Are you sure you're all right?" he asked.

"Can't say that was the best date I've ever had, but it's going to take more than a bunch of shadow-eyed freaks to mess me up." She put her hand on his arm and kissed him on the cheek. "Good job asking, though. I might just get you trained for some lucky girl before you know it."

"Very funny."

Daniel walked Allison to her front door and even got another peck on the cheek.

On the way home, he stopped at a corner near his house. He realized he couldn't wait any longer for an answer to the question that had pestered him since Feng had started talking, and he wanted to see Feng when he asked it.

He turned off the car and got out to stand beneath the streetlight. Feng stood along the ground like a midget version of him. He was glad to see Feng wasn't in helmet mode.

"Why didn't you do it to me? Why didn't you possess me the way the others did?"

I never had any children or a legacy to survive me. To do what we had planned would have made my only legacy an eternity of stolen lives. Feng's head turned to look away. *I am ashamed that I did not recognize this until after you were born.*

He remembered all the times Feng would entertain him and had looked out for him over the years. In many ways, he'd been like a strange blend of friend, guardian angel, and parent.

"You should have said something. You were silent all these years. Why?" His fist curled tightly about the handle of his cane. "Did you feel guilty?"

I made a vow to let you have your life. Shadows are silent.

He didn't know what to say to that. He was angry about all that Feng had kept from him, but would living his childhood in fear of shadow-born attackers really have been better?

"Without a borrowed shadow, I wouldn't have had a life at all, and I would've been really lonely growing up without you. I'm okay with you talking more, but I think I understand why you chose not to."

I am glad.

"So are we all good?"

Feng nodded and even added in a bow.

Daniel climbed back into the car, cranked the stereo and pressed the accelerator.

You drive too fast.

"Don't feel like you have to talk that much."

"Borrowed Shadows" was originally published by Chamberton Publishing as part of the science fiction/fantasy anthology Limelight *in October 2012.*

THE DEADLANDS

The first thing Paul noticed when he woke was the silence. Richmond didn't rank up there with New York where noise pollution was concerned, but the lack of sound was oppressive. He feared he was deaf until he heard his own breathing.

Moonlight, his only source of light, spilled in through the windows, but this wasn't his house. The last thing he remembered was sitting in the den with his parents, watching the TV as they waited to see if the world was coming to an end. Now, he was lying in a bed in some hospital. He wasn't sure how he'd gotten here. His back ached as he sat up, the way it got whenever he slept in too late on a Saturday.

The room felt cold. The stupid hospital gown he was sporting didn't help. He wondered if he could get an extra blanket or put on some real clothes. That was when he saw the shape on the floor near the door. He leaned closer and strained his eyes to figure out what was there.

"Oh crap!" Someone was on the floor, and they weren't moving.

He hit the buttons on the arms of the bed. He couldn't see the "call nurse" button, so he punched as many buttons as he could. Nothing happened, no beeps or lights or anything. "Hello! Help!" He stopped pushing buttons and screaming after a few minutes. No one answered.

Why was he even here, and where were his parents? Knowing Mom, the worrywart she was, she would have set up camp in this place. He couldn't just sit here. He needed to move. As he turned to climb out of the bed and go to the person on the floor, he realized he was wired up like a damn computer. He pulled out the IV first.

The bag it attached to was flat and empty. He also had sensor pads attached to his chest; the kind he assumed went to a heart monitor. He pulled them off; glad he didn't have a lot of hair there. That's when he realized they weren't attached to the same monitor. Two heart monitors? That didn't make sense, did it? And why weren't they turned on? He looked out the window and didn't see a single light on in all of Richmond, or anything on the horizon.

He called out again, not holding out much hope for an answer this time. Still nothing.

The tiled floor half froze his toes as he climbed out of the bed. He crept closer to the person on the floor. The body was dressed in a white coat, the kind doctors wore. He rolled the body onto its back. "Oh, God!" The body fell into a ray of moonlight. It was nothing but a grey, withered corpse with empty sockets of shadow for eyes. The doctor's body was still reaching for the door as if to pull help from beyond the room.

He scrambled back from the body and ran for the door. He flung it open, but he didn't rush into the corridor. Not a single light was on, not even the emergency lights. The moonlight coming through his windows provided him with the only light to be had. His eyes adjusted, granting definition to the dark shapes. He saw a nurses' station with two more bodies behind the counter. Both bodies were dried out and eyeless like the doctor in his room.

Paul shivered, as much from fear as the cold. He tried to remember how he got in this hospital, but he couldn't force a memory where it didn't exist. The last thing he remembered was the news showing images of an ethereal, pink and orange light enveloping everywhere on Earth. The light passed through the walls of his house, not merely through the windows, but through the walls. Mom and Dad didn't seem to feel anything, but his body broke out in goose bumps. Icy pain filled the inside of his chest. Everything went all dizzy. He fell to the floor. A blast of heat, his parents' screams and then... this.

His parents.

He needed to get home. That meant getting out of here, and

he wasn't doing that in the middle of winter dressed like this. He needed some real clothes. He could just make out a door behind the nurses' station and a row of lockers.

"Bingo."

He felt his way around the counter and into the locker room. He found a black turtleneck, some blue jeans and a really awesome brown leather jacket. The turtleneck came from a women's store, but he figured at this point he couldn't really be picky. Besides, who would know?

Now that he was winterized, Paul tried the phones. Every line was dead. He found a few cell phones in the nurse's lockers, but the batteries were drained.

He scored at least two cigarette lighters, and he needed them with the emergency lights out. He singed his thumb a few times trying to keep one of those lighters burning. The first one died on him halfway down the stairs.

He wasn't sure what he expected outside of the hospital. Anything would have been better than what he found. Cars were wrecked along the street with the dead still in the driver's seats. It looked as if everyone died all at once, everyone but him.

He needed a car. Do that and he could get to the West End, where his house was. Bad enough to find the hospital as it was, but now he was wondering just how far all this death went. Was this because of that weird light in the sky? Had it really been the end of the world? That didn't make sense. If it had, then how had he gotten in the hospital? He decided to worry about the rest of the world after he found a car. He ran to the nearest corner and saw a parking garage.

He found exactly what he wanted in the garage, an emaciated body on the ground just between two cars. The man wore a suit and tie and held his car keys in his hands. "Yes!" Paul snatched the keys from the guy. Even with what little moonlight he had, he could make out the VW logo.

"Well, this just sucks." His first time stealing a car, and it was a lousy, lime green Volkswagen Bug. "You could have at least made it a Mustang or a Mitsubishi 3000GT," he said with a look skyward.

Turned out he was bitching for nothing. When he turned the key, he got more silence, not even a cough or click. "Come on, dammit!" He tried to crank it at least a dozen times. Still nothing. Then he tried to turn on the lights, but he just got more, lousy nothing. The car's battery was as dead as its owner.

Paul slammed his fists on the steering wheel. Damn thing wouldn't even honk. He got out and repeatedly kicked and hit the car, screaming every curse he knew. When his hands hurt too much to hit the car again, he dropped to the ground and leaned back against the Bug. He planted his face in his hands, wishing all of this would just go away. He wanted to go home, but a dark thought had started to whisper in his mind, You really think home is still there?

"Well, I'll be damned," someone other than Paul said. "Was beginning to think I was never going to find you."

Paul jumped to his feet and scrambled between the cars. Only after he was there did it dawn on him that he'd just put himself in a corner with no way out except for climbing over the other cars.

"Who said that?" Paul looked right and left. The voice had sounded close, like the guy had been in front of him, but he didn't see anyone.

"Name's Philly."

Paul slammed back into the side of the Bug. "Holy crap!" The voice came from the top of the SUV next to him. There hadn't been anyone there a moment ago.

The guy was crouched on the SUV's roof. He was some pale-skinned guy with a buzz cut, wearing a black leather jacket.

"Sorry, kid, didn't mean to scare you."

Paul stared, unsure what to make of this guy. He was big, but the way he perched on that car made him look nimble like a gymnast. Something about him just felt… wrong, aside from the fact he was the only other person alive in a city full of dead people. Looking at Philly made Paul feel like lunch.

"You were looking for me?" Paul inched his way out from between the cars.

Philly stayed on the SUV and canted his head to watch Paul walk away. "Long story. We'll have time to get to that later. For now, we need to get you somewhere safe."

"How did you get here?" Paul felt a bit more comfortable once he had some distance between him and Philly. He'd always been a good runner, one of the best on his high school's cross country team. He wasn't so sure he could move faster than Philly, though. The guy might be big, but he looked fast. Maybe it was that buzz cut.

"Once I got in this mess, I had to walk until I found a bike. Let me tell you, I was pretty pissed when my car crapped out on me. Damn thing was a rental."

"Just how far is everything…" he paused, searching for the right words, "…like this?"

"Most of central Virginia. Lot farther than I'd expected. All the way north into Fredericksburg and south past Petersburg. Real number on the place, but at least most of the coast is still there. Suppose they'd rather get taken out by a hurricane or global warming… whichever comes first."

Paul felt as if his chest had collapsed on itself. If this grey death had made it that far, then his house was in the middle of all this. Why had it happened at all? Why here? And why wasn't he dead? He sat on the bumper of a car across from Philly's perch.

"So how long have I been out?" Paul asked.

"Out?" Philly's eyes were freaky. The way light reflected off of them reminded Paul of glitter. Philly glanced towards the exit of the parking garage. "Ah, you were in the hospital."

"Yeah." He still wasn't sure how he'd gotten there. "What's the date?"

"The date? Damn, kid, how long you been out?"

"I don't know!" Paul slammed his fist against the car he was sitting on. "If I knew, I wouldn't be asking."

Philly focused those strange eyes on him again and grunted this quiet laugh. "January twenty-eighth."

He did the math in his head. "More than a month."

Philly laughed even louder, which pissed off Paul. "Yeah, would have gotten here sooner, but it's been a real bitch trying to get into the U.S."

"It has? Why?"

Philly's head dropped to give Paul the kind of stare that usually works best over a pair of glasses. "Kid, if 9/11 was some parking lot fender bender, then this," he reached out with his arms as if to define the borders of death with his hands, "was the equivalent of a three hundred car pileup on I-95 at rush hour. People in the U.S. been thinking it's some terrorist, bio-chemical attack, so they haven't been letting anybody in the borders. Then you got everyone else in the world thinking it's some damn plague, so they didn't want to let anyone from the U.S. near their country.

"I was in Britain. Had to wait for the borders to open back up so I could look for you."

"Wait a minute." Paul leaned forward, looking intently for Philly's reaction to his next question. "You were expecting to find me? Why would you think to find anyone alive in here at all?"

Philly didn't answer right away. He hopped off the top of the car. The way Philly stood made being upright look more awkward for him than when he crouched.

Paul got to his feet, ready to run. Everything about this guy set off all sorts of alarms in his gut.

Philly held up his hands, showing he wasn't holding any weapons. Paul didn't think that made a difference with this guy, but at least he stopped walking closer.

"Relax, kid, I'm not gonna hurt you. Hell, I'm here to save you."

"Seems like I'm the only one here who doesn't need saving."

"What's happened here isn't a danger to you or me, but here's the catch. The other guys coming here, the ones who want you dead... this place isn't a threat to them either."

Paul leaned back against the car he'd been sitting on. "Want me dead? Why would anyone want to kill me?"

"You're a threat to them. The very fact you can survive here makes you dangerous."

Paul shook his head, trying to take in all of this in a way that made some sense. "Who are they?"

"Kid, judging from the looks of you, I don't think you're ready for that."

Philly was probably right. Paul's chest hurt. His heart was racing in an unfamiliar way, and he was sweating real bad. Dead of winter, and he'd already drenched the collar of his borrowed turtleneck. Heck, just breathing was getting hard to do. He forced himself back onto his feet.

"Look, thanks for the warning. If it's all the same to you, I'm gonna find a bike and get the heck out of here."

Philly put himself between Paul and the exit to the parking garage. "Hold up, kid. The bicycle is a good idea, but you aren't going to sneak past these guys, and truth to tell... I really can't let you leave the city. Not yet."

Paul heard his mom's nagging voice in his head, reminding him not to talk to strangers. "You tell me there are a bunch of guys coming here to kill me, and then you tell me I can't leave. Convenient." He walked past Philly, going as fast as he could without looking like he was running.

"Bad choice, kid," Philly said. "You need to trust me, or you're going to get yourself killed."

Paul turned around. "Look, pal, I don't know you—" He stopped short as he realized Philly wasn't there.

"Kid, you need my help or these guys will eat you alive."

Paul jumped as he heard Philly's voice. "Crap!" The guy was between him and the exit again. "How did you do that?" Damn, as if his heart wasn't beating fast enough already. "Nobody's that fast!" Nobody human.

"You can relax." Philly smiled as he took a step back. "If I wanted you dead, you'd be dead. I'm here to help you. The things that want to kill you, they're not as fast as I am, but they're just as deadly."

Paul's mind felt numb. Waking up in this death zone was about the most normal thing in his life at this point. Not good. "What do you mean by 'things'?"

"You want answers, and I get that," Philly said. "For now, let's see about those bicycles."

"You don't seem like you need one," Paul said.

"I can move fast, but I can only do it for so long. If I go too far, I get tired and need to get some juice."

Score one for Paul, given he was a long-distance runner. Of course, Paul would need a massive head start on Philly.

Philly walked towards the exit of the parking garage and motioned for Paul to follow. "I stashed a pair of bikes near here. You coming?"

Paul still wasn't sure he really trusted this guy, but Philly was right about one thing. He could have already killed Paul, if he'd wanted to. Didn't take much imagination to see how Philly could just do that super speed thing and crush Paul's windpipe. With that lovely mental image, Paul started walking.

"How much time do you think we have?" Paul asked as they walked back into the moonlight. "I mean before those 'things' you talked about get here." Things more deadly than Philly. Abso-stinkin'-fabulous.

"If we're lucky, we've got until tomorrow night, but best not to assume that."

"I can't decide if you're an optimist or a pessimist, Philly."

"I like to think of myself as an optimistic pessimist, kid. Less disappointment in life that way."

Philly led them down to East Broad Street and headed west. The way Philly walked, like a large cat, made Paul nervous, not that he didn't have plenty to make him that way already. Being with this guy was like being locked in a small room with a large cat.

What Paul wouldn't give for a car that worked. Of course, now that he was walking down Broad, one of the city's major streets, he saw the cars had clogged up the roads pretty good, one wreck after another. Even if he'd gotten that Volkswagen in the parking garage started, he probably wouldn't have gotten far. He'd need a tank to plow through this.

They walked a few blocks down from the hospital and past

City Hall. "Put 'em in here." Philly ran up the front steps to a large building that was all grey walls and large windows.

"What's this?"

"Library, according to the sign." Philly led them through a glass door that had been shattered. From the sidewalk, Paul hadn't even noticed it. There was a small elevator lobby to the right. "Found a bike on the sidewalk here, so I stashed that and mine in here."

"You already had a bike here for me?" Paul found that pretty damn disturbing. "Just how did you know where to look for me? That I was even close by?"

"Could sense you were somewhere near." Philly's tone made it clear he wasn't in the mood to discuss that any further. He picked up a backpack from the floor and slipped it on. Paul was startled to see a pair of swords sitting on the floor. "One of those is for you. Strap it on."

Each sword was in a sheath attached to a really long leather belt. "How fat did you think I was gonna be?" Paul asked.

"Just watch how I do it." He slipped off his jacket and wrapped the brown, leather belt around his waist several times and somehow positioned the sword perfectly on his left hip. The excess belt ran through a metal ring on the other end and down the front of his left leg.

Paul did his best to duplicate Philly's movements, but he had a devil of a time getting that sword to settle on his left hip the way it should. He noticed his belt looked new, whereas Philly's wore plenty of mileage and molded to his body.

"Surprised you left these swords here."

Philly laughed. "Expected you to be freaked enough as it was without the sword on my hip."

"Oh." Paul shifted the sword a bit until it felt more comfortable. "I got this thing on right?"

"That'll do." Philly walked his bike out the door and down to the sidewalk.

Paul followed him outside, pushing his bike by the handlebars west on Broad Street.

"Whoa, kid! Where are you going?"

Paul looked over his shoulder. "I'm going home. That's where I'm going."

"Why?"

"That's where I last saw my parents."

"Waste of time. All you're gonna find is a pile of ash."

"I'm still here, so maybe my parents are, too. What makes you so sure there's nothing there?"

"Because I've already seen what's left of your home. Whole world has."

"Just because this place is like this doesn't mean—"

Philly cut him off. "No, kid, that's not what I mean. Day the Avatar Light arrived, December twenty-first, a few places got wiped out. Your neighborhood was one of them. You were the only survivor. Was checking on another site like that outside of London when Central Virginia got wiped out."

"My parents?"

"Dead... on December twenty-first. Central Virginia joined 'em on January second."

"Everyone but me?"

Philly nodded. Paul's mind was fitting the pieces together, and for the first time, he was stepping back to really look at the big picture. Two disasters... and he'd survived both of them.

"You okay, kid?"

Paul's lips shivered before he could force out another word. "You—you were looking for me. You knew I was here."

Philly stared at him, the stillness of his body as hard as the silence of this place. "Kid, I don't think you're ready to hear this."

"Yeah." Pretty much what he'd expected. Paul climbed onto his bike to ride away.

"Whoa!"

Philly suddenly appeared in Paul's path, same as he'd done in the parking garage. Paul heard Philly's abandoned bike fall to the sidewalk behind him.

"Look, we don't have the time for you to go home and see it

isn't there."

Paul glared at him. "And just where am I supposed to go, Philly?"

"Eventually, we need to go to Washington, but first, we gotta make sure it's safe to take you out of the Deadlands."

"Safe? You mean those 'things' that are coming after me?"

Philly hesitated. "No, that's not what I mean. I mean that if you try to walk out of the Deadlands the way you are right now, you'll never find the borders and you'll just get a hell of a lot of people killed in the process."

The only survivor—twice. Paul didn't want to look at the picture, didn't want to hear what Philly was saying, even as a part of him already knew it.

"There are a lot people dead already, pal," Paul said, "and I don't care to join them."

"Paul, I'm going to say this as gently as I can, but I'm not sure there's a way to do that." Philly placed a hand on Paul's handlebars. "All this started with you."

"What?" He felt lightheaded as he took in those last few words.

"You couldn't help it, and it's not something you can control. Not yet, anyway. All this… it's not your fault, but if you leave here now that you know what you might do, then what happens next will be your fault."

Paul's palms were sweating, but he couldn't make his hands let go of the handlebars. "What do you mean I couldn't control it? What is 'it'?"

"You remember the light in the sky, how everyone thought it was gonna be the end of the world? Turns out it was. Only it's not some snap-of-the-fingers nightmare. That was just the start. Central Virginia, the Deadlands… that's step two. Only gonna get worse from here."

"What does that have to do with me?" He glared at Philly, which wasn't easy with the guy's strange eyes staring back at him.

"The Avatar Light changed certain people and none of them for the better. They can't help what they've become, what they're going to do," Philly said the next part real slow, like he was trying to apologize for what he was saying, "or what they've already done."

"I'm just a normal guy."

Philly laughed. "Yeah? Well then how do you explain being the only person, for a good fifty miles in every direction, to survive this shit?"

"Just shut up!"

"You're not normal anymore, kid. That's all changed. School's over for you." Philly didn't move, just kept his hands on the handlebars. Only thing moving was his mouth. His head didn't even turn. "You know your Darwin?"

"What?"

"Survival of the fittest," Philly said. "Darwinism. Kind of important to you right now, because the food chain in this world has all changed."

"Let go of the bike, Philly." He wanted to get away. He didn't care where he went, just so long as he wasn't here.

"Look, just place your hand on the right side of your chest, kid. I want you to feel for your heartbeat."

"What has that got to do with a damn thing?" He thought back to the hospital and the two heart monitors they'd attached to him.

"Just do it."

Paul placed his hand over the center of his chest. He didn't feel a heartbeat. Then he remembered what Philly had said, to put his hand on the right side of his chest. He shifted his hand right until he felt his heartbeat. It shouldn't be that far right, should it?

Philly was about to say something else, but he must have realized Paul was already placing his left hand on the other side of his chest. Yes, he knew why Philly was asking him to do this, and he knew exactly what he was going to find. He'd hoped he'd imagined it the first time in the hospital, but a second heartbeat on the opposite side of his chest pounded proud and impossible to deny.

Philly nodded, seeing the panic on Paul's face.

"There's only one reason you're still alive in this place, kid, and that's because you're the one at the top of the food chain right now."

"Shut up!" Paul took his hands from his chest and tried to

shake the bike loose, but Philly's grip didn't budge.

"Every bit of life in this place, every soul and more... all of it eaten... by you."

Paul's body went cold as Philly said it.

"You're a soul-feeder, kid... new top of the fuckin' food chain. The Avatar Light awakened—"

"Shut up!" Paul jumped back, off the bike. "You're lying!"

Philly lowered Paul's bike to the ground. "Kid—"

"No! You're lying!"

"It wasn't your fault." Philly stayed down next to the bike, looking up at Paul.

"I said shut up!"

"Paul, it's January twenty-eighth. For a guy who's been sleeping in a hospital for close to a month, you smell pretty damn healthy to me. Last time you probably had any food or water was more than what? Almost a month ago? You should have starved to death by now or damn close to it, but I'll bet you don't even feel hungry, do you?"

He didn't. He hadn't even thought of food, hadn't really needed it yet. He thought of the IV bag—wrinkled, flat, and empty—hanging next to his hospital bed.

He stumbled backwards and landed on his ass. His mom and dad.... He looked over at a wrecked car on the library's steps, saw the driver's dried up body slumped over the steering wheel.

"Oh, God."

Paul cradled his head in his hands and screamed. He didn't want to hear the silence. He tried to drown it out, but he couldn't scream forever.

His throat hurt when he stopped. After that shout, he expected to find his life at an end, but he was still here. Only thing ended here was the world, with him left behind.

When he looked up, he found himself meeting Philly's eyes. There might have been sympathy hiding there, but Paul couldn't swear to it and wasn't even sure it mattered. All the sympathy in the world wasn't going to change that.

"Kid, I'm going to make this simple for both of us. What's coming here for you... That sword on your hip won't save you. Most that'll do is keep you alive a little longer. You want to die, I'll just walk away. Don't care to get myself killed if I don't need to, and after what I just told you, I suppose some people in your shoes might want to end it all.

"You want to live, though," Philly let the offer hang out there a moment, "I'll stick around, and we might just save your happy assets."

The possibility of dying hadn't felt this real even when he'd been sitting in front of the TV with Mom and Dad, waiting for the Light to reach Earth. He'd always thought of people who committed suicide as wimps too scared to get off their ass and deal with it. He wasn't so sure of that now. Some things did seem bad enough to flip the bird at God and say, I'm done.

"What would they do to me?" Paul asked. "What are they, and what'll they do if I just let them kill me?"

Philly didn't nod or blink. "They're called fördröj frånfälle. You'd probably call them zombies, but forget that 'Night of the Living Dead' shit. We're not talking about a bunch of rotting corpses moaning and dragging their way down the street. These bastards are almost as fast as me and a lot stronger. The difference is that they don't have free will, but that doesn't mean they can't think independently. They're just servants to the one who stole their souls. That's the only reason they can survive here. If they get a hold of you, they'll eat you alive... harvest your soul for their mistress."

"Last part sounds poetic." Would hardly even the score, though. He wondered just how many times he'd have to be killed to make things right.

"Never liked poetry. Too morbid for my tastes," Philly said. "The good news? You won't become a monster like them. Doesn't work like that."

"I already am a monster," Paul said. "Isn't that what you're telling me?"

Philly smiled. "Trust me on this, kid. If there's one thing I've learned in my time, you can't be turned into a monster. To become a monster… a beast… that's something you have to choose."

Paul wanted to believe that, just wasn't sure he did.

"All right, kid, what's it going to be? I leave you to become dinner, or we get moving?"

Paul looked down at the sword on his left hip. Probably less painful to kill himself with that than get eaten alive. Could he do that? What if he screwed it up and then was too weak to finish the job? He knew himself better than that; he'd never get up the nerve to do it. He couldn't even stand the idea of getting his finger pricked at the doctor's office. The fear of the pain won out. He just wasn't ready to flip the bird at God, so he'd have to get off his ass and deal with it.

"What do I have to do to make sure I don't kill anyone else when I walk out of here?"

"Good for you." Philly smiled at him. "First thing we need to do is find us a skull, and here's the kicker, kid. You're going to lead us to it."

Somehow, Paul didn't think he was going to like this.

"This should be simple enough," Philly said, "because you've obviously found it before."

Paul took the handlebars from Philly and climbed on. "Found what?"

"It's a crystal skull. All this stuff here, all the damage… you couldn't do this yourself. The skull can enhance your powers, but it also gives you greater control, which is how we get you out of the Deadlands without getting anyone else killed."

"Great, but wasn't like they had one sitting in my hospital room, Philly. I think I would have noticed it."

"Wouldn't need to be. As long as you're close enough to it, you can use it. That means it's probably here in the downtown area."

"So how do I find it?" Paul looked up and down the street, expecting to see those zombies Philly had talked about.

"You just need to listen for it. Same way I found you. I could probably find the skull myself, but being this close to you, you drown it out."

Paul strained to listen, but the silence was all he heard. "Everything here is just so quiet. I'm not hearing anything."

"It's not exactly a sound, more like the breathing of the spirit. Close your eyes."

Paul felt like a glorified idiot, but he closed his eyes.

"Now put that image of a crystal skull in your mind. Your soul's already touched it, explored it. All you need to do is remember its voice and find your way back."

Remember its voice. Easy for him to say. Paul could imagine a crystal skull. That was easy enough, but the picture in his mind somehow seemed wrong. He wasn't sure how to make it right. Hell, he wasn't even sure why he knew it was wrong. The shape was close. That was the easy part, but even that wasn't right. What's missing? He kept asking that question without even really knowing how he was sure it was wrong.

"What color is it?" Paul asked.

"Hell if I know, kid."

Lot of help he was. Paul tried the different colors, beginning with the same eerie blend of pink and orange as the light in the sky that started all this. "No," he whispered. He tried different shades of blue and green before he imagined that skull of translucent rock in a shade of vibrant red. The image settled within his mind along with an undefined whisper. He thought it was like a piano, but one note held without end, so soft he could barely hear it. Just focus on what's wrong, he told himself. The color was right. He knew that, but there was something about the skull that was still wrong. Then he saw the hole in the back of it, the fracture lines flowing from it in a spider web pattern. That lone note swelled, and Paul knew exactly which direction to take.

"Let's go." Paul turned his bike west and headed down Broad Street. They went much farther than he expected. Philly said the skull didn't need to be close, but they'd traveled more than a dozen blocks, eventually even passing the Siegel Center. Dad had promised to take him to a VCU Rams basketball game this season, but no more games were going to be played there. He tried not to think about it, tried to focus on the skull.

That note grew louder as they continued west. The same way the right word sometimes helped him remember a dream, the skull's sound made his mind drift back to his hospital room. A vague image of the room, drenched in sunlight, lifted from the debris of his mind. He saw the doctor standing by his bed, talking to him. He could hear her voice, and he realized the note had been there, too.

The long note of the skull dipped, shocking Paul back to the present. His bike skidded to a stop, and he realized they'd just crossed Boulevard, having passed the Science Museum.

Philly stopped a few feet past him, not expecting the sudden stop.

"What is it?" Philly looked around them. Seeing as there wasn't a red, crystal skull in sight, he had the appropriate confusion on his face.

"Why are you here?" The distraction of Paul's memories helped him step back enough to recognize all the things wrong about Philly being here. "How are you here?"

"Came here to find you." He made that sound so damn obvious.

"Why? I mean, I killed all these people. Plenty of folks would gladly kill me, would see those zombies heading here for me an appropriate punishment. So I gotta ask. Why are you here helping me?" Or am I helping you? Paul didn't have a guarantee that Philly didn't want this skull for some other reason.

He saw Philly considering his words, and that just set Paul off. "Answer the damn question! Don't sit there and think on it, just answer!"

To his surprise, Philly almost jumped off the seat of his bike. Son of a bitch wasn't expecting that, and he spit out the answer plenty fast, too.

"I was sent to get you, because you're not the only one who was changed by the Avatar Light. Remember the other burn spot outside of London I mentioned. That was another awakening. Quite a lot of them around the world."

"More soul-feeders?" Paul got that next question off right away. He figured he had this cocky bastard off-balance, and he needed to press for all the info he could get.

"Some, but others received different powers from the Avatar Light."

"Who sent you?"

"He's gone by plenty of names, but these days, he prefers to be called Organal."

"Or-gahn-all?" Paul said the name slowly, trying to get it straight. What the hell kind of name was that anyway? "And what does he want with me?"

"There are beings now walking this world that will make what you did here seem like nothing. They'll wipe out the people of this world as they feast on your souls. That second heart in you isn't yours. That's another life, the source of your new powers. Most avatars, they no longer have control of their bodies. Their new heart is in the driver's seat."

Paul wasn't sure he believed that. Of course, he didn't want to believe any of this was real. He just wanted it to be a nightmare so he could wake. "And what are you?"

Philly groaned. "Shit, kid. You aren't going to like this answer."

"Haven't liked much of what you've told me so far."

"Yeah, good point." Philly sat up and scratched the back of his head, stalling for the brief moment he could. "You see, I'm a vampire."

Paul felt his blood go cold as he contemplated pedaling for all he was worth. Any other day, he'd have laughed and said, "Yeah, right," but this was about as far from a normal day as a guy could get.

Philly held up his hands in that 'I'm-not-packing-any-weapons' gesture that didn't mean a whole hell of a lot.

"It's all right, kid. Trust me when I say we vampires have gotten a bad rap over the past few centuries. We don't go around killing people every time we get hungry. We can't turn other people into vampires either. Hell, being a vampire is the only reason I'm able to be here to help you. Any normal humans entering the Deadlands, they all die pretty quickly. If Organal could have come himself, he would have, but under the circumstances, you've got me."

That continuous note of the skull distracted Paul. He could hear something else in there now, too, but he wasn't sure what it was. Almost like several, tiny staccato notes at a higher pitch. Did that mean he was getting closer?

He looked back at Philly and decided he didn't have any real options here. Either he worked with Philly, or he took his chances. He didn't know enough about those fördröj frånfälle to risk it alone, assuming they even existed. Maybe they weren't even out there, and all this was some clever lie to make him lead Philly to that skull. He didn't know enough to feel like any choice was the right one, and it was driving him nuts.

"All right, but I'm getting that skull myself. When I decide it's time for you to stay back, then you do it."

Philly nodded. "If that's what it takes to make you comfortable, then that's what we'll do."

That Philly agreed to that so easily didn't offer much reassurance, but what else could Paul do? He needed to know more about everything instead of making all his decisions blindfolded. He tried to consider what he did know... what he knew about Philly and whether he really trusted him. So far, he realized all he really trusted was what Philly had told him, but not necessarily Philly himself. That would have to do for now.

"Let's go then."

Philly didn't say anything this time. He fell in behind Paul as they turned around and pedaled onto the Boulevard.

They only went a few more blocks. He heard the skull sounding to his right from a place he recognized from one of his childhood field trips of all things.

"That's the Fine Arts Museum."

Philly laughed. "Yeah, and I think we can safely say your skull is here." He pointed to a banner hanging on a pole next to the building. A shiver that had nothing to do with winter worked through his back as he looked into the empty sockets of the skull he'd envisioned, its crystal red as blood.

"The Crystal Skull Exhibit." Philly read the banner. "Here through March tenth."

"Guess it's leaving sooner than expected." Paul climbed off his bike and walked it up to one of the many bike racks positioned on the right side of the building. He placed his bike next to a red bike that looked much nicer than his. He considered trading up, but it had one of those u-shaped bike locks on it.

"You got a lighter?" Paul didn't look forward to walking into a dark building, and this place was plenty big. They could have that skull displayed anywhere.

Philly looked disgusted by the question. "Sorry, kid. I don't smoke."

Just his luck... a health conscious vampire. What were the odds of that? He'd just have to make do with the lighter he had left, assuming it would even last. He suspected the fuel was burning up faster than it normally would, another byproduct of whatever had happened to this place.

"Let's go in and get it, kid."

"No." Paul glared at him. "I'm going in alone. You can wait here."

Philly parked his bike and sprawled on the grassy field as he slid on a pair of sunglasses. "Fine. I'll just work on my tan. Have fun."

"Vampire humor," Paul muttered. "Cute."

Philly grinned, giving Paul a good look at his canines, pointed and deadly like a wild cat's. He didn't linger to admire them.

At least whatever had happened took place during the day. Meant all the doors to this place were unlocked.

Thankfully, he didn't need the lighter yet. The walls and ceiling to the museum had enough windows to illuminate the place by the moon. Just inside the entranceway, the floor was littered with bodies, all withered in the same manner as his doctor. At least two dozen small corpses formed a neat row along the right wall. They must have been a school group.

"Just don't think about it," he whispered to himself, a little less thankful now for all the moonlight.

The entranceway opened into the atrium. The ceiling reached three stories high. The front and back walls were all glass, making it much easier to see. He heard the skull better. The note came from above him, but not directly. Was it on the second or third floor? He must have been close, because he could hear those staccato notes more clearly, too.

He wasn't sure which way to go. Two sets of stairs led up from the atrium and to the rest of the museum. He stepped over a body, moving deeper into the atrium. Orange chairs were gathered in the middle of the floor. People's bodies were still sitting there. One body had its back to Paul and had long, white hair.

"Don't think about the bodies," he reminded himself. That was easier said than done with so many. He didn't want to think about how many were dead, how many he'd killed. He closed his eyes for a moment to reorder his thoughts. The desire to make right all that he'd done wrong was noble. He knew that, but he also knew he wouldn't survive to do shit if he didn't focus and find that skull.

Which way? He opened his eyes again and looked at the far stairs and then to the set starting just to his left. Another crystal skull banner was hanging on the wall with an arrow that pointed up the near set of stairs.

"Oh." Made sense the museum would post signs directing people to their star exhibit. He climbed the stairs to the second floor, stepping through the shadows of an overhang and onto a walkway connecting both sides of the second floor. The crystal skull signs pointed left, straight over to a set of sliding glass doors. "Which don't work without electricity. Great." He tried to slip his fingers through the slit running down the middle of the doors, but he couldn't get a good grip. How the hell was he supposed to get through here? He could hear the skull's note ring clear from somewhere beyond these doors. Maybe he could shatter the glass with the sword Philly had given him. He pulled it out, the feel of the hilt in his hand too unnatural to give him any confidence.

His thoughts about the skull, the sword, and those doors

stopped. Goose bumps prickled along his arms as he heard those staccato clicks, but they weren't coming from the same direction as the skull anymore. They were behind him.

He turned around, but he didn't see any movement, nothing that might be a threat, not that he really had a damn clue what to look for.

Fördröj frånfälle. Paul mulled over the term in his head, and he found it odd how it seemed simple for him to use. Foreign languages weren't his thing, and usually something like that would have left him joking, "Frodo Baggins ran and fell?" But "fördröj frånfälle" felt simple for him to handle.

Those staccato notes sounded louder than ever, but this time, he heard something else: the sound of a footfall on the marble tile of the walkway.

A single booted foot appeared from the shadows of the overhang on the far end of the crosswalk. Most of the leg and the rest of the body disappeared into the shadows as if nothing else was there. Then another boot stepped out of the shadows, as if cutting through the darkness until the entire figure appeared. In every aspect, he looked like a normal man, save for the brilliant white of his long, straight hair and the green glow to those eyes. That smile, though... that smile offered nothing human.

He thought the man's appearance from nothingness was a trick of the shadows, but then two more appeared, one on each side of the first.

"Fördröj frånfälle?" Paul's body shivered as he said the name. Only after the fact would he realize what a fool he'd been, letting his fear freeze him to the spot.

The one with the long hair nodded in reply. His arm drew a handgun from his jacket in a motion almost too fast to see. Paul jumped as he heard the trigger click. Surprise flashed in the zombie's green eyes, and he looked none too pleased.

Paul laughed, a weak grunt of relief. The Deadlands, however the hell they worked, must have stopped the gunpowder from igniting. "Sorry, that must be my fault." His legs finally took over.

The zombies blocked his way back down, so he ran up the stairs for the third floor.

He reached the top steps and looked left, the direction he needed to go to reach the skull. More sliding glass doors, but a body had fallen between, just enough room for him to slip through. "Philly!" he shouted as he went through the opening. What were the odds the idiot would hear him?

He ran straight, blind to which way ensured safety or if he could get back downstairs to reach the skull. Was he cornered up here? As he passed a large statue of a bird battling a snake, he looked over his shoulder to see the zombies chasing him. They disappeared and reappeared as their bodies stepped in and out of the shadows.

The skull was on the second floor, and he was on the third. He needed down. Running straight brought him to a set of stairs, but those zombies were gaining. Damn they were fast! Their boots shrieked along the marble floor as they dodged displays to pursue Paul.

He ran down the stairs jumping the last few steps. In his fear, he surrendered to instinct. The skull's note called him, and he raced for it.

"Philly!"

He ran into a room which seemed nothing but shadows. He could only hear, not see, the zombies pursuing him. He heard one of them trip, probably on one of the many bodies on the floor.

Thin moonlight came from a connecting room ahead. The silhouette of a horse blocked his path. He dodged the animal statue and saw more light ahead. Even better, he spotted a sign for the crystal skull, pointing to the left.

Moonbeams cut through a window and filled the room with light. Then he saw it. The red skull rested within a glass display case, glowing in the natural light. That glorious note sang proud and stopped Paul cold. It was like walking in on an angel caught singing in the shower. He suffered for that mistake.

One of the zombies tackled him. Pain shot through his back as he slid across the marble tiles. The sword in his hand clattered to the floor as he lost his grip. The zombie failed to keep hold of him, an angry growl ripping from its throat as it scrambled after him. It was "Long Hair."

Paul grabbed the sword, but the victory was short-lived. Another zombie grabbed him by the throat and lifted him off the ground. He gasped for breath. He thrust the sword into the zombie's chest. He expected an explosion of blood or something equally gross, but the blade just thrust a few inches into the chest and stopped. The zombie grabbed the base of the blade and pushed it out. Dude was strong as hell.

The zombie smirked up at him as he ripped the sword from Paul's hand. Paul shoved his knee up into the zombie's jaw. He heard a satisfying crack of bone, but the zombie didn't flinch, didn't seem to feel any pain. The zombie's face clenched. With an irritated grunt, the zombie tossed Paul down. He landed on his back, giving his spine a rude wake-up call. He saw the zombie reach into its mouth, working the jaw as he seemed to manually right his teeth.

"Oh, hell."

The first zombie, Long Hair, looked down at Paul. He was plenty pissed, too. Paul rolled aside just before the zombie could plant a boot on his face. Long Hair grabbed Paul by the arm and jerked him up off the ground. His shoulder felt like it would dislocate held up like this.

The zombie licked his lips.

"Philly!" Paul shouted.

One of the zombies flew past Paul and Long Hair and struck the wall. As it stood, Paul realized the zombie was missing its head.

Unsure what else to do, Paul stabbed his fingers at Long Hair's eyes. That got a reaction, the closest thing to panic he'd seen from one of these things. The zombie dropped him and wailed as it retreated, temporarily blinded. Thank God. His arm couldn't have taken being held like that much longer.

Paul looked towards the door and saw Philly fighting with the shortest of the three, the one he'd kneed in the jaw.

"Kid, heads up!" Philly kicked the head he'd sliced off to Paul like a soccer ball. "Toss it out the window!"

Paul caught the head in his hands. The face looked at him, the eyes still working and that mouth biting in the vain hope of getting a mouthful of human.

"Out the window!" Philly yelled just before "Shorty" tackled him into the shadows of an adjoining room. "Cack!"

Paul didn't see why he needed to do anything with the head other than drop it until he looked up at the headless body, charging straight for him.

"Crap!"

Paul dodged Deadhead's body as it tried to grab him. Long Hair also swung at him. Paul rolled with the hit to his head, landing just beneath the window. He got to his feet and flung the head at the window, but the glass didn't break. The head just bounced back into his hands.

"Oh, not good."

Paul looked up in time to see Long Hair come at him again and ducked. The jerk didn't get another shot at him. Deadhead's body, chasing after its head, tackled into Long Hair, and they both went through the window. Shards of glass spilled down onto Paul as he dropped the zombie's head and covered his own.

Before he stood, Paul shook off the glass like a wet dog after a bath. Careful not to cut himself on the window, Paul looked down to see the two zombies. Long Hair was already getting up and seemed to be straightening his arms in the same manner Shorty had fixed his teeth and jaw. Deadhead's body flailed on the ground next to Long Hair. "What does it take to kill these things?" Paul almost chucked the head out the window, but then he figured the body might just put it back on.

"Needs your eyes to see what it's doing, huh?" he said to the head on the floor. One of the connecting rooms had some stairs leading down. He flung the head over the railing. Let the bastard's body waste its time trying to find a way back inside the museum and to its head.

He heard Philly struggling with Shorty in the other room, but he didn't run to help. Just get the skull and get out of here, his instincts whispered to him.

The glass box holding the skull looked pretty solid. He tried to lift it, but it was sealed shut. How the hell did they put it in there? He didn't have time to figure out that puzzle. He looked around for the sword and found it along the wall near the window. He glanced out the window again. Only the headless one was out there, stumbling about. Deadhead's body was heading straight in the direction where its head had landed. Weird, but at least that would keep him out of play. Question was how long it would take Long Hair to get back here, probably not long enough.

Paul gripped the sword with both hands and swung it like a bat at the glass case. The first strike didn't shatter the case. What was this stuff? Bulletproof glass? He swung again and again. Cracks appeared in the glass. "Come on!" Another strike and the cracks spread. He heard footfalls drawing closer, someone running in his direction. Long Hair? Paul screamed as he threw all his strength into one last swing. The glass case failed to shatter. Long Hair appeared from around the corner and tackled him. Paul's head cracked against the floor as a cold hand wrapped around his throat, pinning him.

Paul tried to yell for Philly, but he couldn't do more than gasp, struggling for a breath. He saw the zombie's fist pull back, ready to strike.

He'd lost his sword in the fall. He reached for it, but it was too far away! Dammit, he needed the skull, but it was still trapped in glass.

He remembered what Philly had said. He'd used it before, touched it without actually holding it in his hands. He fixed the image of that skull in his thoughts, and it was as if someone poured ice-cold soda directly on his brain—one of those moments where everything but him just stopped. He heard what sounded like thunder, then glass shattering, and the skull leaped to his hand. The red crystal no longer seemed so solid, but more fluid as the eye sockets and shape of the skull vanished, replaced with something else. The new shape, circular and curved outwards, wrapped about his forearm as he swung at the zombie's head.

The edge of that glass circle smashed into Long Hair's head, knocking him off. The screech from Long Hair sounded beautiful to Paul's ears. He'd begun to think nothing could actually cause these monsters pain. Judging from its expression and the way the zombie gingerly touched the place Paul had struck it, the monster was just as surprised. It stumbled back towards the door. Those green eyes narrowed on him, the brief fear passing. Paul felt his courage growing, though. The feel of that reshaped crystal resting on his arm felt better than anything he'd ever known.

Long Hair roared, but just as he charged on Paul, a sword slashed across the zombie's throat from behind. The head bounced along the floor. That didn't stop the body. It was still running straight at him. Paul struck the headless torso in its gut with the reshaped skull. The strike flung the body across the room. The body struggled back to its feet, but not before Philly shoved it out the window to join Deadhead.

Philly slid his sword back into its sheath, and he looked plenty satisfied as he looked out the window at his handiwork. "Nice. Now let's get the skull and run for it."

"Already have the skull." Paul held up his right forearm to display his trophy. He glanced past Philly as he heard thudding from the neighboring room. "Where's the one you were dealing with?"

Philly pointed at Long Hair's head. "Same as that one, only I pitched the head back upstairs." The vampire glanced at the empty display case and then stared at the red crystal on Paul's arm. "That's a shield, kid. Where's the skull?"

"This is the skull," Paul said. "It changed."

"All right then, kid, let's go before these freaks get themselves back together."

That sounded like a good idea to Paul. He recovered his sword and shoved it back into its sheath. "Shouldn't we finish them off before they can put themselves back together?"

"Only way to do that is to cremate the damn things. Sadly, I'm fresh out of crematoriums."

"Oh."

Paul followed Philly out of the museum. He navigated through the place with a lot more ease than Paul, but those glittering eyes probably worked better in the dark. The sliding glass doors where the zombies had confronted Paul were now open. Philly must have forced them.

"Pedal hard, kid. We need one hell of a head start on these guys, and if they catch up before we can get out of the Deadlands, we're screwed."

Paul took him at his word and they rolled for the interstate.

• • •

The night seemed like it would never end. Paul's leg muscles were burning worse than after a three mile race. He wanted a hot bath to soak his legs, but that wasn't going to happen. The temperature just kept getting colder. Thankfully, whoever had previously owned his new jacket had stuffed some gloves into the pockets. He wasn't sure how he would have survived those coldest hours, otherwise, as he held onto the handlebars.

The interstate turned out a lot easier to navigate than the city streets. Most of the wrecks had gone onto the right or left shoulders. Unfortunately, they'd run into a few jackknifed tractor trailers with a few other cars plowed into them that blocked every lane. One pileup was so bad that it forced them to climb over the cars. That would have been tough enough without trying to lift a bike over the mess. Paul's new shield wasn't helping matters either. It was just one more thing to carry, and it must have been at least two-and-a-half feet in diameter. Still, he was surprised at how light it felt, even shoved up his arm enough for his hand to get a grip on the handlebars.

The ride didn't offer a chance for him and Philly to talk, not as fast as they were moving. That left Paul plenty of time to worry about how quickly those zombies would put themselves back together and how long it would take them to catch up.

Thinking on his shield was only slightly less troubling. He

wasn't sure why the skull changed for him or why into this shape. The bowl of the shield was solid. The straps on the inside were made out of the same crystal material, but they could stretch and bend to whatever length he seemed to need. He didn't see how this was going to keep his powers from killing more people, but Philly acted as if he was satisfied. For now, that was good enough for Paul.

"Exit ramp!" Philly shouted as he turned his bike onto the 118 exit.

Paul stirred from his thoughts and wiped his brow before the sweat could fall into his eyes. He wasn't sure how far from Fredericksburg they were at this point. Only thing he knew for sure was that they were north of Ashland. According to Philly, they'd be out of the Deadlands once they made it past Fredericksburg.

"Why are we getting off here?" Paul shouted to make sure he was heard. He was having to do that standing-pedal thing just to get up the exit ramp.

"We need to get indoors," Philly said. "It's almost sunrise."

"So?"

Philly looked back at him like he was an idiot and then pointed at himself. "Hello! Vampire! Moon, good; sun, really really bad!"

Paul rolled his eyes. "Sue me! I was more worried about the zombies that are chasing us. It's not my fault you sunburn so easily."

Philly didn't bother with a clever comeback. Probably a good sign he wasn't exaggerating his fear of sunlight.

They took a right and went down a tree-lined road until they reached the opening to a long driveway on their left. Once they started down the driveway, a two-story house came into view.

"This'll have to do," Philly said.

Paul looked toward the eastern sky and could see the black cover lighten ever so slightly into a dark grey.

Philly ditched his bike and ran for the front door. He kicked it open and ran upstairs. Paul followed him inside as Philly darted into the bathroom carrying a comforter and pillow taken from one of the bedrooms.

"You okay in there?" Paul asked.

"Yeah, just try to keep it down," he shouted through the door. "I'd like to get some sleep."

Paul heard him moving around in there. The edge of a towel stuck out from beneath the door. Philly wasn't taking any chances on sunlight getting in there.

"What about the zombies?" Paul asked.

"Nothing more to do, kid." Philly's voice was muffled. Sounded like he was using the bathtub for his bed. "Just make the house as sun-proof as you can. Otherwise, you'll be on your own if those zombies get here before sunset."

"Great," Paul muttered.

He looked around the house before he did anything else. Place was decorated like some farmhouse, just without a farm. To his relief, he didn't find any dead bodies. Whoever lived here must have been at work when everyone died. "Just don't think about that," he told himself. Instead, he did what Philly had asked. He found a linen closet and pulled out as many sheets as he could find.

He got a hell of a scare when he got to the utility room. Soon as he opened the door, he spotted three roaches on the floor.

"Holy crap!" He jumped back, ready to stomp the life out of them, but they didn't move. None of them scattered for shadow. They just sat there. He mustered up the courage to nudge one of them with his foot. Still no scattering. Paul laughed. The roaches hadn't survived the end of the world, after all. That would disappoint all the scientists.

He kicked the insect carcasses out of the way and searched the utility room until he found a tool box. The best he'd hoped for were some nails and a hammer. He did better than that. He found a staple gun.

Before long, he'd stapled enough sheets over the windows to put the house back into darkness. He had to leave the back door open just so he could have some light. The fireplace looked useable, but he decided against that. The light and warmth would have been really nice, but the smoke from the chimney would lead the zombies straight here. Might as well put up a sign on the interstate that said "Exit Here."

Once that was done, he realized he was hungry. The sensation scared him at first, but then he decided that might be a good sign. If he was getting hungry—normal-type hungry—then maybe what his body wanted was regular food and he didn't need to kill anyone to survive. That meant his new shield was doing something to help him safely leave this place. He didn't want to think about that too much, but he'd take what hope he could get.

Paul looked through the kitchen. The best he found was some seriously stale cereal. He suspected the box might taste better but stopped short of taking a bite out of it… the box, not the cereal (which was gross). He glanced at the fridge, but he sure as hell wasn't going to open that. Probably smelled something pretty nasty in there after almost thirty days without power to keep everything from rotting. He remembered seeing a few convenience stores and gas stations on the other side of the interstate.

After leaving Philly a note, he got on his bike and headed back for the interstate. He stopped on the overpass and tried to sense those zombies, but didn't hear any of those staccato notes he'd noticed back in the museum.

Talk about a damn, dreary sight. From here, he could see a good ways down I-95 North and all the wrecks he still hadn't gotten past. He figured it was well into morning by now, but he couldn't see the sun. The sky was completely overcast. He'd thought the grey look to the world had just been a trick of the night, but now that it was daytime, little had changed. Whatever his powers had done, it was almost as if he'd sucked all the color out of the world along with its life. The only thing that didn't look grey in the whole damn place was the red shield on his arm. Something that had been a skull just a few hours ago was now the most lively-looking thing here. The shield felt as natural on his arm as a shirt's sleeve. He'd used this thing to kill hundreds of thousands, and it felt so right on his arm that he could almost forget it was there. Then just don't think about it and keep moving, he told himself. He didn't want to dwell on what he'd done, all those people, his parents…. Dammit, just stop it and move!

The convenience store turned out to be a good call. He found a bunch of stuff in there. The place smelled something awful. Thank God it was winter. He must have been starving, because even standing in that horrid stench of rotted food and decaying bodies, a hot dog or a sandwich still sounded awesome. He made do with the fruit bars and energy bars he found on the shelves. For dessert, he went with two packs of his favorite candy bar, a peanut butter Twix, washed down with a bottle of "room temp" Mountain Dew which wasn't half bad, thanks again to the cold weather.

Wasn't the best meal, but at least he didn't feel hungry anymore. He hoped that meant he wouldn't need to kill to survive. That's all it was now, wasn't it? Surviving.

He walked past the counter. A man who'd probably stopped for gas was lying on the floor. He leaned over and saw the cashier's body behind the counter. Trying not to think about what he'd done wasn't going to work forever. The shield he carried would be a constant reminder.

Surviving wasn't enough either. He needed a way to make this right, a way to make up for what he'd done, but he didn't see a way to do that. They were heading towards DC, but for what? He didn't know anyone there. He didn't even have any money. At this point, the only reason he had anywhere to go at all was to get away from these zombies.

As he walked outside, Paul heard what sounded like someone stepping on gravel. That was scary enough, but when he heard it a second time, he recognized what he'd really heard, the distant sound of that staccato note.

"Oh no."

Paul scrambled back onto his bike and headed back towards the interstate and pedaled as hard as he could for the house where he'd left Philly. Even with the food he'd just eaten, he wasn't moving as fast as he had been. He could feel exhaustion setting in. You'd think after sleeping for more than a month, he'd be able to go longer without sleep. As he went across the overpass, he looked south.

All he saw were those cars piled up like some psychopath's lego-creations. No sign of the zombies, but he could hear them getting closer, those sharp notes that he was starting to equate with death.

He ditched the bike in the front yard. A thought to hide the bikes had passed through his mind, but he realized that was pointless. Same way he could sense these zombies approach, they must have been homing in on him.

"Philly!" Paul shouted as he rushed through the front door. He secured it as best he could. Philly had splintered the hell out of the door frame when he'd kicked it open. "Philly! Dude, we got company almost here!"

He ran up the stairs and slammed his fist on the bathroom door several times. Philly didn't answer. Must have been one hell of a heavy sleeper. All Paul could think was how irritated he was that he'd bothered trying to be quiet before he'd left the house for some food.

"Crap!" Paul ran back downstairs.

He grabbed the doorknob, ready to pull it open, run for his bike and ride. What was the point in just staying here and letting those zombies catch up to him? He heard them getting closer, though, and he knew there was no way he'd ever outrun them. That was the point, wasn't it? He could run all he wanted to, but these guys were faster and never tired. The only choice was to stand and fight them.

After standing there for a moment, he opened the door and walked outside. He closed the door behind him, in case Philly might come out of the bathroom. If he was going to wait here, then he wasn't going to hide, dammit. The idea of sitting out on the front steps to face these bastards when they showed up scared the hell out of him, but hiding wouldn't save him. It just made his death more pathetic.

He sat on the top step as he waited. His shield, shining in the gloom, rested on his right arm. He supposed he should shift it to his left. He needed his right hand for his sword, but the shield seemed to hurt these things more. "Guess I just need two right hands."

No, he needed to make a choice. It wasn't an insignificant one either, and not just because his life was on the line. He ran his fingers along the curve of his shield. The surface didn't move or change, but something to the feel of it assured him it was alive. The crystal warmed his hand, and he knew that wasn't natural. Nothing about this shield made sense, not that it hurt those zombies; that it felt connected to him... that it existed at all. As that last thought set itself into his mind, he knew that was the real choice. If he decided to face these monsters with this shield, then he was choosing to take a path that made no sense. It reminded him of the Wizard of Oz when Dorothy starts down the yellow brick road. There'd been a red road, too... red like his shield. "Not much of a choice is it?" He couldn't go back to Kansas again. Not now. Never.

When he looked up, he saw the three figures at the end of the long driveway walking towards him. Paul set down his shield and stood. He started undoing that ridiculously long belt Philly had given him. He'd made his choice. When he'd gotten it off, he tossed the belt, sword and scabbard to the side.

"We gonna finish this?" Paul glared at the zombie in the middle, Long Hair.

The zombie nodded and continued walking closer. "Where's your twilight friend?"

That the zombie could speak startled Paul. They hadn't said anything at the museum. He didn't have time to consider it more. He slipped off his jacket and dropped it to the side. "Philly's getting some rest."

The one on the right, Shorty, snapped his teeth in a rapid-fire manner, as if anticipating the taste of Paul's flesh. Paul knew the jerk was just trying to intimidate him. It was working.

He reached out his hand, instinctively calling his shield to him as he had in the museum. The red crystal leaped off the front porch, sliding into its proper place on his forearm. Long Hair and his pals hesitated a step when they saw that. Nice to know he could intimidate them, too, even if another part of his mind freaked at what he'd just done.

"You plan to lie down and die like a proper meal?" Long Hair asked. They'd gotten close, just ten yards away.

"No."

Paul charged at the zombies and threw his shield. The red crystal shot forward, curving to the right to strike Shorty's forehead. Paul cursed. He'd been aiming for the throat, but the short zombie had ducked. Damn, these things were fast. He'd directed the shield's path, though. Somehow, he'd known he could do it, just as he'd called it to his hand from the porch.

Before the shield could hit the ground, it bounced off the short zombie's head and back onto Paul's arm as he swung at Long Hair. The edge of the red shield slit across Long Hair's stomach. Long Hair howled as the cut left a wide, bloodless gash.

The third one, Deadhead, tackled Paul from the left. He'd gotten in under the shield, his shoulder jamming into Paul's side. Paul had played his share of football as a kid, gotten tackled by people twice his size. This zombie hit him a whole lot harder than any of those guys ever had.

Paul scrambled out of the tackle. He retreated on all fours, a graceless and panic-filled skittering that his shield did nothing to assist… but it worked. He made it to his feet before Deadhead could bite him.

Long Hair and Shorty surrounded Paul. Shorty pounced first, coming at him from behind. Paul spun to face him and planted his shield in that ugly, snapping maw. Shorty wouldn't get all those teeth back into place anytime soon. Fingers brushed against the top of Paul's head as Long Hair failed to grab him. Paul struck Shorty again and ran past him.

"You can't outrun me!" Long Hair chased Paul into the trees surrounding the backyard.

Paul had separated the zombies and decided to take advantage of it. He stopped in front of a tree, turned and sent his shield flying for Long Hair's throat. Long Hair dodged it. Paul saw his shield slide across the ground, sending a small wave of dead leaves into the air.

The zombie reached for him. Paul screamed as he tried what might have been the most insane thing he'd ever considered. Just as

Long Hair reached him, Paul grabbed him by the jacket, ducked and jerked him forward, using the tall zombie's momentum against him. Long Hair's head slammed into the tree. Paul's shield, summoned the instant Long Hair had reached him, shot straight through the zombie's throat. The trap worked better than Paul had expected. The shock of the beheading forced the zombie to release his grip and jump back. The shield didn't stop with the zombie's head. It sliced through the tree trunk, too. Paul scrambled out of the way as the toppled tree landed on Long Hair's flailing torso, trapping it.

"Holy hell!" Paul stared in disbelief at his handiwork as his shield returned to his right arm. "Couldn't have planned that if I tried." He glanced down at his shield. What else could it do that he hadn't thought of yet?

Shorty leaped over the fallen tree. He might have looked comical with half of his teeth missing, but the rage on his face more than made up for that.

Paul ran for the back of the house. Shorty chased him like some Olympic sprinter. That probably made the back door the finish line. Paul's body slammed against the door. It flung open just as Shorty collided with him. They smashed into the cabinets. Shorty took the brunt of the impact. The pantry door split at its equator, knocking down the boxes of cereal and biscuit mix. Paul struggled to free himself from the zombie's grip. Just as he thought he might, the iron-grip of those dead hands latched onto the waist of his jeans and the back of his shirt. His feet lifted off the ground as Shorty flung Paul into the den. Pain ripped through his left shoulder as his body shattered the drywall.

He dropped to the floor, on his knees. Paul just saw the blur of Shorty running towards him to finish the job. In his mind, Paul yelled at himself to move, to do anything. Brain and body just wouldn't connect. He forced all his will into his shield arm. He thrust his arm up. The edge of the shield connected with the underside of Shorty's jaw. The zombie lost more teeth. One of them bounced off Paul's head. Shorty's body was knocked onto his back, landing on the kitchen floor.

"Philly!" Now would be a freaking fabulous time for the vampire to wake up.

Paul staggered to his feet and scrambled for the front door. Shorty jumped to his feet and launched across the den. Paul tried to knock him aside with his shield, but Shorty outmaneuvered him. They struggled, bodies slamming against the front door and the stairs until Shorty had him pinned to the floor of the foyer. Shorty had learned his lesson, too. He grabbed Paul by both wrists, the placement of his hand trapping Paul's shield on his arm. The zombie also had Paul's legs pinned like a vice.

Paul felt Shorty's body shiver with his fury. His face just inches from Paul's, Shorty bared what teeth he had left in a cruel smile. "You're going to wish I still had all my teeth, because it's only going to make this take a lot longer." Shorty's jaw widened to what seemed inhuman proportions, ready to bite down.

A roar, a cross between a tiger and a wolf, startled both Paul and Shorty. They looked up to see a shadow fly down the stairs. Before Paul could recognize Philly, Shorty's head dropped from his body, severed by a sword strike, and bounced off of Paul's chest to the floor.

That didn't release him from the rest of the zombie's grip. Philly grabbed the zombie under its arm and flung it into the den.

"Jesus, kid, I can't leave you alone for a minute."

Then the front door burst open. Sunlight blinded Paul. He smelled a putrid burning smell, could taste it in the back of his throat, and felt something hot. His eyes adjusted to see Philly, all ablaze like a human torch, struggling with the third zombie, Deadhead. Paul rolled out of the way and into the dining room. Flames leaped up to the ceiling. Just like everything else in these Deadlands that seemed to require fuel, the fire was consuming the house far too quickly, giving him just minutes to get out of there. The front door was blocked by Philly and Deadhead, both on fire now. They seemed determined to keep each other there so the flames would destroy them both. Paul could already see through the ceiling of the foyer into the upstairs. He considered throwing his shield to behead

Deadhead, but they were struggling too much, dancing in circles. He was just as likely to take Philly's head.

"Get out of here, kid!" Philly shouted.

Smoke filled the downstairs. A memory of a firefighter who visited his elementary school flashed through Paul's head, the warning that it was usually the smoke and not the flames that killed a person.

He ripped down the bed sheets he'd stapled over the dining room windows. The edge of the sheet was burning and spread the flames to the table on which it landed. Paul coughed. Crap, he had to get that window open. "No!" The window wouldn't move. Someone had placed screws there to keep the damn thing shut.

Paul stepped back and threw his shield at the window. The crystal shield burst through the glass. He climbed out, doing his best not to cut his hands. The fire hadn't made it to the front porch, but it was working on it. Flames were already escaping out the door and into the open air, seeking more oxygen to support itself. Paul dodged the flashes of yellow-orange tendrils as he grabbed his leather jacket.

Not that he'd ever seen a house burn, but the way that house caved in on itself so quickly just couldn't be natural. As he watched from a safe distance, Paul wiped the soot and tears from his face with the front of his shirt. To his relief, none of the zombies climbed out of the dead house.

"Thank you, Philly." He lowered his head and took a deep breath to settle his nerves. His entire body was shaking. Not even the feel of his shield on his forearm, nor the warmth of his jacket, seemed to calm his body's jitters.

He lingered long enough to see that the fire was doing its job before he climbed onto his bike. As he got back onto the interstate, Paul saw the smoke curling thick and high, black against the overcast sky to the east.

Killing those zombies didn't grant him any comfort or calm. Instead, he was riding north and feeling more panicked than ever. His shield had helped save him from those monsters, but he still didn't know if he could truly reach the borders of the Deadlands. If what Philly had told him was true, then he had been the center of all this grey.

• • •

The grass turned out greener on the other side. Shortly after passing through Fredericksburg, Paul emerged from the Deadlands. He knew it by the median strip on I-95. The portion of grass within the Deadlands had withered to a drab, lifeless brownish-grey while the portion without remained a healthy, dark green.

Everything about his exit from the Deadlands reminded him of some really bad anime film, complete with his head of shaggy hair which felt like it was going in all directions. At least his bike wasn't making that squeaky sound that anime bikes always made when the young hero was pedaling into the sunset.

Just past the overpass at Exit 136, he spotted a pair of headlights coming towards him. The black limousine turned to park perpendicular to the traffic lanes. Paul stopped just short of it, the first sign of human life he'd seen.

The back door opened and a man with long, white hair, just like the zombies, climbed out. Paul didn't hear the staccato notes or anything, so he felt safe in saying this guy wasn't one of them. He wore an embroidered, white shirt with long, wide sleeves. He reminded Paul of some desert priest.

"Who are you?" Paul asked.

"My name is Organal." Damn, this guy had a super deep voice. "You must be Paul. Although, I expected you to have company."

"Philly didn't make it."

The news was met with a pained look from Organal. "I imagine you have many questions." He stepped aside and gestured for Paul to get into the limo.

Paul considered the offer. Could he really be sure this was Organal? Even if it was, could he trust him? In the end, he knew he didn't have anyone left in this world he knew he could trust without any doubts. He'd have to take the risk. It was that or spend the rest of his life running from monsters.

He sat across from Organal, which had him facing the back of the limo. The inside turned out more luxurious than he'd expected. There was even a mounted laptop.

"A limo?" Paul asked.

"I own a company that builds naval vessels."

"Aircraft carriers?" He'd always wanted to go on one of those.

"Among others, but I would guess your questions have less to do with my 'day job' than how I knew where to find you, just what you are, and the origins of the skull you now wear as a shield."

The air around Organal was relaxed, but that didn't completely put Paul at ease. After his time in the Deadlands, he wasn't sure he'd ever be calm again.

"You're not human, are you?"

Organal smiled. "No, but I am not an avatar like you."

Paul thought about the second heartbeat he carried. "You're one of those," he had to hunt for the word, "parasites?"

"Yes, my kind lives on the life of others. It's what sustains our worlds." He held up a hand to stave off Paul's next question. "The Avatar Light weakens the barriers between our dimensions and the worlds it touches."

"This has happened before?"

"Several times, but it was only in the pass prior to this one that we found your species on this world. Not all of us approved of slaughtering your kind. I was chosen to stay behind and prepare your world for the next pass."

The implication of Organal's last statement took a moment to register. "You mean you're thousands of years old?"

He nodded. Judging by the way his smile widened, he was rather proud of the fact.

"Let it suffice I've walked this world for quite some time. I and my followers, such as Phillip, have spent that time searching for certain bloodlines."

"Such as mine?"

He nodded. "My kind's passage into this world is eased by mixing our bloodlines with those of your race."

"So somewhere in my family tree, there's a parasite like you?"

"I think it safe to assume there's more than one. It's why your mind remains in control of your body. The second bloodline protects you against the parasite's control." Organal pointed at Paul's chest as he said that. "Tell me, how well do you know your Norse Mythology?"

The sudden turn in topic caught Paul off guard, but he recovered enough to shrug. "Suppose I know a little. 'Thor' was one of the comic books I used to collect."

"Most of the mythological figures in this world and many of its religions were inspired by previous avatars. The shield you now carry was made from one of their skulls."

Paul felt something stir within the shield. The idea that this had once been part of a living person sent a shiver through his body, even if he had already come to think of it as having life to it.

"I presume there was a hole in the back of the skull," Organal said.

"Yes, how did you know that?"

"Don't look so surprised." Organal's smile widened. "There are not so many of those skulls to be found within this world, and even fewer that are true skulls. Most of the ones that have found their way into museums are poor imitations created by mortal priests and charlatans. But what makes me so certain I know which skull you found is that you changed it into a shield. This skull belonged to the 'god' named Thor.

"He carried a weapon called Mjolnir. The old myth tellers believed a hammer sounded more impressive, so the fact his favored weapon was a shield crafted from a crystal skull was lost. His shield looked just as that one does, although his was blue. It always returned to his hand and none could destroy it until he was killed from his wounds in battle with Jörmungandr, the Midgard Serpent. That hole in the back of his skull was from that battle."

"Thor's skull?" Paul looked down at his shield. His hand shook as it ran along its outer curve.

"When an avatar dies, the skull is all that ultimately survives, turning to crystal. They can be powerful weapons for other avatars to use and can also be a danger to others." Paul noticed Organal kept his distance from the shield. Probably explained why Philly hadn't gotten his hands on it before Paul used it. Organal didn't bother confirming it before he changed the topic. "I take it you were not awake for some time?"

Paul nodded, uncomfortable with where the conversation was going.

"Some avatars need more time to change. They hibernate," Organal said, then quietly added, "and feast. The Deadlands... you might think of them as a chrysalis."

"Is there a way to undo it?" He wanted his parents back, a way to bring back all of those lives, but he feared he already knew the answer.

"The land will eventually heal itself, but it will take centuries. There are those who would use their powers to wipe out your race and leave this world barren. What happened to your home measures as little more than a blemish in comparison."

"Cheery thought," Paul muttered as he traced the edge of his shield with his fingertips.

"Your gifts are a reason to celebrate, Paul. Thor's name remains one of a great warrior. You have that potential within you now. Hela, the goddess of the dead, knows this. That is why she sent her servants into the Deadlands to kill you." He leaned closer. "You have taken many lives, but you can save many more. The question is whether you are willing to do it."

He looked down at his shield and thought back to the steps of the library. Philly had given him the choice of suicide by zombie or fight to survive. Organal was giving him that same kind of choice.

He'd always been a good runner, but was there really any running from the end of the world? The Avatar Light had left him without a family or a home. Going into hiding now would be little better than killing himself. He couldn't bring back those who were lost, but he could do something to make things right.

It was time to get off his ass and deal with it.

"The Deadlands" was originally published by May December Publications as part of their anthology Four in the Hole *in September 2011.*

THE LIGHT WELL

Eric crouched in the shadows of a tree. Light cut through the slender gaps in the leaves and threatened to expose him. He leaned forward to glance up at the full moon.

"I must be out of my mind."

One in the morning, and he was waiting outside his house for a girl.

The brick tri-level sat on a corner lot. The tree he'd chosen for his hiding place was to the side of the house, less than five feet from the road.

A pair of headlights rounded the turn onto the side street. The white Corvette's high beams exposed him. Thank God there weren't any windows on the side of the house. The car screeched to a stop, and the passenger window lowered.

Rachel waved to him from the driver's seat. "Come on!"

He hesitated. Too many years being the well-behaved, four-eyed, honor roll son had trained him against doing this sort of thing, and yet here he was.

He bolted for the car and climbed into the passenger's seat.

Rachel didn't give him a chance to buckle his seat belt. She grabbed a fistful of his winter coat and kissed him.

She had him dizzy by the time she let go. "Hang on." A mischievous smile warned him just before she slammed her foot on the accelerator. Eric grabbed the door and pulled it shut as the wheels squealed. The Corvette launched down the side street.

"Wasn't sure you'd go through with it," she said.

"That makes two of us." He relaxed a bit after he buckled his seatbelt. "Didn't want to disappoint you."

Four weeks had passed since her parents were killed, the latest "Full Moon Murders."

"I'm sorry you had to sneak out." She took his hand into hers and squeezed. "I just don't think I could do this alone."

"It's all right. I understand." He didn't really, but then he still had his parents. Mom and Dad weren't thrilled about him dating Rachel. Dad's first words after he found out were, "Why would someone like her want to date you?" Even though Mr. Supportive had backpedaled immediately after getting "The Look" from Mom, the words had rooted into Eric's brain.

Hell, Rachel had been homecoming queen. She was a senior cheerleader who'd been dating the top running back on the football team. Less than a week after her parents were killed, she'd broken up with her boyfriend. The next day at school, she'd cornered Eric in the hallway and asked him to take her to lunch. She really told him to take her, but he didn't see a reason to complain.

"I just need to say 'bye' to them." She pulled out of his neighborhood onto Courthouse Road. This late on a Sunday night, even this four-lane road was barren.

Five minutes later, they pulled into the cul-de-sac where her house was. The street lamp on the corner didn't reach her front yard.

"Does your aunt know you're doing this?" he asked as she pulled into the driveway which led to the back of the house.

"Are you kidding? She doesn't have a clue." She turned off the car. When she got out, she stretched out her arms and spun through the moonlight. She closed her eyes and moaned.

She didn't act like a girl visiting the place her parents had died almost a month ago. When she'd asked him to come along, she'd sounded scared by her own idea. A warning siren was blaring in his head, but one look at her cleavage hugging the moonlight tuned it out.

"Let's go inside." She walked backwards towards the rear door.

"I thought the police still had your house sealed off."

He looked past her at the crime scene tape on the door. The bottom right corner had lost its grip and dangled to form an "x" with a limp.

"Come on, silly." She crooked a finger for him to follow.

"Rachel, stop."

"Oh, relax. It's not breaking and entering." She jingled her keychain in the air between them.

"Hold it!" He rushed forward to grab her arm and pointed at her house. "The door's open."

She jerked free of his grip and turned around. "What the hell?"

He pulled out his phone. "I'm calling 911."

Before he could dial, she snatched the phone out of his hand and ran inside.

"Rachel!"

He stopped at the door. She'd ripped down the last of the "x" going in there. The yellow tape remnants clung to the left side of the door. His heart was pounding, making his chest feel light even as everything else in his body clenched.

"Rachel!" She'd disappeared into the darkness of the house.

He looked around for something to use as a weapon before following her. The only thing in the back he could see was a grill. He considered using the lid as a shield, but abandoned the idea as desperate and stupid.

He held onto the doorframe as he peered into what he assumed was the living room. He told himself there was probably no reason to worry. Odds favored that whoever broke in, if anyone did, was long gone. He forced his hand to release the doorframe and entered.

Why the hell didn't she turn on the lights? He reached for the switch by the door, but nothing happened. The electricity must have been cut off.

On the far side of the living room, the sofa and recliner were knocked over. The wooden coffee table was splintered into dozens of pieces. Just enough moonlight cut through the front windows to illuminate the dark stains on the floor. Rachel's parents had died there.

The full moon added to his fears. Police were investigating three different sets of murders, each of them on the night of the full moon. The murders had been in different places throughout Richmond. Was it possible the killer had come back here, like a bad movie cliché?

But why would he? No one was supposed to be here. *Hell, I shouldn't be here.*

He saw the kitchen to the left. The space was small and windowless, but just enough light reached in there for him to spot a wooden knife block on the counter. He ran for it and pulled out the largest knife. The feel of its smooth handle in his hand gave him a bit more confidence, even though the idea of fighting with a knife felt as natural to him as wearing a sundress.

He still hadn't heard or seen any sign of Rachel or anyone else. Now that he was in the house, he was too scared to call to her.

He was about to walk out of the kitchen when he saw the phone mounted on the wall. He grabbed the handset off its mount and clicked the button to turn it on. Not even a beep. *Of course not, idiot. There's no power.*

The silence taunted him as he went into the dining room in the front of the house. A flicker of light drew his attention back to the living room. The lines of moonlight coming in through the front window were more precise and solid than any ray of light he had ever seen. The edge of one moonbeam flickered. No, the longer he looked, the more he realized it wasn't the moon beam. Tiny brilliant dots danced along its edge. The small lights winked in and out as if alive while touched by moonlight, but swallowed whole in the dark.

He walked towards the dancing lights, and as he drew closer, he heard whispers. His ears strained, and a single word gained enough clarity for him to understand. Run!

The warning came too late.

Something dove at him from above as he passed the stairs. A dark shape, the figure of a man, crashed into his body and crushed him against the floor. Pain ripped through his back and stomach.

Darkness obscured his vision, trapping him in shadows. He wondered if this was a sign he was going to black out. He thrashed about and got loose when his fingers stabbed at his attacker's eyes.

The man howled in pain and stumbled back into the dining room, giving Eric his first look at him. He had the shape of a man, but shadows swirled around his body. When the attacker regained his balance, he glared down at Eric.

The eyes were dark voids. He roared at Eric and the shadows took shape around him. Black lines thrust out from the stranger's face to form a three-dimensional sketch of a wolf's snout. The dark storm held more life than the pale flesh of the man within it.

The black, sharp-toothed maw thrust at Eric, who scrambled to his feet.

Just as he was about to run, Eric realized he'd dropped the knife. He looked down and saw it by the front door. The shadow wolf never gave him a chance to grab the weapon. He pounced. Eric dodged the attack enough not to get pinned, but the shadows slashed through his coat and back, knocking him facedown.

He only made it onto all fours before the shadow wolf kicked him in the side. The kick knocked him onto his back. Pain arced through Eric's body from where the monster's claws had drawn blood.

A hand wrapped around his throat and slammed the back of his head against the floor. He tried to scream, but nothing came out. He saw dancing lights again. These bright, floating spots had nothing to do with the strange display he'd seen in the moonlight. He was about to pass out for real. He reached for the shadow wolf's eyes, but the monster held his arm straight, keeping his face beyond Eric's reach this time.

"I knew the Light Well would call one of your kind to this place."

What the Hell was this freak talking about?

"Yes, it did." Rachel's voice came from behind the shadow wolf, whose eyes went wide as she stabbed him in the back. He shrieked and let go of Eric.

Rachel grabbed the man by his hair... no, by the shadows. The tendrils of dark jerked back and forth but couldn't escape her hold. She dragged him away and slit open his throat with the kitchen knife Eric had dropped. The blood that spilled out was black and thick.

The shadow wolf grabbed at its throat as if to hold in its blood. He stumbled back but then dropped to his knees.

Rachel moved in front of him. The dark blood clung to the blade of her knife and moved along the edge as if still a living part of the monster. She plunged the knife into his heart. Light flared from where it pierced his chest. The shadows spun out of control, a tornado losing its shape. As the last shadow vanished into the darkness of the house, the body collapsed.

Rachel left the knife buried in him. She walked to Eric. "It's all right," she whispered as she knelt beside him. Her fingers stroked his hair.

"He was some kind of monster." The words rushed out of him faster than he could think. "You saw it. You had to. You did, didn't you? He was—he was—"

She shushed him. Her fingers caressed his face. Her hand was wet with the man's blood.

"We need to get you into the light." She smiled to him. "You're going to be just fine."

"I don't understand. Why was he here? Why?" He was shaking. Dammit! He needed to get a grip on himself.

She dragged him into the living room. The cuts to his back protested but were forgotten once he was resting within the moonlight. He could feel the light. It wasn't warmer or colder, simply more... real.

"He said something about a Light Well."

Rachel nodded. He looked up into her eyes and saw the small spheres of light swimming around her.

"There are places in this world where moonlight meets the dark, and the darkness gives the light definition and form, like water in a glass." She pointed to the man's body. "He must have guessed what this place was from the news about my parents."

The tiny lights covered her hand, clinging to her body. He saw some of them nestle against her breasts, and he smiled. Damn she was beautiful, and the light made her even more so.

"I don't understand any of this."

She laughed. Her voice echoed and sent ripples through the moonlight.

"Eric, the light of the full moon and the dark of this world cut against each other in some places and rip open a hole for this kind to enter. They need a body attuned to darkness to sustain them, though."

She rubbed his temples, and he took a deep breath, starting to feel steady again.

"How do you know about this?"

"This house is one of those rare places, a Light Well." She sighed as she looked down at the blood-stained carpet. "You know those legends about the full moon turning people into lunatics? Some people can't sustain the light, not like this body."

The lights swimming around her suddenly took on a shape resembling a dragon, just as the shadows had formed a wolf around the man.

"Rachel's parents went mad, so I had to kill them."

Eric tried to get away, but her hand, which was now a talon of light, pinned him down along the edge of the moonbeam, leaving him half in light and half in dark.

"I knew when I saw you at school that you would make a perfect vessel, just like Rachel."

Eric struggled to get free and into the dark. The tiny lights converged on him. A swarm of hot daggers burned into his eyes. He screamed. His agony turned everything white and then silent.

The last words that slipped through his mind were his father's.

"Why would someone like her want to date you?"

THE BIG SNEEZE

My partner Kensington and I were flying the Stonehenge route West of London when we spotted the wreck. The smoke reached for the clouds and contained salty overtones, but the medicinal aftertaste ruined it for me.

"Oooo... that's a big one, Windsor!" Kensington flapped around me in overexcited circles. He's not the best flyer. The British branch of the IBDA had restricted us to non-urban patrols after Kensington smashed into one too many buildings in London. All the reconstructive surgeries on his snout had gotten expensive, not to mention the lawsuits for the property damage. "Can we get a closer look? Pleeeeease!"

"Oh, all right." Traffic jams don't interest most dragons, since we fly everywhere. My partner just wanted a closer look at all the pretty lights which were much brighter than he was.

The flashing blues of the traffic officers and fire brigade distinguished the start of the thirty-car pile-up on the M3 just before the A30 interchange. A long line of stalled, early morning commuters stretched into the receding night. Their headlights stared like wide-eyed children at the coming dawn.

Kensington and I perched on the skeleton of the overturned lorry which had started the mess. An ambulance screamed past us. The hot steam from where the fire hoses had beaten down the flames coated my green scales in a pleasant mist.

Kensington worked his jaw and snapped his forked tongue as if to spit a bad piece of meat from his mouth. "This air tastes funny, Windsor."

"Hey there, you two!" A police officer waved for us to get

down. Fellow must have had pretty good eyes, because my partner and I aren't the biggest dragons.

We floated to the ground just beside the officer. We stood just a little short of his knee caps. "Morning, officer. Special Agents Windsor and Kensington with the IBDA."

"International Bureau of Draconic Affairs?" The officer smiled when I nodded that he had it right. "I'm Officer Bilkins. What brings you boys down here? Um, you are both boys, right?"

"Yes, we're both 'boys'." I rolled my eyes. Humans. "Just flying our beat. Figured we'd drop in for a look was all."

"Bloody lorry kissed the crash barrier an hour ago," Officer "State-the-Obvious" said. "Turned the motorway into a right nice car park."

I sniffed and recognized the odor of cooked meat. "Just the one fatality?"

"Fortunately, but a right strange one." The officer scratched the side of his head with his pen. The clipboard in his other hand held the initial sketches of the crash report.

"What's the puzzle, officer?"

The human pointed to a group of people with more pens and paperwork gathered around a body on the left shoulder. "Well, the driver flew through the windshield and landed over there."

Kensington scratched his brow with his long blue tail. "Um, I don't get it."

I pointed to the lorry's cabin which was facing the opposite direction. "What he means is that the driver landed on the wrong side of the road."

"Ohhhh."

"Someone drag the body over there?" I asked.

"Can't see how that's possible. Poor bastard was burning like Guy Fawkes when the first responders got here."

I took another sniff. There was something familiar mingled in with that distinctive smell of burned human. "Mind if I get a closer look?"

"Not a bit."

I kept to the air as I flew over to the body. One of the forensics ladies winked at me over her facemask and offered a muffled, "Hi."

"Don't mind me," I said. "Just doing a quick reccy." Was true enough until I saw the empty bottle of malt vinegar to the side of the body.

"Hey, don't disturb that!"

I ignored her and sniffed at the bottle.

"Officer Bilkins, he's disturbing the scene!" She waved her clipboard as if she could dispel me like a whiff of smoke.

I swatted away her clipboard with one of my wings. "Actually, you humans are disturbing my crime scene."

"What's that?" Officer Bilkins asked as he ran over to us. "What do you mean 'crime scene'?"

I hovered a little higher to be eye-level with the humans. "You ever see those bumper stickers that warn not to meddle in the affairs of dragons?"

"Oh, I love those," the forensics lady said. "How's that go? 'Because humans are crunchy and good with ketchup,' right?"

"Actually, most dragons in Britain prefer their human with a bottle of that." I pointed to the malt vinegar. "What was in the lorry, officer?"

"Just pharmaceuticals headed for some stores in London. Wouldn't think you dragon folk have any interest in those sorts of things." Officer Bilkins was scratching his head with his pen again. "You thinking some dragon came after the driver for a quick brekky?"

"Not likely. You humans aren't that tasty. Probably why this chap brought along the condiment."

Kensington landed next to the bottle and sniffed it. "Smells good. Makes me hungry." The officer stepped back from Kensington as if he might go feral and take a bite out of him. Stupid humans.

I scowled at my partner. "We can grab a lamb on the way back into headquarters—later. For now, call into dispatch and let them know what we've got."

"Aw, okay." He pulled out his radio.

"Where did he get that from?" The forensics lady leaned right to left as if looking for a hidden seam in Kensington's scales. "I mean, he doesn't have any pockets?"

"Dimensional-portal pockets, actually." I pulled out my radio, too, just to show her.

"I'm sorry. A what?"

"It's a dragon thing. Don't worry about it." I put some distance between me and the humans as I flew back to the wreckage of the lorry. I sifted through the debris and spotted a half-burned, blue box cover with the word "Loratadine" in white letters.

The lorry's cabin contained the most useful clue, though. The rays from the rising sun distinguished my find from the shards of the windshield. Dragon scales have rainbow-like ripples in them. This one was no different, even though it was predominantly purple. Our hungry thief had left a bit of himself behind. I just hoped this dragon was registered in the database.

• • •

The IBDA occupies the twenty-first through twenty-third floors of New Scotland Yard. You can't ride an elevator to those floors either, so don't plan any visits unless you have a pair of wings.

I was watching the lazy rotation of the London Eye from the view of my boss's office. Inspector Merlin wasn't my first supervisor since joining the Bureau, but he was the best. He's headed up the London Branch for five centuries, and while he has a deductive brilliance to shame Sherlock Holmes, he's gotten a bit distractible in his old age.

The inspector flew into his office and landed behind his desk. He tossed down a manila folder like a practiced gambler dealing cards.

The only one playing a gamble was me. I hoped the scale I found at the crime scene would point to a suspect and give me a one-way ticket back to London from my rural exile. "Sir, what did they fi—?"

"Wait!"

He crouched down until his black eyes were almost level with the desktop. He reached over to a set of pendulum balls decorating his desk and pulled back one of the suspended silver orbs. "Hmmm…" Then he let it go and watched as the ball collided with the other four, sending the farthest one into the air, the process going back and forth.

"Fascinating." Going by the inspector's whisper, I couldn't tell if he was talking to me and Kensington or to himself.

"Um, inspector?"

"Hm? What? Oh, yes! No time to waste!" He sat up and flipped open the folder. "Top chop work, lads. You've given us a break in one of our biggest cases."

"Which case would that be, sir?" This was why I hated patrolling the farms and motorways. I couldn't track any of the ongoing investigations while I was in the field. I'd petitioned for a transfer for three years, but since I was the only one who seemed capable of working with Kensington, they weren't moving me anywhere until he learned to fly straight.

"We only recently started to connect the dots, but it seems someone is targeting all the allergy medicines in the British Isles. A series of heists and arsons throughout the UK have all but wiped out the available supply." He slid a series of pictures from the open folder. "So far, we've seen factories burned down, pharmacies robbed and your lorry attack makes for the third in as many weeks. It's bad, lads. Things are getting dicey out there."

The list of events chilled the fire in my gut. "When you say 'dicey,' you don't just mean these attacks, do you?"

The inspector rifled through the folder and placed a list in front of me. "It's only within the past week that our 999 center noted the sudden rise in accidental flamings. We've seen a jump from an average of five a week to almost fifty."

"Sir, what do accidental flamings have to do with—?"

A deep breath from the inspector cut me off. He crouched behind his desk, his eyes on the pendulum balls. "It stopped."

"Um, sir? I'm pretty sure it's supposed to do that."

Kensington crouched on our side of the desk like a mirror for the inspector as our boss set the balls in motion again. He went for two this time.

I cleared my throat as loud as I could manage. "Sir, the accidental flamings?"

"Hmmm." He leaned back and stared at the balls as if watching a murder suspect confess. "What? Oh, yes. The flamings." He settled into his chair. "You see, an inordinate number of dragons who live in predominantly human-occupied regions tend to develop severe allergies. Whether it's an allergy to the humans or their waste products or whatever is anybody's guess, but one thing we all learn at an early age is to never stand in front of a sneezing dragon, not unless you enjoy getting torched."

The inspector tapped at his rounded snout. "Hmmm... Wait. What was—?" Then he slammed one of his talons on the desktop. Kensington screamed and fell onto his back as the inspector shouted. "1666!"

"I'm sorry, sir. What?" My head ached as if my stubby horns were digging into my skull.

"The Great Fire of London was in 1666," he said. "Rather bad day at the office, I can assure you. Haven't seen the like since, but at the rate these accidental flamings are escalating, London might turn into a cinder box. We have only two courses open to us. That's why I'm tasking all our resources with hunting down the devil targeting the nation's allergy medicines."

"I take it that's the first course of action. What's the second option?"

"To stock up on marshmallows." The inspector capped off his answer with a nod of total certainty.

"I'm sorry, sir, but how would marshmallows prevent a massive fire in London?"

"Don't be daft, Special Agent Windsor. Marshmallows won't stop a fire, but they're excellent when roasted over an open flame. I have my secretary working on that."

"Can we get chocolate and graham crackers, too, sir?"

Kensington jumped around on all fours. "I love s'mores!"

"I'll pass that along to my secretary." The inspector rifled through his desk for a pen and some paper to write down the suggestion. "Yes, now then, where was I? Oh, yes. To the break in the case. We've identified the owner of the scale you recovered from this morning's crime scene. Tell me, Special Agent Windsor, what do you know about the Dug?"

"Douglas Rand? That dragon is the most dangerous hoarder in all of England."

"Let me assure you, Agent Windsor, the Dug is the most dangerous hoarder in the world."

My wings quivered enough to lift me an inch out of my chair. This case was huge, enough to save me from the Stonehenge route for the rest of my career. "I heard he caused the 2009 spike in gas prices."

"Quite. Took a fancy to oil barrels that year."

Kensington scratched his brow. "He was hoarding oil?"

"No, just the barrels. Cost the oil industry millions to replace them." The inspector paused to set his balls in motion again. "Once even took an interest in bellybutton lint."

That one made me throw up a bit in my mouth. "Not that I understand why he'd want to do that, but I don't see why that would bother anyone."

"He didn't leave the previous owners of the lint around to complain." Inspector Merlin turned to look out his window, and his profile faded to a dark green shadow backlit by the sunset. "All our kind feel the urge, that need to hoard something we cherish. Most of us find a single passion. For me, it's Ferraris—such lovely cars. The Dug—I once thought it was a matter of surrendering to that urge, leaping from one thing to the next in hopes of finding what it is he desires but never able to. Now, I believe he hoards something you cannot lock in a safe, store in a warehouse or stuff in a mattress. What he hoards is chaos."

Kensington and I followed his gaze towards the London skyline, the fiery rays of sunset a foreshadow of what the Dug's deeds might do to this city.

"I collect croutons." Kensington spread his lips into a wide smile. "Garlic herb is my favorite."

The more I heard my partner run his mouth, the more I feared my chances of running this investigation might turn to smoke. I'd waited too long for this chance. "Sir, I'd like to fly point on this case."

Inspector Merlin chuckled. "Tired of chasing hungry sheep thieves on the Stonehenge route, eh?" He smiled at me and cast a curious glance at my partner. "Very well. I'm temporarily reassigning you both to investigations and relieving you of your patrol duties. Prove yourselves, and we might consider making the arrangement more permanent."

Kensington flew in a circle. "Oh, goody!" That is, until he slammed into the wall. "Ouch!"

"Inspector, does he have to go with me?"

My question came too late. The inspector waved us out and returned his attention to the pendulum balls on his desk.

• • •

Sherly's Pub has drifted from one London rooftop to the next for the past three centuries. These days, it rested atop a grey, four-story monstrosity near the intersection of Northumberland and Craven. As any investigator worth his coin can tell you, information floats. You just need to know the right place to perch to find it. The hotter the info, the better the odds it would float to Sherly's.

We could hear a pair of dragons crooning about love and charcoal coming from inside the small pub. Sherly's didn't look like it could stand up against a small shower in April, but the dark brown, enchanted wooden boards that appeared to lean against one another had survived far worse. I hadn't been here since it moved six months ago. I was glad to see its new home was on a flat roof. The gable roof of the previous address forced you to hold onto your drink the entire time and made walking around quite tricky when you started feeling squiffy. Soon as we went inside, I realized we'd picked a busy night to visit.

"Well cover my wings in cement and call me a gargoyle, I haven't set my beady eyes on you two in months!" Miriam wobbled her pale pink girth around the bar and crushed me and Kensington with a hug. She inherited Sherly's from her husband two centuries ago. Rumor had it the old sot was still digesting in her belly after getting caught rubbing wings with one of the hired help.

"Sorry, Miriam. The Bureau has been keeping us busy." I'd done my best to keep our banishment to the Stonehenge route from public knowledge.

"Busy, is that?" She scratched at one of the silver horns jutting down from her jaw as she issued a contemplative growl. "Heard you two got shafted with hunting down sky-diving sheep stealers."

So much for protecting my reputation. Time to go for damage control.

"We're done with that." I perched on a stool in front of the bar. "Been reassigned to investigations. Got a big case, too."

Kensington hopped onto the stool next to me. "It's a temporal assignment!"

Miriam laughed and wobbled back behind the bar. "You two must be needing something strong then. Fire water?"

"No, we're on duty. Better stick with blood tea." Good stuff that. Brewed from tea leaves soaked in sheep's blood and then—well, you probably don't want the finer details about that. Nevermind.

"So, big case, eh?" Miriam hefted her round body to the back of the bar and prepared our tea. "You two must be after those allergy pill bandits."

"Gotten that bad, has it?"

"Straight up! Had to add a rule to the bar because of it." She pointed to the blackboard hanging on the wall behind the bar. In white chalk, rule number fourteen proclaimed in all caps, IF YOU FEEL A SNEEZE COMIN' ON, TAKE IT UPSIDE! "Had one girl, drunk up to her back scales, nearly do in the whole pub the other night. Right bitch, she was. She burned my bar top. My poor Sherly's ashes would be turning in the wind if he could see these scorch marks." She patted the far end of the bar where the twin lines of blackened wood stood out against the pale varnish. "Taught her a thing or two."

"What did you do to her?" Kensington asked.

Miriam's tummy gurgled, and she quickly concealed a burp with one of her talons. Her bright green eyes widened. "Don't you be interrogating me in my dead husband's pub, Kensington. I didn't do nothing to that little trollop." She busied herself with placing our drinks in front of us and then muttered, "Nothing she didn't deserve."

"Relax, we've got bigger dragons to torch." Not that there are many dragons bigger than Miriam, but I wasn't going to say anything lest I pay a visit to her late husband. "Don't suppose you've seen the Dug."

"Dropped in for a drink just last week." She picked up a napkin and fanned herself. "Such a naughty thing that boy is, the way he flicks his pointy tail, and he's got that long, slender neck I could just nibble on all night."

I did my best not to let that mental image take form. Good thing blood tea is a natural antiemetic.

"So, any idea where he's holed up these days?"

"No, but I hear he took Analiese home with him that night. She'll dive with anything that has wings, scales, and a tail. Between you and me, I hear the scales part is optional for her." Her pink hide rippled with disgust. "Stick around long enough, and you can ask her. She's usually in about this time. Just look for the girl with pale green scales and a lavender belly, one of them exotic types."

An hour later, the crooner in the far corner had moved onto a tune called "Raw Deal." The lyrics provided an overly clever analogy between an uncooked piece of lamb and the misrepresentation of dragons in the human media. I was working on my second mug of blood tea and Kensington was near the bottom of a bowl of Mongolian unicorn. That's when she flew into the pub. Exotic fell five stories shy of describing her. Her scales shimmered like green gold.

"Kensington," I slapped him on the back with my wing to get his attention, "that's her."

He turned on his barstool for a better look as she sashayed her slender tail over to a table near the stage. "Yep, that's a her." He leaned closer to me and whispered. "So who is she?"

"Analiese... the girl the Dug was hanging out with."

The horns on his head rubbed against each other as his brows furrowed in total confusion. If his memory was a knife, it couldn't cut a stick of butter.

"Just follow me and try not to talk." I hopped down to the floor and made my way over to her. "Analiese?"

Her forked tongue slipped out to lick the edges of her cool smile. "Yes?"

"Special Agents Windsor and Kensington." I displayed my ID. "We'd like to ask you a few questions about Douglas Rand."

"Don't know him." She pulled out a smoke made from faery tree leaves and placed it between her slender lips. "Would you?"

I was about to answer when I realized she wasn't looking at me, but over my shoulder at Kensington.

"Huh?"

"She wants a light, idiot," I said as I sat at her table.

"Ohhhh." He leaned forward, placed a finger on his snout to close one of his nostrils and shot out a flame with the other.

She blew out a stream of smoke, its scent sweetened by the faery tree leaves, that all but groped his face. "You have a nice, long tail," she said.

"Yeah, I trip on it a lot."

Her chuckle resembled a purr. "I bet you do."

"Ma'am, I'm told you spent some time last week with a dragon known by many as 'The Dug'."

Analiese ignored me. If her violet eyes had fingers, I could have charged her with felony groping of my partner, not that he'd noticed. Odds favored she'd mistaken his vacant stare for being smitten instead of stupid.

"Here's a picture of him." I slid a mug shot of the Dug across the table top. She glanced at it, flicked it back at me and then returned her attention to Kensington with a salacious wink. "Ma'am, he's wanted in connection with a long list of larcenies and a series of injuries related to accidental flamings."

That got a reaction out of her—but not the kind I'd expected. "Ha! Accidental flaming is right. His flame shot a little too early for me that night."

"So you did spend time with him that evening."

She tapped her smoke on the edge of the table, knocking its ashes onto the floor. "Not long enough for my satisfaction."

"Yes, got that. Were you with him long enough to know where he's holed up?"

"Perhaps." She exhaled a tight stream of smoke into my face. This had more of a "bitch slap" quality to it compared to the sex offense stroking she'd given Kensington. I knew what she was really saying.

"Just what is it you want to change that 'perhaps' into a 'yes,' Miss Analiese?"

The scales of her neck rippled as she stroked Kensington's chin. "What is your friend here doing later tonight?"

"I usually go to bed at ten." He laughed. "That tickles!"

"If the information's good, consider him yours for the night." I figured I better get the goods before she found out he didn't have the brains to put his tail to the kind of use she wanted.

• • •

Analiese's tip led us to Brick Lane where folks go Sunday mornings for the Up Market. No crowds were searching for bargains this time of night, though. The warehouse where she claimed the Dug was holed up was near the intersection with Quaker Street. So much graffiti had overwhelmed the outside that it was the vandal equivalent of white noise.

Kensington and I flew the perimeter, looking for any signs of activity. Someone had painted the windows black, so I couldn't even tell if any lights were on inside. Perhaps the Dug was out searching for more easy tail to dive with.

"You do know to wear protection later tonight, right?" I asked as I pressed my face up against a third story window, trying in vain to see something through a crack in the black paint.

"Um, I don't think they ever replaced my Kevlar armor after I crashed into the Prime Mister's bedroom."

"That's 'Prime Minister,' idiot, and I was referring to—oh, forget it. You hear anything in there?"

"Nope."

I could feel this was the place, though. Problem was we couldn't just break in the window or door and search it. Regulations dictated probable cause. I'd considered having Kensington fly in circles around the building in hopes he'd accidentally smash through the wall, but knowing my luck, he'd smash into the coffee shop across the street, sending us back to the Stonehenge route for good.

We landed and walked the sidewalk. I prayed for something suspicious, but the only thing suspect was that a pair of dragons would be walking down this street at night.

"We gotta get this guy's attention, make him peek his head out of this door, if he's even here."

"I usually knock." Kensington stepped up to the door and banged his head against it three times. "That hurts."

"Don't do that! If he sees us out here, we'll never get him to—"

I shut up when the door pulled back, and a small, narrow head with a floppy ear poked out. It was the Dug.

"What?" He snapped at me as if he meant to bite off my snout.

I stammered like an idiot stuck on repeat. When my mouth put together a solid word, the only thing I managed was, "Allergies."

The Dug smirked in the finest fashion of the sleaziest of salesmen. "You here to buy?"

"We were looking for you." Kensington jumped in place with the exuberance of a hatchling. "And we found you!"

"Hey, if you got the sniffles, I got the cure." He pulled the door open enough to let us in.

"I don't have allergies," Kensington said.

I grabbed my partner by the snout before he could say anything to ruin our chance. "That's right. I'm the one with the allergies." I rubbed my nostrils and tossed in a long series of sniffles.

"Well, get in here, friend. Be quick about it."

I kept a grip on Kensington's snout and walked into the warehouse. How perfect was this? Not only had we found the Dug, but we were about to catch him peddling the stolen goods. The inside reeked of pharmaceuticals and dust. It smelled like a promotion.

"How much you needing?" the Dug asked.

"Um, enough for a month." I didn't even know how much that was.

I'd never worked with the narcotics unit. The last time I'd worked a drug deal was back in my training days, some fifteen years ago, and that was part of a mock exercise.

"You prefer the twenty-four hour or twelve-hour stuff?" he asked.

"Um, twenty-four."

"I got what you boys want in the back."

He led us down an aisle bordered by two long rows of box-shaped piles covered in dark tarps.

"Wow, that's a lot of medicine." Kensington's voice surprised me. I didn't realize I'd let go of his snout.

I remembered my part and sniffed a few more times. All the dust in this place made staying in character simple enough. The one thing I couldn't remember was when to make the takedown. Could we do it yet? I didn't think so. Figured if I waited until he took my money and handed me the product, we'd be good to go, though.

Unfortunately, I was so focused on figuring out the whole process that I didn't think to wonder why the Dug was leading us to the back of the warehouse when he had the stuff up front, too.

"Now then." The Dug stopped at the far end of the warehouse and turned to face us. "Let's talk money."

"Oh, yeah." I shoved my hand down into my personal dimensional-portal pocket and dug around for some cash. "You got change for a twenty pounder?"

The Dug laughed. "Twenty pounds might get you through the next twenty-four hours. If you want a month's worth, you better have three hundred pounds."

"Draco's scales! Three hundred pounds?" My payday wasn't until Friday, and I'd gone on a huge iTunes binge last night. I knew buying Duran Duran's greatest hits was a mistake even after I'd downloaded it and danced through my flat screaming the lyrics to "Hungry Like the Wolf."

"Just how much do you have?" The Dug stepped up to me, close enough to lick my snout if he'd wanted to.

"Um, I think I've got twenty…" My voice trailed off as my fingers rooted through my pocket for some change. My fingers snatched onto something circular and pulled it out. "And a—oh, um—a button?" Bugger.

"What about your friend?" The Dug hadn't asked that question. Kensington and I turned to see a trio of dragons behind us. That's why he'd led us to the back of the warehouse, to trap us. The three dragons looked like they'd hatched from the same weyr. The only difference was in color—one red, one blue, and one green.

"Yeah, empty those pockets, pal." The tall, blue dragon pushed Kensington from behind.

"Okay." His talons dug deep and croutons flew out. The pile of stale bread challenged the Dug's stack of stolen meds.

The Dug growled. "What the hell is this?"

"Croutons!" Kensington giggled. "I love croutons, especially the garlic and herb kind."

"We want cash, you fool," the red dragon shouted right into Kensington's ear. "Where's the money?"

I felt my throat go dry and the scales on the backs of my talons quiver. We had to get out of here. Forget busting the Dug. I just wanted to get out of this warehouse alive. Even if we had the money, we didn't have the backup for taking down four dragons, three of whom were twice as big as us. The Dug's growing irritation steamed against the back of my neck. Every second made our situation worse, and to top it off, I now had Duran Duran's "Wild Boys" stuck in my head.

"You two better make with the cash. I've torched a lot of people and property to stockpile all these pills." The Dug's talon gripped my throat. "Fandral, show these fools what will happen to them if they don't give us the money we want."

"Sure thing, Dug." The green one jumped forward and shot twin jets of fire from his nostrils. The flames engulfed the pile of croutons, overwhelming my senses with a combination of burned oregano, garlic, and basil.

Then I heard Kensington's scream. "My croutons!!!"

The next moments whistled by me in loud, panicked screeches. Kensington, now a scaly airborne pinball shooting flames, bounced off the walls of boxes. The Dug barked commands at his hench-dragons as big, white pills rained on us. None of them had a chance to react. The instant a lick of realization struck my brain, I shouted, "Halt, in the name of the IB—!"

My partner's large body collided with mine before I could say more. I got a face-full of his purple belly, and then everything went black.

• • •

I woke up an hour later on the sidewalk. My eyes opened and found Inspector Merlin's face inches from mine.

"Good show! He's awake." He slapped me on the shoulder. "How do you feel, lad?"

"Baked." My face hurt worse than anything else, but I ached all the way to the outer tips of my wings. I thought I was squinting, but then I realized I simply couldn't open my eyes all the way because of the swelling.

The inspector pulled me to my feet. The street was buzzing with activity. A human fire brigade was sifting through the ashes of the warehouse. The Dug and his hired wings were cuffed and sitting on the sidewalk just down the street. At least a dozen agents were standing guard over the prisoners.

"Top chop work, lad." The Inspector placed a hand on my shoulder. "You boys found the stolen goods and bagged the Dug and his whole gang. Top chop!"

"Uh, yeah." I looked around and realized my partner was missing. "Where's Kensington?"

"Debriefing a young lady at Sherly's, I believe." He pulled out a notepad and flipped through the pages. "Name of Analiese."

"Lucky bastard." I tried to walk but fell on my hindquarters as I took my first step.

"You need some time off, lad?"

I shook my head. "I'll be fine in the morning."

"Very good, because I'm putting you two on the London investigative team. You'll be reporting to your new supervisor at 0800 sharp!"

"New supervisor?"

"I know you'll enjoy working for this chap." He elbowed me in the ribs. "You and Kensington make an excellent team, after all, and that lad has all the makings of a great leader."

"Kensington? You're promoting Kensington?!"

"Exciting, isn't it!"

I wanted to throw up, and that had nothing to do with the multiple concussions I'd probably taken from Kensington's pinball routine.

"Oh, you should hurry to the back of the warehouse before you go." The inspector flew ahead. "Thanks to your partner's quick thinking, we're having s'mores. Seemed a shame to let all those marshmallows, graham crackers, and chocolate bars go to waste."

"I'll be there in a moment, Inspector."

I sat there and chewed on the ashes of my success. All that wingwork I'd done, and Kensington was getting the promotion and the girl. At least I'd seen the last of the Stonehenge route. For tonight, I'd have to settle on some s'mores and dancing solo in my flat, howling "Union of the Snake" with Simon Le Bon.

ACKNOWLEDGEMENTS

I resisted writing short stories for a long time. That might seem a strange admission at the end of a collection of short stories, but it's the truth. For a long time, my only ambition as a writer was to be a novelist. For anyone reading this who hopes to see a novel published, I can't encourage you enough to write short stories.

My time with James River Writers in Richmond is what pushed me to try my hand at short stories. I'm certain I never would have gotten my first novel *Gidion's Hunt* published if not for the experience and skills I gained from working on many of the stories gathered in this book.

Each story owns a long list of acknowledgements. I can't possibly list all of those people here, but among the people I gladly owe my thanks are Kristi Tuck Austin, Katharine Herndon, Shawna and Mike Christos, Leila Gaskin, Lana Krumwiede, Phil Hilliker, and especially my wife Sheri.

From Diversion Books, I want to thank Chris Mahon, Sarah Masterson Hally, and Lauren Szenina.

Most of all, I want to thank my editor Laura Duane who proposed the idea of this collection. Unbeknownst to her, I'd been considering for some time the idea of assembling these stories as a self-publishing project. As I worked with Laura, I realized many times how fortunate I was to have her calling the shots instead of doing this alone. Perhaps the biggest thanks I can give her is that my experience with *The Deadlands: And Other Stories* has left me eager to work with her on future projects.